M

P9-EKE-779

A
Proper
Proposal

Dawn Lindsey

A SIGNET BOOK

NEW AMERICAN LIBRARY

1

"Lady Holland writes that Kinross attended her ball last week," remarked Mrs. Chudleigh to her young companion.

They were enjoying a quiet evening at home as usual, for Rosemullion, to Mrs. Chudleigh's lasting regret, was far too isolated to encourage frequent parties or casual drop-in visitors. Mrs. Chudleigh, a stout and effusive widow of some fifty-odd years, was occupied with her voluminous correspondence. From time to time she good-naturedly shared some interesting tidbit from one or another of her letters, in blithe disregard of the fact that her young relative had never met any of the fashionable people whose names figured in the latest amusing *on-dits* from London, or indeed set foot out of Cornwall in her twenty years.

"She says he is easily the handsomest and most charming man in London," she added with simple satisfaction. "Lady Holland assures me that Kinross's manners are so delightful that one would never guess he's one of the richest prizes on the Matrimonial Mart. She says he doesn't arrive late or refuse to dance with any but the most beautiful girls present, as so many young men seem to do nowadays. He even danced a pair of country dances at her ball with quite the plainest girl in the room, when there were any number of far more eligible beauties longing for a chance to stand up with him."

Miss Nicola Lacey looked up from her frowning attempt to reproduce on paper the intricate whorls of a seashell. She was a slender young woman with a quantity of dark hair and a countenance that was rescued from mere prettiness by a pair of extraordinary green eyes shadowed by unexpectedly long dark lashes. She had grown inured over the past months to hearing Lord Kinross's praises sung, but she said now, in a rallying tone, "Good gracious, ma'am, neither you nor Lady Holland can have thought seriously, if you consider that a kindness in Lord Kinross. Next we shall no doubt hear that the unfortunate young lady in question has developed a *tendre* for him and gone into a decline, as Lady Jane Fox did last summer, or taken to haunting his residence as that Miss Williams did. Really, I am persuaded you should prefer him to be rude, and ogle the company in a condescending manner before retiring to the card room before the evening's half over. From everything I've ever heard, not even Lord Byron before his unfortunate departure for the Continent seemed to rival your nephew's fatal charm. And Lord Kinross doesn't even have to write poetry."

Then she was promptly ashamed of herself. She had, admittedly, developed a hearty contempt for the absent Lord Kinross, whom she had never met, but that did not excuse being unkind to her benefactress. From everything she could tell, Lord Kinross seemed to live an entirely frivolous life devoted to nothing but his own pleasure, but she was well aware that his aunt derived immense satisfaction from following his fashionable career.

The fact that Lord Kinross was also in some way Nicola's benefactor, she was far more easily able to overlook. It was highly improbable that that fashionable peer was even aware that she had been residing with his aunt in his principal seat for the better part of the last year, and in fact far more likely he was totally ignorant of her very existence. Mrs. Chudleigh had certainly written to inform him of the fact when she had first invited Nicola to come and live with her on the death of Nicola's father some ten months before. But since Lord Kinross seemed to pay almost no attention to his aunt's frequent letters, and seldom bothered to answer even direct appeals for decisions about his estate, Nicola did not flatter herself he was likely to have remembered their remote connection—

or cared if he had unwittingly acquired still one more dependent. In any event, his wealth, based on the fabled Trelowarren mine, was so vast it could scarcely matter to him if he supported an army of indigent relations.

Even so, under the circumstances Nicola had been hesitant to accept Mrs. Chudleigh's kind invitation. Her connection to the notable Kinross family was admittedly remote, and she had feared some possible awkwardness when Lord Kinross at last returned to his principal seat.

But it had quickly become borne in upon her not only that Lord Kinross never set foot in Cornwall but also that she could do him a real service, however little he might be aware of the fact. He had, no doubt in an idle moment, commissioned his aunt to restore Rosemullion to a livable condition again after a great many years of neglect, but Mrs. Chudleigh, though kind enough, was both indolent and ineffectual, and had no real love or understanding for the historical beauty that was Rosemullion's. She thought it inconvenient and isolated, and had quite happily handed over the reins to Nicola shortly after her arrival.

Nicola, herself capable and looking for something to occupy her time, had quickly fallen in love with the Elizabethan gem, and regarded the restoring of the vast and criminally neglected pile as a real labor of love. It was Nicola who managed the house, and even the estate, and was gradually bringing it back to warmth and life again.

It was therefore unfortunate that she should have taken so unexpected a dislike to her absent host. If Mrs. Chudleigh's correspondents were to be believed, not only was Lord Kinross the biggest matrimonial catch in the country, as well as one of the wealthiest peers in London, but was also famous for his charm and good nature. He seemed to be as well-liked among the gentlemen of his acquaintance as among the ladies, and was reputed to be a leader of sport and one of the best whips in the country. Any party that lacked his presence was clearly a failure, and he seemed to have to do no more than speak to an impressionable young lady to have her fall hopelessly in love with him. The hapless Lady Jane Fox was just the last in a long line to have gone into a decline after he flirted with her a few times, then abruptly dropped her.

Nicola, admittedly straitlaced, thought him spoilt and shallow, and further resented him for his total neglect of his local responsibilities.

That was bad enough, but even more unforgivable, in her estimation, was his neglect of his aunt, who plainly doted on him. Beyond giving her a *carte blanche* to do as she wished at Rosemullion, he showed little interest either in her or in the repairs taking place there.

Mrs. Chudleigh, perhaps not unnaturally, turned a blind eye to these many slights and defects, and had fondly convinced herself that Kinross was restoring his home in preparation for receiving his bride. The fact that his name was constantly being linked with a series of highborn beauties and that he showed no inclination to settle down with any of them, she conveniently managed to overlook.

Not even the disgraceful Lady Jane Fox affair had been sufficient to shake this optimism, and she said now, foolishly, "Oh dear! I do hope you're wrong, for that was most unfortunate. Not that anyone blames Kinross, as I hope you know, for Lady Holland assures me it was that wretched girl who was wholly at fault. She seems to have pursued him quite brazenly, though I don't mean to sound hard. And while I'm sure she imagined herself in love with him, everyone knows the Foxes are all to pieces, and I can't help thinking his fortune had a great deal to do with it. And as for going into a decline, I'm sure it was no such thing, and she just did it to make herself interesting! Not that *that* sort of notoriety is what any decent girl should desire."

Nicola's mouth twisted a little cynically, and not for the first time she found herself feeling sorry for the unknown Lady Jane. But she could not resist glancing up rather involuntarily at the full-length portrait of his lordship that hung over the mantel.

Even she was forced to acknowledge that it would have been difficult to find a more handsome man than Lord

Kinross. His portrait revealed a tall, indolently elegant figure with a classically handsome countenance, made more vital by a pair of vivid, laughing blue eyes. His hair was guinea-gold, belying his Cornish roots, and even on canvas his portrait exuded a charm that was almost palpable, making the portrait one of the first things one noticed on entering the room.

Nicola critically thought him too good-looking, and frequently resented his dominance of the room. Everywhere else in the house, it was possible to forget, for hours or even days at a time, that Rosemullion and its wild, isolated setting were not hers. But however little Kinross might value his inheritance, his portrait, laughing down at her every evening after dinner, easily made a mockery of that foolish deception.

"My dear ma'am, I fear I've seen no indication that Lord Kinross has any intention of settling down anytime soon," she said honestly now, "despite installing you here and spending a fortune on restoring Rosemullion. But he must have done that in any case, you know, for it would be a crime to let such a jewel fall into ruin, particularly one so closely connected with his family's history."

"Well, as you know, I am far from agreeing with you on *that* score," returned her benefactress frankly. "Rosemullion was always absurdly remote, and the rooms are either far too large or too small and dark for comfort. Papa was wishful to tear it down and rebuild something more modern even when I was a girl, but of course there was never enough money then even to think of it. But it would be far more comfortable set closer to Falmouth, where we could at least enjoy an active social life. And as for the sea you love, I am sure the endless sound of it is the most dismal thing I have ever heard. I only know it never fails to depress me."

Nicola wisely forbore to pursue this old argument, knowing it was useless to point out that Rosemullion's remote setting and dramatic perch overlooking the sea were half of what made it so wildly beautiful. But then, as Mrs. Chudleigh pointed out, Nicola loved the sea, and could not imagine living without the sound of it always in her ears. Papa had been used to tease her and say she must be part mermaid, for with her black hair and incongruous green eyes, she was the epitome of some ancient Celtic witch, as her great-grandmother had once been accused of being.

So she said merely, returning her attention to her sketching, "Well, there is plenty of money now, but at least Lord Kinross has had the sense to value Rosemullion for what it is, one of the most beautiful Elizabethan manors in the country, and certainly in Cornwall."

But Mrs. Chudleigh was evidently no longer listening, for a sudden cry broke from her. "Good Lord, ma'am, what is it?" Nicola cried in alarm, half starting up from her chair. "Not bad news, I hope?"

"No, no! Or rather, Lady Holland writes to warn me that Kinross's name is everywhere being linked with Judith Layton's these days, which is quite bad enough," wailed Mrs. Chudleigh.

Nicola subsided again, her brilliant eyes not quite able to hide their scorn. "Good gracious, ma'am, is that all? Lord Kinross's name is continually being linked with one woman's or another's, so far as I can tell. You must be used to it by now."

"Yes, but this is very different! The woman is married already, and Eugenia fears there may be a dreadful scandal. Everyone knows the creature married a man twice her age merely to obtain an entrée into the *ton*, but Eugenia says Lord Layton is foolishly jealous. Really, I can't imagine what Kinross can be thinking of!"

"I think that, at least, must be obvious," Nicola pointed out dryly.

She might have saved her breath. "Dreadful woman!" exclaimed Mrs. Chudleigh, looking genuinely upset. "Eugenia Holland reports that she is scarcely discreet, and fears Layton may in the end be forced to divorce her. If so, no one will blame Kinross, of course, for everyone knows what she is. But even so, the scandal will be unpleasant. Unfortunately Lady Holland also writes that she is quite depressingly lovely, and wholly without principles. I only hope she does not mean to try to trap Kinross into marrying her if Layton does divorce her, for nothing could be more disastrous.''

Nicola found herself studying Lord Kinross's picture again with a cynical eye, finding it difficult to feel any particular sympathy for him. Even if she were inclined now and then, in a weak moment, to acknowledge the striking resemblance he bore to a Greek god, or even a knight of the Round Table, so dear to Cornish legends, it did not take Mrs. Chudleigh's almost continual revelations of his conduct to remind her that there any resemblance with an ancient hero undoubtedly ended. If he were indeed carrying on an affair with a married woman under her jealous husband's eye, she thought he deserved to be caught in a scandal. No amount of charm would likely weigh with an enraged husband.

In fact, he could ruin himself with her goodwill, so long as he remained far away from Cornwall. She might long have wished to make Lord Kinross's acquaintance, if only to give him a piece of her mind, but she was selfish enough to know that as long as he remained safely in London she was free to restore Rosemullion with a loving hand, and need not share it.

And since, from the sound of it, there seemed no immediate danger that he would either settle down or suddenly remember he possessed a home and a devoted aunt in Cornwall, he might have his name linked with a dozen Lady Laytons for all she cared.

That decided, she realized with some irritation that she was still staring at his portrait, and abruptly turned back to her sketching. But even so, it was some time before she was able to dismiss the annoying Lord Kinross from her mind.

2

At almost the same moment, in London, the Honorable Gideon Harewood was feeling equally annoyed with Kinross. He had grown bored with a negligent game of macao and wandered back to the hazard table, beginning to think longingly of his bed, but to his disgust found Kinross still lounging in his chair, evidently engrossed in the play.

The candlelight turned his fair hair to gilt, and his blue eyes were faintly sleepy, but a pile of rouleaux and scribbled vouchers before him seemed to attest to a current run of good luck. A half-empty bottle of burgundy also stood at his elbow, but after a shrewd glance Mr. Harewood thought the level had not gone down any in his absence.

The same could not be said of the other two players, for Lord Gayland's cherubic countenance was slack, and he seemed to have some trouble in casting the dice, and even Sir Guy Percival's heavy-lidded eyes seemed even more mockingly unpleasant than usual.

Abruptly Lord Gayland shouted for another bottle of brandy. Percival looked annoyed and remarked in his faintly sneering way, "My dear Gayland, I will remind you you are holding up the game."

"Good God, I'm in no hurry!" insisted Kinross, yawning and stretching a little. "In fact, I'm about ready to call it a night."

"No, no!" objected Gayland foolishly, hiccuping a little. "Night's young yet. Might make my chance! Five, is it? Aye, that's bad. Devilish bad! But stranger things have happened. What's the main? Seven?"

12

Since he had been punting on tick since before Harewood wandered off an hour before, it didn't look likely. But to the latter's disgust Kinross said nothing, merely yawned again and glanced up at the newcomer a little mockingly.

"Macao no longer hold your interest, Gideon?" he asked in amusement. "Do you care to sit in?"

"Not if you're winning," replied Mr. Harewood frankly. "I've something better to do with my money than throw it away, thank you!"

Then he could have bitten out his tongue when Percival laughed unpleasantly. "I'm beginning to agree with you. His luck has certainly been uncanny tonight, at all events. But allow me to point out that Gayland was—I profoundly trust—about to cast the dice at long last."

Harewood cast the other a glance of acute dislike, wondering suddenly if the rumors he had been hearing lately were true. Percival was said to have suffered a series of bad reverses at the tables recently. If so, and he had hoped to mend his fortunes tonight, it might explain his present bad temper. Not that Percival seemed to need any excuse to be unpleasant.

In fact, Kinross was a fool to play with him. Gayland was always gloomy on settling-up day, for his bad luck was notorious, but at least he was good for his losses. But if Percival were indeed facing ruin, Harewood wouldn't put it past him to cause trouble of some kind. His birth was respectable and his *ton* excellent, but his tongue was biting and his manner always faintly sneering, so that he was far from being a general favorite. Harewood thought him an ugly customer and generally steered clear of him.

For that reason, though he was nearly asleep on his feet, he resignedly settled down to watch the play, abruptly calling loudly for a pot of coffee to help himself stay awake.

Kinross, as if aware of his motives and amused by them, shot him a mocking glance, and offered him a glass of burgundy instead.

"No, no, I'm half-foxed already," Harewood said

truthfully, thinking he might need a clear head before the night was over.

"Then go home to bed, for God's sake," answered Kinross a little impatiently. "You're three-parts asleep."

Harewood denied it, though not very convincingly. Kinross shot him another half-exasperated glance from under his golden lashes, but Percival remarked unpleasantly, "You are indeed fortunate to possess so devoted a nursemaid, Kinross. But I would have said I was the one in need of protection tonight, not you."

Harewood flushed, but decided to ignore the gibe. Gayland, unaware of any undercurrents in the room, threw a seven.

"Burn it! That's nicked me!" he said gloomily, rapidly scribbling another voucher and shoving it across the table. "I'll confess you've got the devil's own luck tonight, Kinross."

Kinross received the voucher indifferently. "If so, it's not likely to last long," he pointed out philosophically. "In my experience it never does."

"Aye, so I usually think! Unfortunately my luck is usually phenomen . . . phenom . . . uncannily bad," complained the other, beginning to slur his words a little. "Damme if it ain't unfair, now that I come to think of it. Ought to be a law against a man of your wealth winning so consis . . . consistently. Spread some of it around, is what I say."

Gayland was too drunk to mean anything by it, but Percival laughed unpleasantly. "Much as it pains me to agree with anything our drunken friend here has to say, your luck certainly has been phenomenal tonight, Kinross," he agreed insolently. "But then, like most women, I've always found Luck a notoriously mercenary jade."

When Kinross merely shrugged, Percival abruptly took up the dice. He cast a two.

"Ames-ace!" groaned Gayland sympathetically. "Told you Kinross can't lose, by gad! He's made a tidy pile tonight off us. In fact, I don't know about you, but I've had enough. How much do I owe you, blast you?"

He accepted the total philosophically enough, however, and promised to pay him at the end of the week. "Won't be before, for I'm run off my legs," he added frankly, yawning and getting uncertainly to his feet.

"Don't worry. There's no hurry."

Percival's brows rose, and he observed in an amused tone that did little to rob his words of their offensiveness, "That's damned decent of you, Kinross. You will forgive me for thinking that for Gayland to redeem his vouchers is a little like carrying coals—or should I perhaps have said copper?—to Newcastle. But then, your mines are in Cornwall, not Newcastle, as I remember. I must confess I've always thought one place as impossibly uncivilized as the other."

The insult was unmistakable and Harewood stiffened, but Kinross remained lounging in his chair. "Probably. I've never been to Newcastle, so I couldn't say," he answered indifferently. "But I've had enough for the night as well. I make your total two thousand, Percival."

Percival abruptly downed the contents of his glass, confirming Harewood in his opinion that he had been suffering deep doings of late. "I admire your enviable detachment, my dear Kinross," he remarked sneeringly. "But then, I don't doubt I'd feel the same if I had guineas being pulled night and day out of the ground for me."

"Not guineas! Not pulling guineas out of that mine of his, Percival," interrupted Gayland, whose attention had momentarily wandered. "I'm sure I heard it was copper. Not that it don't amount to the same thing, in the end."

"Precisely the same thing," agreed Percival. "Unfortunately we lesser mortals are not so fortunate. I believe you at least owe me my chance for revenge."

"Good God, I've never heard such rot!" exploded Harewood, unable to keep silent any longer. "Whatever his fortune, he don't owe you a thing, and you know it, Percival."

Kinross frowned him down. "Very well, Percival," he agreed evenly at last. "You can have your revenge, but I warn you I don't sit past four. I'm riding to Newmarket tomorrow morning. Will you take the bank this time?"

"Unfortunately, like our annoying friend here, I am also run off my legs," replied Percival with his brusque frankness. "But I've had a surfeit of hazard for one evening. If you've no objection, I suggest we switch to something that requires slightly more than blind luck for a change."

Kinross merely shrugged and agreed without a blink to the other's suggestion of piquet at five-pound points.

But Harewood frowned at the stakes, for this was plunging recklessly indeed. He was well aware Percival had the reputation of being a noted card player, and suspected it was Percival who meant to do the fleecing this time.

But he knew better than to say anything more, for Kinross wouldn't thank him for his interference. He was tempted once more to go home to bed, but distrusted Percival too much to be able to leave with a clear conscience. Instead he contented himself with retiring to a chair in a dark corner for a brief nap, knowing that if he stayed to watch the play he would be unable to hold his tongue.

But it seemed clear to him by now that Percival was indeed run off his legs. His expensive habits and his propensity for high stakes had no doubt caught up with him at last. Harewood found himself quite unable to feel the least sympathy for him, but resented the fact Kinross had clearly been marked to repair his opponent's shattered fortunes.

But when at last he wandered back an hour later, yawning, it was to find the score unexpectedly tied, and Percival's mood far from improved. "You should not have had that capot," he said abruptly, pouring himself another glass of brandy and downing it. He glanced up rather impatiently as Harewood returned and added, "What, are you still here? I thought you'd gone."

"I'm like the bad penny," agreed Harewood cheerfully,

ignoring the dislike in the other's eyes. "Who's winning?"

"We've both had one rubber apiece," answered Kinross easily. "You're in time for the deciding rubber. But I'll admit I had slightly better cards that last hand. Your deal, I believe, Percival."

Percival cut the cards toward him with something of a snap.

Harewood settled down to watch the last rubber. It was apparent almost immediately to him that Percival's nerves were on the stretch, however much he tried to hide the fact. He was no longer even bothering to maintain the facade of goodwill, and played with a concentration that showed how determined he was to win. But how much of that was due to his unfortunate financial troubles, and how much to the born gamester's dislike of owning himself beaten, was hard to say. Percival had seldom made any secret of his dislike for Kinross, and Harewood suspected he had long since forgotten everything in his determination not to be beaten by one he considered his inferior in wits and skill.

It was equally obvious that Kinross's own indifference to the outcome of the game galled Percival even more. His dislike and desperation must have made it difficult to forget everything but the play, as he must do to avoid costly mistakes. But he was a seasoned gamester, and obviously still considered Kinross a negligible threat. He might know that Kinross possessed sometimes uncanny luck, but piquet had less to do with luck than skill, and Kinross in addition had the reputation of being far too easygoing to be a serious gamester, as Percival was no doubt counting on.

But as Harewood watched the first game in the rubber go to Percival, who relaxed slightly and poured himself another drink at its conclusion, he began to wonder if Percival had reason to be quite so confident. He thought that despite his control Percival was letting his need, and his contempt for Kinross, affect his game. He was playing recklessly, taking obvious risks on the slim chance of spoiling a point or two for his opponent, and relying on his superior skill to fluster Kinross.

If so, he was not succeeding. Harewood began to grow a little uneasy when Kinross swept the board in the next hand. The cards had seemed to be roughly even, as well, so that Percival couldn't blame the other's phenomenal luck this time.

Percival seemed to recognize it, for he downed the brandy in his glass before remarking grudgingly, "Damn you, I shouldn't have given you that spade guard."

"I doubt it will happen again," remarked Kinross indifferently.

Percival laughed harshly, then abruptly pushed away the bottle of brandy at his elbow. "That's generous of you!" he acknowledged. "Your deal, I believe."

They played for some moments in silence after that. For a while no great points were made on either side, nor any obvious mistakes. Then Percival said a little gloatingly, "My point is good, I think, Kinross. and my pique."

"Yes, but not your repique."

A small muscle jumped in the other's cheek, as if he had not expected that, but he said merely, "Also my quint. And, I think, a tierce."

Kinross gave his deceptively disarming smile. "I'm afraid not," he said gently, and spread out his own cards.

Percival stared at them for a moment as if stunned, an ugly red color suffusing his cheeks. Then he said offensively, "I should have known better than to challenge your damnable luck. My own is obviously completely out lately."

Kinross merely shrugged. "I warned you I don't sit past four. I make it four thousand you owe me."

But Percival had himself well in hand again. "I presume you will afford me the same courtesy you did Gayland?" he said with his sneer. "Particularly considering how little such a sum must mean to you. I fear it will take me some days to raise it."

Then his expression changed abruptly. "Unless . . . What the hell! I had intended this for another purpose, I must confess, but unfortunately my present need must hold precedence." He plunged his hand into one pocket and produced a jewel case. He snapped it open to reveal an emerald necklace of some size that glittered dully in the candlelight. "It is worth something over five thousand, but I won't quibble over the value with you."

Harewood whistled and raised his quizzing glass to get a better look. "Good God! A strange bauble to be carrying about with you! But perhaps you keep it for just such emergencies?" he added nastily.

Percival cast him a look of intense dislike, then shrugged. "I assure you it's genuine, and recently appraised at something over five thousand pounds, as I've said. Well, Kinross? Will you accept it in place of my vouchers? It's either that or wait for your money. And I tell you frankly, much as it annoys me to do so, that I have suffered enough reverses lately to make it doubtful that I can have it soon, if ever."

"Good God, don't do it! What the devil do you want with an emerald necklace?" exclaimed Harewood in exasperation.

But Kinross's eye seemed caught by the necklace, for he picked it up from its case and regarded it interestedly. "I don't doubt I could find something to do with it. But I don't like to take it if it's an heirloom. There's no hurry to repay me if you're temporarily short, you know."

Percival laughed without amusement. "I doubt if 'temporary' is the right word. But I've no sentimental attachment to the piece, if that's what you mean. Take it, by all means."

Still Kinross hesitated. "You say it's worth something over five thousand? Make it six, in round numbers. You owe me four. I'll lay you double or nothing, the necklace against your vouchers, to be decided by one cut of the cards." He was showing more interest than he had all night.

Harewood snorted in disgust, but Percival hesitated only a moment, his eyes taking on the reckless gleam of the true gamester. "Done! I've always said you were a fool, Kinross," he added. "But I'll beat you yet, damn you! I own that the dislike of being bested by such a fribble as you almost outweighs even the money involved, little though I can stand to lose it. But even your luck can't last forever.''

Abruptly he reached down and cut the deck. He turned up a knave of hearts.

Kinross smiled and negligently leaned forward. Harewood held his breath, then expelled it loudly as he turned up a queen.

There was a moment's silence, then Percival began to laugh a little wildly. "I should have known a woman would turn up to save you," he said offensively, and tossed the case down on the table. "It's obvious we were born under opposite stars, you and I. I can only hope to see the tables turned one day.''

He strode out without another word.

As they strolled home through the pale, chilly dawn sometime later, Harewood vainly attempted to remonstrate with his old friend. "Why the devil did you stay and play with him?" he demanded irritably. "You know what he's like, and it's obvious that rumors are true and he's badly dipped.''

The other shrugged unrepentantly. "Good God, what excuse did I have for not playing?" he asked unanswerably. "And if you thought you were protecting me, by the way, you quixotic fool, let me tell you I am more than capable of taking care of myself.''

"Aye, it looked it!" agreed the other bluntly. "He had every intention of fleecing you, you know.''

A streetlamp revealed a hint of amusement in Kinross's handsome countenance. "He certainly meant to, I'll agree.''

Harewood eyed him suspiciously, but then shrugged. "What I'll never understand is why you allow such fools to impose upon you. Owed him his revenge, indeed! I've never heard such nonsense.''

"Yes, so you said," answered Kinross, sounding a little impatient for the first time. "But what *you* won't understand is that he was right, in a way. It means nothing to me whether I win or lose— When it obviously matters so much to others, it seems churlish to refuse to play. At any rate, I'm unpopular in either case, for if I refuse, I'm accused of being arrogant, and if I play and win, it's even worse. I've thought of giving it up completely, but I'm damned if I'll do that. And I can scarcely refuse to play for money, for that would be considered condescending.''

Abruptly he shrugged again, and seemed to dismiss the subject. "At any rate, at worst it costs me nothing but a few hours of boredom.''

"It would have cost you a damn sight more, if Percival had his way!'' insisted Harewood doggedly. "And is that your excuse as well for tolerating all the unstable women who imagine themselves in love with you? It don't do your reputation any good, believe me, and you don't do them any favors either.''

"Good God!'' exploded Kinross. "You know as well as I do it's my fortune they imagine themselves in love with, not me. But I refuse to go through life either apologizing for my wealth or becoming a prisoner of it. I'd sooner give it away.''

"And which is Lady Layton in love with?'' demanded Harewood dryly.

But Kinross had abruptly recovered his usual even temper. "Probably neither!'' he admitted flippantly. "But we understand each other. And as you just pointed out, I have no more than to smile at an eligible young lady to foster in her breast ambitions of squandering my fortune. You should be delighted I have taken your lectures so much to heart.''

Harewood sighed, suspecting that his old friend had merely jumped from the frying pan into the fire. But he said more mildly, "I'll concede—reluctantly—that possessing such a fortune is more complicated than I'd ever have imagined.'' Then, as Kinross burst out laughing, he smiled grudgingly. "I know—I daresay it's a small enough price to pay. But you're too easygoing, if you ask me. Percival's not the only one to resent you for your wealth. Worse, you accomplished nothing by tonight's little demonstration of tolerance. Now you're stuck with a necklace you've no use for, and he hates you anyway.''

"Oh, I can find a use for the necklace, I don't doubt,'' said Kinross easily. "And as for Percival, he'd had too much to drink. Good God, do you expect me to care for what's said after the third bottle's been broached? If so, I should have called out poor Gayland as well, no doubt.''

Harewood, who knew exactly what was likely to be done with the necklace, refused to be talked out of his present ill humor. "If you ask me, Percival don't need to be drunk to be unpleasant,'' he said bluntly. "He's got a damn sharp tongue in his head at any hour. Can't abide the fellow, if you want the truth! I only hope you haven't made an enemy out of him for your pains.''

Kinross laughed again. "I don't fear Percival. I confess I don't like him any more than you do, but I daresay he's harmless enough.''

Harewood shook his head over this willful blindness, but they had reached his lodgings in Duke Street by that time. Kinross wished him a cheerful good night and strolled off whistling, in blithe disregard of the fact he carried a fortune in jewels in his pocket, easy prey for any footpad who might be lurking in the shadows at such a deserted hour. And as Harewood had suspected, he also was headed in quite the opposite direction from his own residence in Berkeley Square.

Harewood, who knew full well that Lord Layton's town house lay in that part of town, and that he was away on business for a fortnight, gave it up and went resignedly up to bed.

3

Sir Guy Percival arose late the next morning, and in a sour mood that was not helped by an aching head and an unpleasant memory of the events of the night before.

Harewood was right that he had indeed been having deep doings of late, and last night's fiasco had done nothing to help matters any. He had thought Kinross an easy pigeon for plucking—he still thought him so, as a matter of fact—but he was obliged to own he had reckoned without the other's uncanny luck.

But Harewood was also right that he had persisted, long after reason had told him it was folly to throw good money after bad, because it galled him unmercifully to be obliged to own himself bested by such a fashionable fribble. He disliked such handsome, charming men on principle, but had Kinross been of modest means, Percival was honest enough to admit his dislike would have gone no further. But such good looks and charm, when allied with one of the largest fortunes in England, were a very different matter, and never failed to rouse his resentment, particularly since he himself was generally perilously on the brink of ruin.

In fact, he was cynically conscious that the contrast between himself and Kinross could not have been greater if an unkind providence had planned it. Kinross was handsome and well-liked, blessed with wealth and charm and popularity, as if an indulgent heaven had smiled on his christening. By contrast Percival knew himself to be consistently dogged by evil fortune. Whatever he touched turned to dross in his hands, and he knew that unless he was extremely careful he would shortly be facing complete

ruin. Certainly another evening like the last would leave
him with little choice but flight to the Continent or blowing
his brains out.

Nor was his mood improved by the unpleasant task that
still lay before him. Typically he chose to carry it off with a
high hand, saying abruptly as soon as his valet entered with
his shaving water, "By the way, I'm afraid our arrangements regarding the necklace have been altered somewhat.
I lost it at play last night."

Clavering was a sullen, unpleasant-looking man, barely
held in check at the best of times by his fear of his
employer. Now his face suffused with ugly color and he
demanded shrilly, "You *lost* it? What d'you mean, you
lost it?"

Percival yawned. "The words don't seem to invite any
particular confusion. It is a common enough occurrence,
God knows!"

The servant set the water can down, his voice becoming
menacing as he started toward the bed. "I'll remind you
them sparklers wasn't yours to lose! That's what we get for
cutting a flash into our lay. Well, you won't tip us the
double, see? You'll dub over the possibles you owe us, or
my friend will have something to say about it."

"My dear fool, I will remind you that you didn't cut me
in on your 'lay,' as you call it, I cut myself in. And as for
'dubbing over the possibles,' another evening like the last
one, and I'll be lucky to keep the shirt on my back. But
don't worry. I'll make it up to you. I'm still exceedingly
useful to you and your mysterious friend, don't forget."

"Aye, so you keep reminding us. But for all your break-
teeth words, the joke's on you this time," said the other
with a certain satisfaction. "You'll share more'n you've
bargained for if we're snabbled. I was coming to tell you
that the sparklers've been missed, and are too hot to
handle just now. We're all likely to go up the ladder to bed
for last night's bungling."

Percival's expression changed on the instant. "*What?*"
he demanded furiously. "You fool! You told me the old
lady wouldn't miss them for months!"

"So she wouldn't have," said Clavering sullenly. "My . . . friend had an in with the old crone's chambermaid, and she assured him she was as good as gone to roost, and never went nowhere. Only, as luck would have it, she took it into her head to inspect all her sparklers afore making her will, and that whiddled the scrap. The chambermaid was lucky to escape with her job. But if you've spouted the baubles, we're all likely to end on the nubbing cheat."

"I should have known better than to throw in with such fools," said Percival, coldly furious now. "But you are overconfident, I fear. I had no hand in stealing the goods, and you may be sure the world will hardly take the word of an admitted thief over mine. At worst I will appear a foolish dupe, whereas you and your accomplices will undoubtedly end on Tyburn, as you say. But so long as none of us loses our heads, the affair doesn't have to prove fatal. I shall have to redeem the necklace before Kinross can dispose of it, of course, but he's such a fool it shouldn't be too difficult. Unfortunately I can't raise five thousand pence let alone five thousand pounds at the moment, so you and your 'friend' will have to come up with it."

"Why should any of us come up with it?" demanded the other resentfully. "Why don't we just mill this cove's house like we done originally?"

"Because, my buffleheaded friend, that will arouse precisely the sort of attention we most wish to avoid. Two such necklaces stolen in London within a fortnight is stretching credulity just a little, don't you think? Fortunately, as I said, I should have no difficulty in getting it back. The fool hasn't even the wits to realize how much I dislike him. But I warn you I must have the money immediately, before he has time to dispose of it."

The other grumbled, but at last agreed to see what he could do. In the end he reluctantly came through with the money, as Percival had known he would. But when Percival called on Kinross later in the day and spun him some tale of having had a lucky bet pay off and regretting pledging a family heirloom, he was dealt an unexpected blow. Kinross betrayed no particular suspicion, but revealed carelessly that he no longer had the necklace.

"You *what*?" It had not occurred to Percival that he could possibly dispose of it so soon. Then, realizing he dared not arouse even Kinross's easygoing curiosity, he abruptly made himself swallow his anger. "I must congratulate you. May I ask what you did with it in the last twelve hours?"

"Good God, you should know better than to ask such a question, Percival. Chivalry naturally prevents me from revealing its present whereabouts," said Kinross cheerfully. "I'm sorry. Had I known you meant to redeem the piece, I would naturally have held it for you. But I'm afraid you're too late."

Percival's previous formless dislike against such an easygoing fool crystallized into actual hatred in that moment, but he had no choice but to accept that answer and withdraw with what grace he could manage.

But like Mr. Harewood, he had little doubt who had the necklace now. Kinross's name had been linked with a number of expensive bits of muslin over the years, but Percival was well aware that his most current inamorata was the beauteous and grasping Judith Layton. And if so, the game was not totally lost, for she would scarcely dare to wear the necklace openly. It was well known her elderly husband was growing increasingly jealous, and since Layton was as ungenerous as he was elderly, his suspicions would instantly be aroused if his wife were to be seen flaunting such an expensive trinket not of his bestowing.

He thus managed to temporarily calm his servant's fear, but once more Percival had reckoned without his own wretched luck. At a dinner party not two days later, almost the first thing he saw upon entering the room was the emerald necklace sparkling around Judith Layton's beautiful white throat.

She was a statuesque brunette whom Percival knew to be vain, shallow, and wholly without scruples. It had amused him to follow her career, for she had successfully managed to barter her considerable charms for the entrée to the *ton* she most craved. But as most such bargains, she had quickly learned how deceptive was her victory, for though she enjoyed a certain success, particularly among the men, she was stuck with an aging and jealous husband, and one, moreover, whose fortune quickly proved to be inadequate for her needs, even supposing he had been willing to expend it on her behalf. Since he was a notorious skinflint, and had quickly grown disillusioned with his expensive new bride, she had not wasted much time in seeking consolation elsewhere.

Until now, however, she had been reasonably discreet, no doubt knowing an open scandal and possible divorce would scarcely further her ambitions. But either she was growing careless, or else expected more of her liaison with Kinross than Percival thought was likely, for she was openly wearing the emeralds tonight. Kinross was admittedly a fool, but he would hardly forget his ancient name and title to marry a woman already his mistress, and one, moreover, who came to him only at the expense of a messy divorce.

No, Percival suspected she had allowed ambition to overcome her usually well-developed sense of self-preservation. It mattered little to him whether she ruined herself, and Kinross with her, but if she were to flaunt the necklace all over town, it was inevitable it would be recognized eventually.

In fact, he could cheerfully have wrung her beautiful, treacherous neck, and cursed his own fatal luck. But he was not one to admit defeat easily, and so took the first opportunity of approaching her when she was momentarily alone.

When he congratulated her maliciously, she raised her brows in question. For answer he fingered one of the emeralds and said mockingly, "Am I mistaken? Surely these are new? You must be cleverer even than I suspected, my dear, for I would have thought Layton's devotion would long since have worn thin."

She looked briefly annoyed, but then could not quite

resist preening herself a little. "As a matter of fact I . . . won them, at play. Do you like them?" she asked.

He smiled unpleasantly. "If so, I congratulate you even more. Your luck must be improving, unlike mine. But do you really expect Layton to swallow such a story for long? You must know your own business best, of course, but I would have thought it far too easy to disprove."

She flushed, but then shrugged her beautiful white shoulders. "And if I don't care? I find my husband less than amusing these days, I must confess."

"Speaking for myself, I have always thought there ought to be a law against all husbands. But you will perhaps forgive me if I speak frankly. Oddly enough, I have your best interests at heart, which is unlike me. How much nauseating interference is perpetrated under that pious guise, by the way! But in this case my advice is quite disinterested and even well-meaning. I would merely hate to see you make a fatal mistake, my dear."

She frowned, then glanced involuntarily across the room, where Kinross stood chatting with their hostess, a raddled matron in puce satin. She did not pretend to misunderstand him, but said confidently, "What will you lay me you are mistaken? If I can land Kinross, I care nothing for Layton. And divorces are not unknown these days."

He smiled. "If you can land Kinross, I would be your most fervent admirer, my dear. I own I would like to see him taken down a peg or two. But I fear you are overconfident. He won't marry you."

She could not hide her complacency. "Men always think they're so clever," she said throatily. "But I still have some tricks up my sleeve. What will you bet me I can get him to propose?"

Percival's eyes gleamed. "These?" he said, touching the emeralds again. "Against my matched grays you have been coveting?" He didn't tell her that unless his luck improved quickly he would have no grays to stake, for they would almost certainly have to be sold. At any rate, he would have to retrieve the necklace long before then, if his neck were to be saved. But he couldn't resist the irony of the wager.

She readily agreed, and since dinner was announced then, there was no further chance for conversation. Over dinner, however, when she deliberately turned the conversation to Cornwall, where Kinross's estates were located, he began to acknowledge her undoubted skill as he recognized her purpose.

"Is it really as barbarous as they say?" she demanded in her throaty voice. "The tales we hear of murderous pirates, and even more murderous wreckers, makes my blood run cold, I must confess, my lord."

Kinross shrugged, but answered good-naturedly. "I haven't been back for a great many years, I fear, so I can't answer that. My stepmother certainly refused to live there any longer after the riots in the last century, but I've no idea what conditions are like now."

Their hostess, one Lady Fitzhugh, shivered dramatically. "For myself I fear I would be afraid to set foot there! I well remember those disgraceful riots, though I am no doubt betraying my age by confessing it. And you haven't been back since, Kinross?"

"No, but not because I fear riots. I believe the county is peaceful enough now."

"You surprise me, my lord," Percival drawled. "I would have thought you had every reason to brave any number of dangerous Cornishmen. Or don't you count the richest copper mine in the country inducement enough to return?"

Judith Layton regarded him assessingly, as if wondering at his motives, but said brightly, "Yes, the famous mine! What is it like, my lord? I confess I've never seen one."

"You haven't missed much," Kinross said ruefully. "My father would seldom let me near it when I was a child, for they can be dangerous, so I fear I know little more than you. I mostly remember the depressing gray color and the huge engines."

"But you have a house there, surely? Don't you ever feel the need to visit it?" she persisted.

"Not particularly. Rosemullion is—or was—falling into ruin, for it has not been lived in for nearly twenty years, and had been neglected for nearly twice that time before that. I have installed an aunt there now, to do what she can to restore it, but I don't hold out much hope."

"I'm sure you exaggerate, my lord. In fact, I'd love to see it," said Judith, still more brightly. "I must confess the whole sounds extremely romantic."

"You wouldn't think so after catching your death of cold in the damp rooms, or having broken your leg by putting a foot through a stair, as I almost did as a boy," Kinross insisted in amusement. "I've been thinking of buying an estate in a more accessible part of the country, but there seems no hurry. Perhaps when I marry I will."

Lady Layton cast Percival a triumphant look. "You should hold a house party!" she exclaimed, as if the idea had just occurred to her. "It would be a considerable adventure, if what you say is true, and surely it is time you went back, if you haven't seen it in all these years. At any rate, you know how boring London is this time of year. I am sure I will soon die of tedium."

"Good God, I can think of better ways to relieve tedium," answered Kinross.

Judith Layton eyed him with a half-smile playing about her beautiful mouth and deliberately fingered the emeralds about her throat. "Oh, I have a feeling it would be an adventure, my lord. I have always thought Cornwall sounded so romantic, with its tales of ruined castles and pirates and smugglers."

He frowned, as if by no means pleased by the direction the conversation was taking, but said pleasantly enough, "I've no idea what state the house is in, or even if it's habitable. I suspect you would soon find it more adventurous than you'd bargained for."

Percival had been an appreciative audience of this performance. He had no real reason to further her ambitions in that direction, but it had occurred to him that until he could think of a plan for retrieving the necklace, it would be far safer out of London and Cornwall seemed remote enough that almost anything might happen there.

So he said deliberately now, "I must confess I, too, would be curious to see the source of so much . . . I almost said 'obscene wealth,' but I am the first to admit that no wealth, whatever its origins, is to be despised. But perhaps Kinross has no desire to be reminded of his . . . somewhat unconventional roots, my dear Lady Layton. After all, the Cornish are reputed to be little better than barbarians, or so I am led to believe."

Kinross's handsome face flushed, but he said shortly, "By all means come if you want to. I can promise very little, but it's probably past time I went home myself. Only don't blame me if you find the place more picturesque than you're obviously imagining. It was going to rack and ruin twenty years ago, and has scarcely been lived in since."

Satisfied with her victory, Judith Layton immediately began planning dates and guest lists, obviously meaning to have the ordering of the party herself. Percival had every intention of seeing that he was included on that guest list, for it should be far easier to retrieve the necklace at his leisure in so benighted a place, if everything he had ever heard about Cornwall were to be believed.

But his contempt for Kinross grew, since he obviously had no idea how easily he had just been manipulated.

4

The Honorable Gideon Harewood seemed to be of the same opinion. "What queers me is how you ever let yourself get roped into such a devilish party in the first place," he complained, not for the first time.

They were completing the last leg of the long journey into Cornwall, in advance of the rest of the party, which was traveling more slowly by chaise. In Mr. Harewood's opinion the trip had been long and uncomfortable, nor was he in the best of humors.

"You needn't have come, you know," retorted Kinross unsympathetically. "I am aware you did it in the mistaken notion you were helping me, but I warned you it was likely to be deadly dull—not to mention deucedly uncomfortable. Unless my aunt has worked miracles in the last two years, Rosemullion is almost certainly uninhabitable. Far worse than the inn that so unjustly earned your scorn last night, you shameless snob. This is Cornwall, not England, and in fact the Indian Queens is one of our more luxurious accommodations."

Mr. Harewood almost shuddered, both at the memory of the inn they had graced with their patronage the night before, and the ordeal that still lay before him. Kinross might assure him the roads were admirable now, and the journey had used to take three weeks when he was a boy, but Mr. Harewood had found the Cornish countryside to be oddly unsettling, and the inns inferior. The sheets last night had been decidedly damp, the inevitable result, no doubt, of the cold, creeping mist that came in off Bodmin Moor, and the food leaden and unfamiliar. He might almost have imagined himself in another country, except that the inhabitants spoke at least a form of English, however unintelligible it might be to the untrained ear.

He said a little bitterly now, "Someday I'll take you at your word and abandon you to your fate. And you can save your breath and stop trying to humbug me this party was your idea! I know exactly what happened. Someone made it impossible for you to refuse, and as a consequence you're stuck with returning to a place you've no desire to visit, and entertaining a houseful of people you've no interest in."

Kinross laughed. "Good God, what a fool you must think me. The truth is, if you must know, that I was not particularly enthusiastic over returning, but this party has forced me into belatedly remembering my responsibilities. It was time and past that I returned to see how my aunt is proceeding, and to look over the old place. As for this house party you so disapprove of, I have a strong hunch my guests won't remain long, once they realize the shortcomings of the hospitality I'm offering them."

Harewood was less convinced that any of the ill-assorted party following behind them would allow a little discomfort to deter them. Judith Layton he frankly suspected of being up to mischief of some sort or another, and her husband was too parsimonious to quibble at being housed for a couple of weeks at someone else's expense. Miss Siddings, the only other female of the party, was a bosom bow of Lady Layton's, and had no doubt been included merely to throw dust in her husband's eyes. As for Percival, Harewood had no idea why he had consented to come along on such a dreadful journey, unless his financial difficulties were so acute that he, too, preferred to be spared the expenses of London for a while. But whatever his reason, Harewood had no wish to be forced to live in close proximity to him for several weeks.

But one of Kinross's predictions was soon fortunately proved to have been overly pessimistic, for the grounds of Rosemullion, at least, betrayed no visible signs of neglect. The drive was freshly graveled, the rhododendrons flanking the carriage drive neatly trimmed, and the sweeping lawns freshly scythed. In fact Harewood, used to the autumn colors they had left behind in England, had been pleasantly surprised, ever since they reached sight of the sea, by the rich green of grass and trees, as though it were still high summer in Cornwall.

Even Kinross raised his brows a little, remarking in surprise, "My aunt must be a better chatelaine than I had expected."

So indeed it seemed. The house and the sea had been hidden from view, but as they topped a little rise, both burst dramatically into view at the same time, the house clinging picturesquely to the wild cliffs as if in danger of dropping into the sea at any moment. Rosemullion was clearly Elizabethan in origin, its red bricks and fanciful chimneys and towers made airy by the setting and the large expanses of leaded-glass windows. But despite its obvious age, it looked unexpectedly beautiful against the vivid blue of the sea. Mr. Harewood began to suspect that Kinross had greatly exaggerated its drawbacks, but then, he had long suspected it was more than mere uninterest that had kept him away from his home for so many years.

Kinross, too, seemed to be thinking something of the same thing, and was frowning a little. He had been surprised ever since they had crossed the Tamar at how familiar everything seemed, for he had thought he remembered very little of his boyhood there. He had gone away to school in England at the age of eight, and returned only infrequently since, for the journey was long, and his stepmother had preferred to spend as little time as possible at Rosemullion. But for some reason the wild, beautiful scenery appealed to him, and Rosemullion itself struck a strange chord in his memory.

It was absurd to credit it to some ancestral link, nor did he feel particularly as if he were coming home. But he was pleasantly surprised at how much better-cared-for it all looked than he had anticipated, or indeed had any right to expect.

He was realistic enough to know that his impression on a clear, sunny day, and from a distance, was probably misleading, for Rosemullion was very old-fashioned. He had a vivid memory of the rooms being low-ceilinged and dark, the public rooms, on the contrary, too vast and thus impossible to heat, and the passages low and uneven. His stepmother had used to complain endlessly of the work required to keep the intricately carved paneling, of which Rosemullion was liberally supplied, cleaned and polished, and the army of servants it required to maintain such a rabbit warren of rooms.

But then, she had never liked the place, and had been delighted with a legitimate excuse for moving permanently to London. He abruptly shrugged and dismissed the problem, reserving judgment until later.

As they approached the curving drive to the house he saw a curtain at a window on an upper floor pull back, and a figure appear. He was too far away to recognize whether the watcher was male or female, one of the servants, or perhaps his aunt, watching out for him; but even as he glanced up curiously the curtain fell again and the figure disappeared from view. He pulled his team to a halt before the freshly painted door, and promptly forgot it as the front door opened immediately, as if someone had indeed been on the watch.

At the upper window Miss Nicola Lacey drew back with slightly reddened cheeks, humiliated to have been caught spying. She was also a little startled and by no means pleased, for some reason, to discover that Lord Kinross in person was even more striking than his portrait had led her to expect.

In the meantime Kinross was rendered acutely uncomfortable by the effusiveness of his greeting. He had not expected to recognize any of the servants, after so many years, but the ancient butler who hurried out and almost tearfully welcomed him seemed to have changed very little in the last twenty years. "My lord! Oh, my lord!" he cried. "I had given up hoping to live long enough to see this day!"

"Good God! Poole? Can it really be you?" exclaimed his lordship in astonishment. "I had thought you must have retired years ago!" He abruptly thrust the reins into Harewood's hands and sprang down to shake the butler's hand, saying with his easy charm, "How have you been keeping? And Mrs. Poole? Don't tell me she's still house-keeper here as well?"

"Very well, my lord, very well! All the better for seeing you at home where you belong, at long last!" said the butler fervently, clinging to his lordship's hand, his eyes suspiciously damp. "Mrs. Poole will be flattered that you should remember her after all these years, my lord. She's not as spry as she once was, but both of us could never leave Rosemullion, as I hope you know. And now that Miss Lacey is here to take over some of the responsibilities of so great a house, we both manage to go along well enough, despite our ages. But, my lord, you should have come back sooner. You have been sorely missed. Sorely missed."

Kinross was a little embarrassed by the urgency in the other's tone, and wondered whether something was seriously amiss there. But more than likely the words were merely prompted by the natural attachment of an old family retainer convinced there should be a Kinross at Rosemullion, as there had been for centuries. He also wondered briefly who Miss Lacey might be, but had no time to pose the question, for the butler was urging him inside, saying that Mrs. Chudleigh, his aunt, was eagerly awaiting his lordship in the crimson saloon, which his lord-ship might remember from his boyhood.

As they stepped into the great hall, Kinross halted, a little startled despite himself. If the truth be known, Rose-mullion had played little part in his memory, for his years there had not been particularly happy ones. Certainly he had forgotten that it was quite so beautiful. Or perhaps, as an indifferent child taking it for granted, he had never noticed. The entrance hall was darkly paneled in carved oak, in an old-fashioned style he did not much care for, even now, but the great floor-to-ceiling leaded windows more than made up for any gloominess there might other-wise have been. The beautifully carved staircase branched gracefully at the half-landing, and was constructed so that it seemed to float in the sun-moted air that poured in through the great windows behind it. Again his opinion of his aunt's unexpected wizardry increased, for everywhere was the gleam of well-polished wood and rich rugs, warmed by a huge bowl of golden flowers arranged with deceptive simplicity.

He had half-feared that after his butler's near-tearful greeting his entire staff would be gathered to meet him, but it appeared he was to be spared that, at least. As Poole explained apologetically, they had not known quite when to expect his lordship, for his letter had said only that he would be arriving on or about the ninth. And at any rate, Miss Lacey had feared such a reception would be too over-powering. And then, of course, there were very few of the old guard left who remembered his lordship, which Poole obviously considered close to being sacrilegious.

Kinross found himself grateful to the unknown Miss Lacey, and again wondered who she might be. But Mrs. Chudleigh, alerted by the voices, trotted out then, nearly as tearful as her butler, and again he forgot the matter in her breathless greeting.

Mrs. Chudleigh was a plump, easily flustered little woman, who did almost everything but fall on his chest, to his slight discomfort. Certainly her mannerisms would never have led one to believe she was as efficient as all signs seemed to indicate, and in fact he had invited her to take up residence there merely on a whim, having no particular expectation of achieving any noticeable results.

Mrs. Chudleigh welcomed Mr. Harewood with seeming real pleasure as well. Kinross had feared she would resent being obliged to entertain a houseful of strangers, but it quickly became apparent that she had received the news, if she were to be believed, with excitement bordering on delirium. As she said, it had been far too long since Rose-mullion had been opened for entertainment as in the old days, and usually they were so dull there that she some-times thought she would go mad with nothing but the sea to listen to. She only hoped he wouldn't be disappointed, for doubtless he had forgotten how inconvenient the place was, and how distant some of the guest bedrooms were from the main part of the house.

"On the contrary, I am almost overwhelmed by all you have managed to achieve here," he said truthfully. "I don't remember the place appearing half so welcoming, or warm, in all the time I lived here. You have achieved miracles, in fact, ma'am."

She blushed rosily, and disclaimed a trifle disjointedly, "Nothing will ever make it really comfortable, of course, for it is far too old-fashioned, but even I am surprised at how well it is looking. And of course I have dear Nicola, who has been an enormous help to me."

"Is that Miss Lacey? If so, that's the third time I have heard her name mentioned," said Kinross in amusement, beginning to think the matter something of a mystery. "Who is she? A new housekeeper?"

"Oh no! I wrote and told you when I meant to invite her to come and live here, I'm sure I did, for I would never dream of doing such a thing without your permission. She is related to the Kinrosses, though I am never exactly sure just how. She ought to be here to greet you, but unfortunately she is laid down upon her bed with a bad headache. I know how disappointed she must be."

"Well, I'm sure she'll soon recover from her disappointment. But you have made a liar of me, ma'am! I have been regaling Harewood all the way here with tales of rotting floorboards and damp ceilings. I do hope you haven't managed to abolish all the old inconveniences, for he will be sorely disappointed, I fear. I know he is expecting no less than smugglers appearing in the middle of the night, or perhaps an attack by marauding Turks."

Mrs. Chudleigh earnestly denied that there was any local smuggling done nowadays, though when she was a girl it had been quite notorious. And as for the house, doubtless Alex remembered that the bedchambers were all dreadfully low-ceilinged and gloomy, and no amount of modernization could change that. "I have always suspected, in fact, that the Elizabethans must all have been much shorter than we are today, for there's no denying the rooms are all decidedly cramped. Dear Alex has grown so tall, I fear you will be in constant danger of bumping your head."

She insisted upon escorting them upstairs herself, despite the still-hovering Poole, who obviously hoped for further conversation with his long-absent master. She took Mr. Harewood to his bedchamber first, apologizing for its size, and once he was left behind, proudly showed her nephew to his own, throwing open the door with something of a flourish.

Kinross's heart sank as he recognized she had put him in his father's old rooms, but he had not the heart to disillusion her. The truth was that he would have preferred almost any other room, no matter how small, to this vast and heavily furnished and paneled chamber, with all its accompanying memories. She also seemed disposed to linger to talk, but he soon gracefully got rid of her by pleading a need to change his travel-stained clothes.

As he was shrugging himself into his own coat in the absence of his valet, following behind with the bulk of his baggage, and ruefully regretting the impulse that had brought him here after so many years, Harewood wandered across from his own room down the corridor. He inspected the outdated magnificence of his friend's room with a jaundiced eye, and remarked in amusement, "It's obvious they've prepared the fatted calf for you, dear boy. Mrs. Chudleigh a favorite aunt, I take it? She clearly dotes on you."

"Good God, no!" said Kinross, hastily arranging a fresh cravat. "In truth, I scarcely remember her. As I recall, she lived in England when I was a boy, and her husband was still alive. I've seen very little more of her since. But I tell you frankly, I hadn't counted on being greeted quite so profusely. Or being obliged to sleep in my father's old bedchamber. In fact, I'm almost sorry I came. How is your room, by the way?"

"Not nearly so bad as you had led me to expect," conceded Mr. Harewood graciously, insensibly cheered by the small fire he had found burning in the grate in his bedchamber, and the inviting arrangement of flowers. "In fact, you were unnecessarily gloomy in your warnings, dear boy, for so far the place seems quite charming. It ain't London, of course, and I've never cared much for the sound of the sea, as your aunt said, but I don't mean to quibble. Did your father really use to sleep in this room?" he added, looking around interestedly.

"Yes, and call me in regularly for disapproving lectures. But I must confess my aunt must be far more capable than she appears. I did almost bump my head on the doorway as I entered, and I've a strong suspicion Fletcher won't approve of the distance he has to come from the servants' quarters, but so far I'm pleasantly surprised by all I've seen."

As it happened, he was soon to discover that it was not Fletcher, his august valet, however, who most disapproved of Rosemullion's amenities. When, sometime later, he strolled down to see how his groom was faring, he found that critical gentleman far from pleased by the deficiencies of the stables.

"Yes, I know, Trotter," he said sympathetically. "Do the best you can. And at least you must admit the country-side promises some good runs. It seems to be flat and largely empty."

"That's all very well, my lord, though the ostler at the last posting house was telling me how treacherous them hidden mine shafts can be," answered his groom repressively. "Apparently you're on them before you've had a warning, and if you should have the misfortune to fall into one, you may never be heard of again. But the stables are outdated, and from what I can tell, the fellow who calls himself head groom here is not one I'd hire as stable lad at home. But since he seems to have nothing under his care but a fat cob and two underworked carriage horses, it's perhaps not so surprising. What I'd like to know is what we're doing here, my lord."

"What, don't you agree the country is beautiful?"

His groom spat expressively. "I suppose it's pretty enough, if you happen to like rocks and the sea." His tone clearly indicated his opinion of the matter. "But what I've seen of the people so far, they're scarcely English, and far from appreciating us, neither. What I say is, we should have gone to Leicestershire, as usual, and forget all this nonsense."

Kinross laughed. "Don't forget, I'm one of them, however much I may have forgotten my origins. And we needn't stay long. But having shown my face, I can scarcely leave immediately, so you will have to suppress your English snobbery, at least for a little while."

Trotter had to be content with that, but he thought privately that far from seeming one of the dark, suspicious strangers he had met with so far in Cornwall, his lordship seemed to be wholly English. It was no wonder, in fact, that he never returned to his home, for a stranger, less hospitable place it would have been hard to imagine.

5

The rest of the house party seemed to share that opinion. They arrived around four, and at dinner that evening Miss Siddings, a spinster of indeterminate years and a somewhat strained air of girlishness, praised the beauties of Rosemullion lavishly, but playfully complained of the inns they had stayed in along the way, and the quaintness of the Cornish servants.

"Well, my bedchamber is charming, but I wonder if I'll be able to close my eyes," agreed Lady Layton in amusement. "It looks as if it must be haunted, and I expect any moment to see a robed monk appear through the paneling."

"Oh no!" exclaimed Mrs. Chudleigh, sincerely horrified at the notion. "At least we've never had any trouble of that kind, thank God. And even if it were haunted, I'm sure it wouldn't be monks who appeared, for all the Kinrosses have been staunchly Protestant, you know."

"Not to mention scarcely civilized, from all I've ever been able to tell," put in Kinross. "If a monk haunts the house, it is doubtless out of horror at my noble ancestors' godless ways."

Even with the presence of Miss Siddings, the numbers were uneven, since the unknown Miss Lacey had not recovered enough from her headache to come down to dinner.

When the ladies retired to the drawing room after dinner, Miss Siddings professed to be very much struck by his lordship's portrait over the mantel. "It's so particularly lifelike, isn't it, my dear Lady Layton?" she said archly.

"Really, the artist has captured dear Lord Kinross's expression to the life."

"Good God," exclaimed Kinross, coming in with the gentlemen in time to hear this. "I had forgotten that was ever done. My stepmother insisted upon it, but I certainly don't care to be obliged to look at it every evening while I'm here. Have Poole banish it to some dark attic, Aunt, preferably permanently."

Both Miss Siddings and Mrs. Chudleigh cried out against that, the latter swearing fondly that it was her favorite portrait in the house. "It makes you look so very much like your dear father, though of course I don't mean to imply he was ever as handsome as you, my dear."

His lordship looked acutely unwell, and retorted promptly, "In that case, I make you a present of it, ma'am. I shall have it carried up to your sitting room first thing tomorrow."

The rest of the evening passed uneventfully enough, and the tea tray was brought in early, since Mrs. Chudleigh, a very bad traveler herself, was convinced that everyone would wish to make an early night of it.

As Kinross carried her cup to Lady Layton, she said under her breath, "I see we keep country hours here. That should prove . . . convenient. I had to bring Miss Siddings to allay Layton's suspicions. She's a fool, but is devoted enough to me to be discreet, I assure you."

"And Percival?" inquired his lordship curiously, handing her her cup. "Why did you invite him?"

She shrugged her beautiful white shoulders, the emeralds he had given her sparkling dully in the candlelight. "He wanted to come, and will give Layton someone to play cards with in the evenings. Needless to say, my husband plays for nothing but chicken stakes," she added contemptuously.

"Then he will scarcely care to play with Percival. But are you sure your husband suspects nothing? What did you tell him about that necklace?"

She leaned back and smiled seductively at him. "That I

won it at play. He's far too greedy to object to so expensive a trinket. At any rate, don't worry. I can take care of Layton. Your aunt is more of a problem, for she obviously doesn't approve of me.''

He looked his surprise. ''I think you're imagining things. How the devil could she know anything about us?''

She merely shrugged again, obviously amused by his naiveté. ''In either case, it hardly matters. Will you come to me tonight? You needn't fear my husband, for he never travels well, and will be only too happy for an early night.''

After a moment he agreed to it, but added fairly, ''We can't always count on his being so exhausted. And if my aunt suspects something, I won't have her insulted. We must be discreet.''

''Darling, I am always discreet,'' she drawled provocatively. ''At any rate, I have said you needn't fear my husband. He values his reputation far too highly to risk a public scandal, even if he did suspect anything.''

Kinross moved away then, fearing to cause too much remark, and made vaguely uncomfortable by the position he had placed himself in. He did not, in truth, fear Layton, who must have some inkling of the affair between his wife and his host and obviously chose to be complaisant about it. But he disliked dissimulation, and began to wonder if it was time to bring the affair to an end, however beautiful Judith Layton might be. Then he dismissed the matter from his mind with his easy insouciance, and went to chat with his aunt.

Only Percival, his unpleasant eyes alert, observed this brief exchange. He suspected that an assignation had been made for that night, and wondered what Judith was up to. But since he had his own reasons for not wishing to end such an ill-assorted house party too soon, he hoped she wouldn't stir things up prematurely.

But it amused him to keep Kinross late playing cards, knowing he was too polite to refuse. For once even Harewood, who was unaccustomed to country hours and expected to be kept awake most of the night by the sound of the sea outside his window, made no objection, and so it was past one before the game at last broke up.

Kinross hurried belatedly up to his room, cursing Percival's insistence on playing cards and wondering if Judith would long since have grown bored and gone to sleep. He found his valet sleepily waiting up for him, and demanded his robe quickly, then sent him on to bed, pausing only to ask if everything was to the valet's satisfaction.

Fletcher bowed, and held his lordship's brocade robe for him, refusing to abandon his post until he had seen his master made ready. "As to that, my lord, the company in the servants' hall is a little strange, but congenial enough, I daresay," he said ponderously. "Which reminds me, I found this on your lordship's floor when I came in." He held up a folded sheet of paper. "Did your lordship drop anything?"

"No, not that I know of. Never mind. I'll attend to it later. Wake me early, for I wish to ride in the morning. That will be all."

Fletcher hesitated, then bowed and placed the paper on a convenient table before retiring.

Kinross waited only a moment or two before following his valet out, a little annoyed at the necessity of skulking about the corridors of his own house. When he had handed her her bedroom candle, Judith had managed to indicate to him which was her bedchamber and he reached it without incident, grateful that a low lamp had been left burning in the passage.

At her door he knocked lightly, then turned the handle and went in without waiting for an answer, having no desire to be found lurking outside her room at such an hour.

Everything was quiet within, and only a lamp left softly burning on the bedside table indicated that she was still expecting him. Her bed lay in shadow, the bed curtains undrawn, and he could see her form lying beneath the quilt. She seemed to be sound asleep.

He smiled and approached the bed. "Am I in complete disgrace, my love? I apologize, but Percival would play cards half the night and I couldn't get away."

Still she didn't stir. He wondered if she were annoyed with him, and merely feigning sleep, and sat down on the edge of the bed to remark teasingly, "This is ardor indeed! I may as well be your husband, I fear, for the romance has clearly gone out of our relationship if I am so easily forgotten."

There was still no movement from the bed. Despite the burning lamp there was little light in the room, and her face was turned away from him so that he couldn't tell if she were merely feigning sleep. But he noted the demureness of her nightrobe with amusement, suspecting she had been forced to don it in protection against the cold room. Her usual preference, as he well knew, was for diaphanous silk.

He was tempted to withdraw without disturbing her, but then was damned if he would scurry back through the halls so soon. He reached for the ribbon fastening at her neck and began to untie it, saying in amusement, "I begin to think you are more knocked up by the journey than your husband, Judith. Shall I go away again and let you get some sleep? Or can I make you forget your exhaustion for a little while?"

At last she stirred, mumbling something in her sleep and turning her head a little. To his astonishment, he found himself staring into the face of a perfect stranger.

Then before he could gather his scattered wits and withdraw, she opened her eyes. For a moment they were blank and still clouded with sleep. Then, as consciousness returned, she jerked up in alarm and opened her mouth to scream.

6

Kinross reacted instinctively, managing to get a hand over her mouth before she could wake up the house. But it was a mistake, he soon ruefully discovered, for his unknown bedmate proved to be a remarkably formidable opponent. Despite her slight size and having just been waked from a sound sleep, she fought like a wildcat, using her nails to good effect.

He swore as she managed to bite his hand, and caught one wrist, half-amused despite himself at the ludicrous situation. *"Ouch!* Hey, you little hellcat! I'm not going to hurt you! Good God, this is absurd. If you'll stop fighting me, I'll let you go."

His words must have had some effect, for abruptly she stilled, her breast rising rapidly under her demure nightdress and her eyes straining in the dim light above his hand. He began to feel guilty for frightening her, and added quickly, "I'm sorry! This is indeed unforgivable, but I didn't dare risk letting you wake everyone up. If you promise not to scream, I'll take my hand away. All right?"

She hesitated, then abruptly nodded. Gingerly he let her go, wondering what he would do if she tried to scream again or gave way to hysterics, as he deserved. He had seldom felt more of a fool.

Fortunately she was as good as her word. She pulled sharply away from him, still breathing a little fast, but she seemed to have lost her earlier terror, for she scrubbed at her mouth as if to remove the feel of his touch, and said scathingly, "I regret to inform you that Lady Layton elected to change rooms with me at the last moment, Lord Kinross. Unhappily for me you are in the wrong room."

47

He was surprised and rather intrigued by her unexpected self-possession. "That at least seemed obvious, or else I remembered less of the house than I thought I did. In fact, that must have been what was in the note that fool—" Then he remembered himself and broke off, to add quickly and with sudden curiosity, "But who are you? And how is it you know me?"

"I have lived with your portrait for almost a year, my lord. I believe it is a very good likeness," she answered dryly, sitting up more fully to begin to chafe her mangled wrist. "I am Nicola Lacey. I believe we are related, though the connection is admittedly slight. And I certainly had anticipated a more formal setting for our first meeting."

He couldn't help laughing. "You're mighty cool, I must say that! I'm grateful, for I feared to be faced with hysterics at the very least. Are you always so self-possessed?"

She flushed a little, and retorted tartly, "It's as well for you that I am, my lord! But it would help neither of us for me to carry on like a threatened virgin. Only I would have thought the first necessity in such an intrigue is to make sure you have the right room. Lord Layton's is only two doors down, after all. You would have looked even more ridiculous if you'd stumbled into his room instead."

He laughed again and said cheerfully, "Oh, then I would have pretended to be sleepwalking. And you are a most remarkable girl, Miss Nicola Lacey. I begin to think I should have come home a long time ago. Exactly how are we related?"

Abruptly she seemed to remember the extreme impropriety of the current situation, for she belatedly pulled the quilt up around her shoulders and drew her knees protectively up to her chin in a childish gesture. Both amused him, since it would have been difficult to have found anything more prim than her voluminous nightdress. She was not precisely to his taste, for usually he preferred more opulent women, but he admitted that her calm in the face of so unusual a situation intrigued him.

In addition, she was both younger and prettier than he

had expected. He had, admittedly, almost forgotten his aunt's protégée, but he had not expected her to be a self-possessed young woman with a striking mane of black hair and remarkably clear green eyes.

"Not close enough to permit midnight visits, I assure you," she answered dryly.

For answer he turned up the lamp, wanting to get a better look at her. He saw immediately that despite the childish posture, she was not as young as he had first thought her. But perhaps her oddly self-possessed air had something to do with that. Her body was slight beneath the demure nightrobe, and her face small and delicate, and she possessed a straight little nose and a well-molded mouth that combined to give her an odd gravity.

Her clear, deep green eyes were almost the color of the sea, and fringed by unexpectedly thick black lashes. They also seemed to have a habit of looking out in a slightly challenging way, as if she had not found life exactly easy or pleasant until now.

Nor was it only her eyes that made her remarkable, he saw now, for her hair was black and very thick, and, unbound, tumbled wildly about her face and shoulders in a way that was both beautiful and unexpectedly provocative in one of her matter-of-fact nature.

In fact, her face struck an unexpectedly familiar chord in his memory, though he was sure he had never met her before. He frowned, briefly chasing the elusive memory, amused to see she was looking him over almost as thoroughly, and with a great deal less approval, if her expression was to be believed.

"Guinevere!" he exclaimed suddenly, having captured the elusive connection. "That's who you remind me of."

Miss Nicola Lacey looked as if she suspected he was a fugitive from some madhouse. "Exactly how much did you have to drink tonight, my lord?" she demanded suspiciously. "I begin to think you are drunk as well as mad."

"Less than half a bottle, upon my honor. I'm not jug-bitten, if that's what you fear. But I've suddenly remembered who you remind me of. There was an illustrated book of Malory that was used to be in the library here. I wonder if it's still there? I was too young to be very interested in the stories, for I must confess at that age I found Malory dashed hard going, but I was fascinated by the illustrations. There was one picture I remember of Guinevere that I liked particularly. She looked a little as you do now, with her hair flowing romantically around her and her eyes a mysterious and bewitching sea green. I must remember to look for it tomorrow. But I am beginning to suspect none of this is real, and I'll wake up in the middle of an empty field in the morning with my pockets turned inside out, and no idea how I came there."

She had to resist laughing, he could see it in her eyes, and he liked the way she primmed up her mouth to keep from giving herself away. "I'm no knocker, if that's what you fear, my lord."

"What's a knocker?" he asked curiously.

She shrugged. "Mischievous elves who are said to cause trouble in the mines. Most Cornishmen are very superstitious, as you may remember. But I believe I am a common enough Celtic type, though one of my ancestresses was admittedly almost burnt as a witch in a much earlier age."

"If she looked like you, I can believe it," he said in amusement. "Which reminds me, I have yet to discover exactly how we are related. I don't remember my father mentioning any Laceys."

"Hasn't it yet occurred to you, my lord, that this is hardly the time or place to go into a detailed discussion of our respective family trees?" she asked with dangerous restraint. "I will remind you that you are in my bedchamber, at a highly improper hour, and moreover, that Lady Layton is no doubt waiting for you. Pray don't let me keep you any longer."

"No, no, I'm done with skulking through the halls for one night! At any rate, she's doubtless been asleep for hours now. And hasn't it occurred to *you* that my remaining is far less dangerous than my going? You will hardly wish me to be caught coming out of your room at such an hour," he added.

Then as she frowned in sudden alarm, he regretted teasing her. "I'm sorry! I shouldn't tease you. But you must admit the situation is an intriguing one. And don't pretend you're either shocked or alarmed by my presence, for you know I'm perfectly harmless. At any rate, I've a strong hunch that very little manages to alarm you, Miss Nicola Lacey."

"You should try waking up with a strange man looming over you if you think that, my lord," she grumbled. "At the very least I'm sure I'll have bruises tomorrow."

"Yes, but you're forgetting I'm no stranger, for we're related. And you shouldn't have fought me so hard. I probably bear teeth marks myself. But if I really have bruised you, I apologize. Here, let me see."

Abruptly he captured one of her wrists and raised it to the light to inspect it, then dropped a light kiss on her wrist before releasing it. "I didn't see any bruises. And still you haven't told me how we are related."

"I begin to understand your reputation, my lord," she responded wryly, safely tucking her hand away under the covers. "If I tell you, will you promise to go away? I fear I am not used to the sophisticated hours you keep, and would like to get some sleep at least before morning."

"Yes, I'd forgotten my aunt spun me some tale of your having a headache and being too ill to come down to dinner. You don't look particularly ill to me."

She hesitated, then shrugged. "I thought you would prefer to enjoy your first dinner without strangers present. And keep your voice down, for God's sake."

"Don't worry. No one can hear us. I *do* remember that from my childhood here. The walls are all half a foot thick," he retorted irrepressibly. "I do remember my aunt writing me your father had died. Who was he?"

She sighed and gave up the struggle. "His name was Nicholas Lacey," she explained in the voice of one humoring a lunatic. "But our connection, such as it was, is on my mother's side. *Her* mother was a Kinross, your grandfather's cousin, I believe, so you can see how remote is the connection. Certainly not enough to allow me to claim your aunt's—or rather, through her, your—protection.''

"Good God, my aunt may do as she wishes! I'm delighted she has the company. But surely you must have had some nearer relations to appeal to, ones able to provide you with a livelier existence? My aunt was bemoaning the isolation and lack of entertainment here only this evening at dinner.''

"I assure you I'm grateful for your aunt's kind invitation, and have no particular desire for a livelier existence. And I am used to solitude. I was born not five miles from here, and have never set foot out of Cornwall.''

He found it difficult to imagine such a parochial existence, and said with ready sympathy, "But you are far too young and pretty to bury yourself here! At your age you should be attending balls and flirting and enjoying yourself.''

"Since my father has been dead less than a year, I would hardly be attending balls and flirting and enjoying myself under any circumstances. But you would no doubt be surprised to learn that not everyone considers it a penance to live here, my lord.''

He found that difficult to believe, for in his experience all women craved excitement and almost constant entertainment. But he was beginning to think Miss Nicola Lacey indeed wholly out of his experience. She had at first been genuinely afraid, he knew, and later had pretended to be angry, but once her fear had subsided he thought she had betrayed almost no shock or embarrassment, as if finding a strange man in her bedchamber at such an hour were by no means out of the ordinary. The women he knew would either have feigned hysterics or turned coy, and all of them would have attempted to use the situation to their advantage. Kinross was remarkably lacking in the vanity most people expected him to possess, but he had reason to be familiar with the power his fortune had over women. But Miss Nicola Lacey, as if unaware of the opportunities inherent in so absurd a situation, instead tucked her knees under her chin and made no attempt to attract his interest.

"If you grew up within five miles of here, how is it I never heard of you before?" he asked curiously.

"We were hardly in the same social circles, my lord," she answered frankly. "At any rate, my father was considered something of a radical—at least by yours, or so I understand. My father held extremely unfashionable notions about the necessity of feeding the poor and maintaining Cornish traditions in the face of increasing Anglicization, you see, which was far from being popular with the local landed class. And since you went away to school before I was born, and have seldom bothered to return since, it is hardly remarkable you never heard of us."

He frowned, wondering if he had imagined the faint criticism in her tone. He had suspected it once or twice already, and was mildly curious what he could have done to offend her. But he answered easily, "No, my stepmother never cared for the place, and it was frequently too far to travel just for the school holidays. Nor did there seem any particular reason to come back in the last years. But how is it my aunt knew of you, then?"

She colored once more. "I was still at school when my father died and I was faced with the necessity of taking care of myself. My headmistress, who had a kindness for me, knew that I was related in some way to the great Kinrosses of Rosemullion, for it had used to be a joke between my father and myself, and wrote to your aunt without my knowledge. Your aunt disliked living here alone, and so was kind enough to offer me a home. But I am very aware that I must be grateful to you as well, my lord."

He wondered if that were the reason she resented him, and said immediately, "You are my aunt's guest, not mine, for you must know I've given her *carte blanche* to do as she wishes here. I am only grateful to have the place lived in—and restored beyond my wildest expectations. I remembered the place as falling down. I'm astonished at the changes she's achieved so quickly."

She hesitated, then shrugged. "You should have come

back sooner, my lord. But then, as you say, so long as Trelowarren mine continued to produce your livelihood, you had no real reason to come back after all.''

This time he was convinced he had not imagined the criticism in her tone. For some reason Miss Nicola Lacey did not like him. The fact amused rather than offended him, and merely added to the mystery she was assuming in his mind.

Then a faint sound outside caused him to stiffen, and drove all thought of her from his mind.

He was unsure of exactly what had alerted him, but he had very acute hearing, and a strong instinct for survival, and began to regret giving in to the impulse to remain once he had discovered his mistake.

She, too, as if sensing his sudden alertness, lifted her head and said sharply, ''What is it? Did you hear something?''

He made himself relax. ''No, nothing. Probably only a mouse. But I should undoubtedly be going. I assume you're not expecting someone else tonight?''

''Not unless another of your guests is roaming and finds the wrong room!'' she answered sarcastically. ''Or Lady Layton is out looking for you.''

He grinned despite himself, and tried to remember whether he had locked the door behind him.

Then as a floorboard creaked distinctly in the passage outside, he stiffened again, and made a lightning decision. As the door was thrust open he reached for Miss Nicola Lacey and kissed her thoroughly.

7

Kinross caught her with her mouth agape, so that it was far from being a romantic kiss. She was rigid in his arms, and he began to fear she would ruin everything by fighting him again.

Lord Layton took one look at the entwined couple on the bed and cried out in triumph, "Aha! I've caught you at last!"

Kinross, his besetting sin a liking for the ridiculous, as Mr. Harewood had frequently pointed out to him, stopped kissing his undemonstrative partner and exclaimed in disgust, "Good God, Layton, if you can't think of anything more original than that, I wash my hands of you. This is not some Cheltenham tragedy, you know—though I will admit it has all the elements of a two-penny farce."

Lord Layton was naturally thrown a little off his stride by this unexpected criticism, but he rallied quickly. "I have no doubt you consider it a farce to brazenly seduce a man's wife under your own roof, my lord! You thought I was a fool, but I was too smart for you. And if you think I'm going to support my wife while you have the use of her, you have another think coming. I'll divorce her, that's what I'll do, and then you'll have the pleasure of supporting her extravagances."

Kinross said in genuine contempt, "What a disgusting muckworm you are!" He moved, so that his companion was no longer in shadow, and added, "But as revealing as these confidences no doubt are, I fear you are in the wrong room. Now, I suggest you apologize and withdraw before you make any more of a fool of yourself than you have already."

Lord Layton gaped at Nicola as if he had seen a ghost. But the realization that his wife was not cheating on him did not seem to afford him the relief that might have been expected. "It's a trick!" he cried shrilly. "A trick, I tell you! You think to make a fool of me, but you won't succeed! Where is she? What have you done with my wife?"

"Well, she certainly is not under the bed, if that's what you're implying," retorted Kinross, fast losing all amusement in the scene. "Come on, admit you've made a mistake and withdraw with some dignity."

But he might have spared his breath. Lord Layton had long since fallen out of love with his expensive young wife. Marrying her had been his only act of folly in a life devoted to jealously husbanding his minor fortune. In a moment of weakness he had given in to the lure of her beauty, but he had very soon come to regret his bargain. Not only was she foolish and vain, and once the ring was on her finger wasted little further time in catering to the vanity of a husband who frankly bored her, but she was outrageously extravagant, and seemed likely to run through in a few years what it had taken him a lifetime to amass.

Lord Layton, himself an extremely thrifty man—his housekeeper said more truthfully that he was the biggest lickpenny of her acquaintance—had not taken long to awaken to the extreme nature of his mistake. His fortune was not large, but might have lasted him comfortably for the rest of his life if he were careful. He paid his servants extortionately low wages, pored over his housekeeper's accounts every month with a fine-tooth comb, looking for any signs of unnecessary extravagance, and was as a result cheated unmercifully whenever his servants thought they could get away with anything. He certainly had soon come to bitterly resent his new wife's expensive habits far more than her increasingly blatant infidelities.

"You can't pull the wool over my eyes!" he shrieked. "This is obviously some trick or other. What I want to know is, who is this?"

Nicola had been sitting there in frigid outrage, but she

said now, icily, "Lady Layton elected to change bedrooms with me, since she objected to the chimney's smoking in this one. I believe you will find your wife in the next room, probably sound asleep by now."

"Yes, but who the devil are you?" demanded Layton, almost beside himself with fury.

"Not that it is any concern of yours, but this is my cousin, Miss Lacey," Kinross said grimly. "She also happens to be my affianced wife. Now, having satisfied your curiosity, and assured yourself your own wife is in her bedchamber asleep where she belongs, I would suggest you take yourself off before I forcibly remove you. Do I make myself clear?"

When he started up deliberately, the other, by no means a courageous man and well aware that Kinross had the advantage of both youth and years of training in sport and self-defense, began to edge nervously toward the door. But he cried furiously, "Don't think you've heard the last of this, my lord! An unknown fiancée is mighty convenient—mighty convenient! But perhaps she doesn't know how you have lived in my wife's pocket for the last six weeks, making you both notorious."

Nicola spoke up again in tones of unmistakable contempt. "Your problems with your wife are hardly any concern of mine, sir. But perhaps you would care to search the room before you go. I hadn't thought even Lord Kinross capable of entertaining two ladies at the same time, but perhaps I underestimated him."

"That won't be necessary!" said Kinross, his blue eyes kindling. "His lordship is just leaving."

As Kinross started toward the door, Layton defied him only a moment longer, then scurried cravenly out the door.

Kinross took the precaution of locking it behind him. "What a mawworm," he said contemptuously. "I'm sorry for that, but thanks for not betraying me."

But the oddly self-possessed creature of a moment before had turned into an outraged virago. "I didn't do it for you, my lord. And at least now I begin to understand Lady Layton's insistence on a change of rooms!"

"Good God, you don't think I planned that, do you?" he demanded in astonishment.

"That is precisely what I think, my lord," she answered contemptuously. "You may have managed to pull the wool over that poor man's eyes—though even that is doubtful—but I am not quite so easily duped, I fear."

An unaccustomed flush stained his cheeks. "In case you're interested, that 'poor man,' as you call him, is one of the most pompous fools in London. And as for pulling the wool over anyone's eyes, I will admit I kissed you once I guessed what was happening, but it didn't change anything. He wouldn't have believed my visit innocent at such an hour if I'd been wearing Church of England vestments. I'm sorry, but neither one of us could have foreseen this chapter of accidents."

"Oh yes, I will admit you have been very clever, my lord!" she said bitterly. "But then, I should be surprised by now at nothing you do to get your way. I knew once you returned to Rosemullion everything would be ruined."

"Now, just a minute!" he protested in growing annoyance. "I've admitted I made matters worse, and everything that has happened tonight has undoubtedly been my fault. But I might equally accuse you of having planned the whole, for I have only your word for it that Lady Layton chose to change rooms, after all. And a lamp was left deliberately burning, as if in expectation of my visit. I still maintain my error was a natural one."

"I have no doubt it's very natural for one of your morals, my lord. But your effrontery passes all bounds. I have had my reputation ruined, and you dare to accuse *me* of planning the whole?"

"I'm merely trying to point out that appearances can sometimes be misleading. Why did you leave a lamp burning, by the way?"

For the first time that night she seemed oddly thrown out of countenance for some reason. "Because I'm afraid of the dark, if you must know," she acknowledged furiously at last. "Does that satisfy you, my lord?"

It was the last thing he'd expected. "You're *what*?" he

repeated incredulously. Then at her outraged expression, he couldn't help laughing. "You needn't be ashamed of that, you know. I used to be afraid of the dark myself, as I recall."

"Yes, as a child of ten, no doubt! And if you dare to laugh at me again I will . . . I will . . ."

"Cast a spell on me?" he asked in amusement. "After this disastrous night, I begin to think you are indeed a witch. Look, I realize you have ample reason to be angry, but you should know by now it does no good to rail against things you can't help. I learned long ago that it only exhausts you, and seldom makes any difference anyway. The trick is to try to make the best of a bad situation. I promise I won't let you suffer for my sins."

"I begin to think the whole world suffers for your sins, my lord," she answered contemptuously. "Certainly Lord Layton, his wife, and I are all your victims. Now, I am aware this is your house, but if you will have the goodness to vacate my bedchamber—however belatedly—I would be grateful. And you may be sure I have every intention of locking the door behind you to prevent a recurrence of this ridiculous scene!"

He saw that she was beyond reason at the moment and judged it wisest to say no more for the present. But he could not resist retorting, "If you had done so from the beginning we might both have been spared this ridiculous scene. We will discuss it again tomorrow, when you are more prepared to be reasonable."

"I have no desire ever to set eyes on you again, my lord!" she cried. "And I will certainly take care to lock my door from now on—or at least as long as your party is here from London."

He had to prevent himself from laughing as she rose, trailing her quilts behind her, to stalk to the door and open it. Still he hesitated, but then at her furious expression shrugged and gave up. True to her word, she turned the key loudly in the lock behind him as he went out.

He half-feared Layton would still be lurking about in the

corridor, but fortunately the passage was deserted. He shrugged again and returned to his own bedchamber, conscious of seldom having shown to worse advantage.

Once there, he went first to the table where Fletcher had laid the paper he had found. As he had suspected, it held a few cryptic lines in Judith Layton's sloping handwriting. "L. is suspicious," it said dramatically. "Don't come tonight!"

It was unsigned, but could hardly have been more damning, had Layton found it, if she had tried. He tore it up, annoyed with her cheap turn for histrionics, and even more by the scene he had just endured and the absurd figure he had cut. Then he went belatedly to bed, ruefully hoping the spirit of his father did not linger in the ornate room to haunt his dreams.

If so, however, he was unaware of it, for he went almost immediately to sleep and didn't stir again until his valet roused him in the morning.

Miss Nicola Lacey, not so lucky, would undoubtedly have envied him his repose, though it probably wouldn't have surprised her. She herself sat up in her chilly room for a long time after she at last had her bedchamber to herself again fighting a strong, if foolish, urge to burst into tears.

But if she were honest, she knew bitterly that she had no one but herself to blame for the undeserved loss of her reputation and the humiliating scene she had just endured. If Lord Kinross had proven more charming and handsome in real life than even his portrait had led her to expect, he was also undoubtedly even shallower and more self-centered. It should have come as no surprise to her that he was capable of sacrificing anyone in order to protect himself from the consequences of his own actions. Whether or not he had planned the whole, he had certainly been quick to take advantage of it to serve his own ends and to try to hide his affair from his mistress's jealous husband.

But what was far more inexplicable was why she, knowing what he was, hadn't sent him away immediately instead of giving in to the pull of his undoubted attraction.

It was that bitter thought that had kept her awake for some hours after he had gone.

Well, she would pay dearly for her few minutes of folly, for even if Kinross did not send her away, she could not remain under the same roof with him. She clearly would have to leave Rosemullion, and that was the bitterest pill of all to swallow. She had allowed herself to become too attached to it, and even to pretend that it didn't belong to Kinross at all, and that was her supreme folly.

But Kinross was right that it seldom did any good to rail against fate. She had known she was dreading his arrival, however much Mrs. Chudleigh had been looking forward to it, but not even in her wildest dreams had she imagined he could create such havoc in so little time. It was perhaps as well she would be leaving before he could cause her any more trouble.

That decided, she firmly turned down the lamp and went to sleep. But after so disastrous a night she shouldn't have been surprised that Lord Kinross managed to haunt even her dreams. Her troubled sleep was full of a handsome, irresponsible countenance and a pair of laughing blue eyes.

8

Since his mysterious new cousin didn't come down to breakfast, Lord Kinross also began to wonder if he might not have dreamed the whole of last night's absurd scene. But Lord Layton's unpleasant manner and his wife's remarkable efforts to speak privately with her host showed that the night's events were all too real.

Kinross pretended to misunderstand both Layton's scowls and Judith's broad hints, and did not linger long over breakfast. He rose as soon as decently possible and asked his aunt if Miss Lacey was still confined to her room with a headache.

Mrs. Chudleigh looked surprised at the question. "Oh no. She always breakfasts early. Did you wish to speak with her, my dear? I'm sure she's about somewhere. Shall I send for her?"

He declined this offer and excused himself, merely recommending to his guests that they enjoy a quiet morning. He added a little grimly, "Layton, I'd like a word with you later, if convenient," and strolled out without another word.

He was fortunate enough to find Poole outside the breakfast room. The butler seemed as surprised as Mrs. Chudleigh by the question, but was able to inform his lordship that Miss Lacey was presently in the drawing room arranging flowers.

Kinross once more declined an offer to go and fetch her, and went immediately across to the drawing room. There, sure enough, he found her artistically arranging an armful of red roses in a warm copper bowl.

Momentarily distracted by the attractive domesticity of

this scene, since he had wondered who was responsible for the imaginative use of flowers throughout the house, he said appreciatively, "So that explains it! Whatever her other virtues, and I must confess they seem considerable, I found it hard to believe my aunt was also the genius behind the beautiful flower arrangements to be found everywhere. You could easily make your fortune in London with such arrangements if the necessity should ever arise, for I haven't seen anything half so original there."

She had blushed a little at his entry, but now calmly continued with her task. "Thank you, my lord. If ever I am in need of employment, I'll remember that. But I doubt I would be happy to live in London."

He noticed that she was a very different woman this morning from the provocative creature of the night before. She was still in mourning, for her gown was of a demure gray, made high up to the throat and trimmed with a knot of funereal black ribbons. Her hair was confined in a severe style which still didn't manage to wholly hide its luxuriance, and she kept her eyes steadily downcast on her work, effectively concealing their unusual color. But the crimson splash of the roses she was arranging, and her obvious pleasure in them, somehow belied the drab image she was evidently trying to create.

He noticed that her hands were small and unexpectedly capable-looking, unlike the helpless white hands of the women he knew, designed to do no more than show off a jewel or flirt with a fan. But there was little sign of the oddly unconventional, or even icily contemptuous, damsel of the night before.

"Under the circumstances, I hope you're mistaken, Miss Lacey," he remarked. "But why weren't you at breakfast? Or do you still suffer from your mysterious headache of the night before?"

She raised her eyes briefly, the color startling in the pale background of her face. "I didn't get much sleep the night before," she reminded him deliberately. "But I always breakfast early."

"Ah, I can see you are going to be an excellent example

for me. Up early, already hard at work by ten o'clock. Under your influence I shall no doubt soon be a reformed character.''

"I doubt I shall have either the time or the desire to reform you, my lord," she said shortly, and returned her attention to her work.

"That is but one of the things we have to discuss. But much as I admire your artistic talent, Miss Lacey, do you think you could leave your work for a moment? I find it disconcerting to be obliged to talk to the top of your head."

She seemed to stiffen for some reason, then made herself relax again. "I don't believe we can have anything to discuss, my lord. In fact, whatever it is you wish to say to me I would prefer you to reconsider. Believe me, there is no need."

"On the contrary, there is every need. Tell me, are you always this difficult to propose to, Miss Lacey?"

For the first time that morning she betrayed a flash of the woman of the night before. Her green eyes jumped to his, unmistakable shock in their depths, and sudden color flooded her cheeks. Then the color as quickly departed, leaving her waxy pale, and she carelessly pricked her thumb on a rose thorn.

She dropped it immediately, saying in agitation and annoyance, "Oh—the devil! You have succeeded in surprising me after all, my lord."

There was speculation in his blue eyes, but he insisted on taking her hand, over her objection, and regarding the bright drop of blood that oozed from the small wound. "It doesn't look fatal. Do you always swear when you're surprised, Miss Lacey?"

She tried again to withdraw her hand. "Yes, an unfortunate relic of my unconventional upbringing, I fear. Oh, for heaven's sake, my lord, leave it! It's nothing but a small scratch."

He smiled, but insisted upon wrapping his handkerchief around the wound before adding lightly, "May I ask why you believed I'd come, if not to propose, Miss Lacey? Forgive me, but it seems the . . . obvious solution, under the circumstances."

She hesitated. "To buy me off, my lord!" she answered bluntly at last. "That seems the far more logical solution, believe me."

He raised his fair brows. "Dear me. You do dislike me, don't you?" Then as her eyes flew quickly to his own in surprise, he added mockingly, "I haven't forgotten you said something similar last night, to the effect that everyone else but me usually suffers for my sins. And you obviously believed me capable of having planned the whole to protect myself and Lady Layton at your expense. But I must confess I'm curious. Since we met for the first time last night, may I ask whether your obvious contempt for me springs from general prejudice against men of my type, or just men in general? Or do you have some basis for believing me so wholly devoid of conscience and honor?"

Nicola, thrown off her guard by his unexpected acuteness, was nevertheless obliged to admit that he was full of surprises that morning. She had braced herself for this interview, prepared to repudiate with contempt his dismissal and expected offer of money, but the very last thing she had expected was an honorable proposal of marriage from him. She did not need Mrs. Chudleigh's intelligence network to know he might have any bride he chose for the mere lifting of a little finger. It certainly had never occurred to her he might so far forget what was owed to his wealth and position as to throw himself away on a poor relation, whatever the provocation.

"It is not mere prejudice, my lord," she said evenly at last, resenting the position she unexpectedly found herself in, of being thrown on the defensive. "We may not have met before yesterday, but I know more of your activities than you might suspect. Your aunt follows your career with interest. In fact, she receives almost daily reports of your activities from her various friends in London."

His expression lightened. "In that case I don't blame

you for disliking me," he said ruefully, his eyes crinkling attractively at the corners. "In fact, I can think of few worse penances than being obliged to listen to secondhand reports of people you've never met. But is that your only reason for disliking me, or have I unknowingly offended you in some way?"

She flushed a little and said bitterly, "How could you have offended me, my lord, since I doubt you were even aware of my existence? At any rate, I have it on the best authority that you are the most popular man in London."

"Ah! I have offended you!" His expression was still pleasant, but there was a fixed look about his eyes, as if he were making an effort to hide his anger. "I think I have a right to know why."

She began suddenly to wish she had never begun this absurd conversation, but would not draw cravenly back now. "I have reason to believe I am more . . . strait-laced than those of your class, my lord," she conceded stiltedly. "At any rate, it is hardly my place to disapprove of whatever you may choose to do."

"And that is no answer at all. You obviously do disapprove. You should at least have the courtesy to accuse me to my face."

Thrown on the ropes, she said hotly, "That's unfair and you know it! My position as your dependent makes it so, if nothing else does."

This time he didn't quite manage to hide the flash of anger in his eyes. "And that is even more unfair, Miss Lacey. Unless you believe me so contemptible as to be likely to send you packing if you dare to anger me. And if so, no assurances of mine will serve to convince you I wouldn't."

She shrugged, refusing to back down. "Wouldn't you, my lord? In that case, I apologize."

"Tell me, does my aunt share your . . . dislike of me?" he asked evenly. "I must confess I hadn't guessed it."

"You must know she is highly attached to you," Nicola pointed out bitterly. "You seem to have the ability to charm people effortlessly wherever you go."

He smiled, though the expression did not quite reach his eyes. "But obviously not you, Miss Nicola Lacey. I must remember that. But you still have not told me what I have done to earn so much enmity. I must confess I also have never suspected my reputation was quite so unsavory."

"It is not so much what you have done, my lord! And this is a ridiculous conversation. I had no intention of saying any of this to you."

"Until I threw you into confusion by asking you to marry me," he said easily. "I must apologize. I really had no intention of insulting you."

She realized that he was indeed angry despite his smile and surface charm, but merely shrugged. "I'm sorry if I've offended you, my lord," she said stiffly. "But I will remind you it was you, not I, who insisted upon continuing this absurd conversation. I told you from the beginning it was pointless."

Abruptly he laughed, looking more himself. "No, no! Don't apologize. You are no doubt excellent for my vanity, if nothing else. You must meet my friend Harewood, by the way. You will have a great deal in common, for he agrees with you that I'm a hopeless case. But you have yet to tell me what I have done to deserve such contempt. I'm curious, for while I'm certainly no saint, I had never believed myself quite as black as that."

She could not resist pointing out dryly, "I believe no one ever does, my lord." Then when he laughed again, acknowledging the hit, she added deliberately, "And I have no intention of giving you any more excuse to make a fool of me, my lord. But I will give you one example only. Did you or did you not buy off Lady Jane Fox last summer in almost the same circumstances?"

For the first time he looked thunderstruck, which gratified her for some reason. "Good God! If my aunt's intelligencers told her that, it's no wonder you have such a low opinion of me. It seems a waste of breath, under the circumstances, for you obviously have no intention of believing me, whatever I say, but I give you my word I did not."

She looked her skepticism. "I think you should know, my lord, that the information came from Lady Holland, who had it directly from Lady Jane's mother herself."

His brows rose, but still his smile remained, as if he were merely entertained by the conversation. "And that of course makes it more reliable than my word? In that case there seems little more to be said."

She did not like the feeling of being on the defensive, as if she, not he, were behaving badly. But she said as calmly as possible, "Indeed, I warned you so from the beginning, my lord. It would have been far better had we never had this conversation. But it obviously will not surprise you when I tell you that under the circumstances, I must . . . decline your highly flattering offer, if indeed you were serious. In fact, I had already made up my mind to leave Rosemullion."

"I see. You are refusing an offer designed to save your own reputation because of some supposed slight done to some lady long before I met you? Forgive me, but that seems to be carrying principle a bit too far."

She had the absurd desire to hit him, for he made her feel a fool. "Not only because of that," she answered stiffly.

"I see. There are still more crimes you have laid at my door. May I not know what they are?"

"You have made your point, my lord," she said through her teeth. "For one of my position to refuse an offer from one of the biggest prizes on the Matrimonial Mart is no doubt laughable. Just chalk it down to my being one of the wild Cornish you so much despise."

His eyes narrowed abruptly. "Now we are getting closer to the truth, I suspect. Come on. Out with it!"

"Very well, my lord! If you must know, I disapprove of almost everything you stand for!" she said, goaded at last. "Your neglect of your local responsibilities, your frivolous dedication to nothing but your own pleasure, your repudiation of your origins, even your neglect of your aunt—all I find unforgivable!"

He had been looking astonished, but now he burst out, "My neglect of my *aunt*, did you say? I am not necessarily disputing the rest, but that at least surprises me."

Her lips twisted. "Your very surprise betrays you, my lord. It is clear you seldom remember her existence, when she is so painfully devoted to you." When he looked even more astonished she added unwillingly, "Do you really pretend you didn't know?"

"I don't pretend anything. I merely find it somewhat astounding, considering that I haven't met her above five times in my life," he pointed out sardonically.

It was her turn to be thrown into some confusion. "Five times? I can't believe that! She talks of little else but you."

"That may be so, Miss Lacey, but she lived in England when I was a child, and once I was at school I can recall meeting her only a handful of times. If she was indeed the doting aunt you describe, she managed to hide it very well, for I had no notion of it."

"Oh . . . oh well! Perhaps I misunderstood," she acknowledged unwillingly, embarrassed despite herself.

"I won't bother to point out that you might be equally mistaken about other things as well. But I must admit I have yet to see what any of this has to do with the question at hand, which seems a straightforward enough proposition."

She threw up her hands. "And that explains the difference between us more than anything I can say, my lord. I have told you I disapprove of you and everything you stand for, we don't know or even like each other, and you still expect me to leap at your offer."

"I expect you to be sensible, Miss Lacey," he said calmly. "I may be all those things you say, but if you are as straitlaced as you claim, you will prefer even my inadequacies as a husband to total ruin. And if you are relying upon Lord Layton to do the gentlemanly thing and keep his mouth shut, you are an optimist, believe me."

Then, as she paled, he grimaced and abruptly possessed himself of her hand. "Come, this squabbling gets us nowhere," he said persuasively. "As you so rightly pointed out, this unfortunate situation is my doing. You must allow me to make what recompense I can by offering you the protection of my name. Beyond that, if I am so distasteful to you, I give you my word I won't trouble you."

She could not resist saying with irony, "That, at least, I had little doubt of, my lord. I am hardly to your usual taste. But it is you who are being impractical, for I hope you won't try to convince me you are not concerned with the succession, at least. You will need a son sooner or later, which argues that you can hardly keep your promise not to trouble me."

He abruptly burst out laughing. "I suspect we shall do better than you believe. It was already obvious last night that you're hardly conventional. As for children, we'll deal with that when the time comes. What do you say? Shall we bury the hatchet and cry a truce?"

She stared up into his handsome face, a little surprised to discover how suddenly tempted she was to give in and accept his unexpected offer. She did not for one moment believe that if she were foolish enough to marry him he was capable of being faithful to her or of contributing to a marriage between two equals as she understood the term. But at least she thought he would betray her with charming insouciance, never be deliberately cruel, and probably always treat her with the easy charm that seemed to be second nature to him.

More, she would have to be blind not to realize that he would undoubtedly be delighted to leave her in possession of Rosemullion, returning only infrequently while most of the year quite happy to forget he even possessed so inconvenient a wife. It would mean she could live at Rosemullion for the rest of her life and not be faced with leaving when Mrs. Chudleigh grew bored and moved on, or he eventually married. Even more important, as Lady Kinross, however nominally, there was a great deal of local good she might accomplish, with or without his cooperation.

But weighed against that must be the fact that the

picture such a bloodless marriage conjured up, with him being charmingly unfaithful and content to leave her in the background, was an exceedingly depressing one. He would almost certainly come to resent her in time, and begin to chafe at so restrictive a marriage—particularly if he should ever fall in love at last. His proposal had certainly startled her, and he seemed resigned enough at the moment, but he could desire the marriage even less than she did. He had nothing to gain, after all, and everything to lose by so unequal a match.

Worse, the thought of being thrust into intimacy with this handsome stranger even on so limited a basis almost made her shudder. If it was disconcerting to feel as if his portrait had come suddenly to life, Lord Kinross in the flesh was admittedly even more formidably charming than his painted image, as she had already learned to her cost. To be obliged to face him over the breakfast table, if no more, as his wife, knowing that he must inevitably compare her unfavorably with the beauties he had known, and be bored by her lack of conversation and ability to sparkle, was oddly depressing.

Something of all this must have shown in her face, for he was looking down at her with discernment. "Don't think so much," he said persuasively. "It's a damnable muddle, I know, but I warned you it never does any good to rail against the inevitable. At any rate, don't you ever do anything on impulse, Miss Nicola Lacey?

She thought with sudden insight that that was a good part of his charm, and no doubt his weakness as well. He did seem to have the ability to ignore the consequences of his actions, and if that made him oddly attractive, and others like herself seem plodding by comparison, she had to remind herself that it also accounted for his charming irresponsibility as well, the consequences of which she was all too familiar with.

"Very seldom," she admitted truthfully. "I fear it's not my nature to ignore the consequences of my actions. I would no doubt bore you within a sennight."

She had made up her mind to refuse him. But fate, for

the second time in as many days, seemed to mock her, for at that moment the door to the drawing room opened, and Mrs. Chudleigh's shocked voice exclaimed from the doorway, "*Nicola!* I couldn't believe it when my maid just told me—oh, you wicked, ungrateful girl! But I should have known it was too good to be true when you pretended all these months to be so uninterested in my nephew!"

9

Nicola snatched her hand away as if it had been scalded, and Kinross swore under his breath. "I would advise you to say no more, ma'am," he said warningly to his aunt.

But Mrs. Chudleigh was too upset to be so easily deflected. "And to think that I could have nursed such a viper in my bosom all these years!" she wailed. "Pretending to be uninterested in him, when all the time you were no doubt planning this! But then, I suppose I shouldn't be surprised, for I have no doubt you were raised on immoral principles, just as people have tried to warn me. And this is how I am repaid for refusing to believe such things of you. Well, you may pack your bags and leave today, miss, for I won't have a . . . a *strumpet* in my house!"

Nicola had stood stiffly under this onslaught, making no attempt either to intervene or to try to defend herself. But Kinross flushed darkly and thundered, "*Aunt!* I think you should know that Miss Lacey has done me the honor of consenting to be my wife."

Both ignored Nicola's stiff gesture of repudiation. Mrs. Chudleigh gasped as if she had been struck. "Your wife?" she cried in disbelief. "Oh, she has been cleverer than I thought! You, who might have had a duke's daughter for the lifting of a little finger, to be trapped into marriage by such a little . . . Oh, it makes my head spin!"

"That's enough! I will speak to you later." Kinross almost physically thrust her out of the room, despite her protests, and closed the door behind her before turning back to say apologetically, "I'm sorry! I had no idea—"

"Don't apologize," Nicola snapped. "It is only what everyone will be saying soon enough. Or did you expect people to believe you had fallen desperately in love with me?"

"I don't particularly care what people may believe," he retorted grimly. "And if necessary I will make it plain that it was I who trapped you—as I intend to do with my aunt. But you may believe that as my wife you will be treated with all the respect due to you."

"While you are around!" she countered contemptuously. "And do you think I wish the real story to be made the property of every malicious gossip any more than your aunt's version? Either is an unconscionable intrusion on my privacy."

"Very well, then." He was evidently controlling his temper with an effort. "What is it you're suggesting instead? You saw my aunt. Unless we are indeed to be married, and that quickly, it is clear she will no longer protect you. And while I can give you enough money to support yourself, obviously, you have already repudiated the suggestion I might buy you off. And at any rate, I think you would find such a life very lonely."

She was surprised at his unexpected insight, but said stiffly, "I am not penniless. If I gave you that impression I didn't mean to. My father left me a small inheritance, and the house we had always lived in, which returns a small rent at the moment. I have enough for my needs."

"And where do you intend to go? Not to Falmouth, I fear, or even Truro, for such gossip has an unpleasant habit of following you. Believe me, I know."

She had in fact intended going to her own old school, where she had a standing offer of employment, but she saw bitterly that he was right, and Mrs. Berryhill could not afford to hire her under the circumstances. Mrs. Chudleigh would never be able to hold her tongue, and if even the servants knew, it wouldn't take long for such gossip to travel. She said more stiffly still, "I shall find employment somewhere. Perhaps in London."

"That will scarcely be any better. If my aunt has the

wide correspondence you say, you may be sure you will be found out sooner or later. I regret it, but that's the way of the world."

"In short, someone is again paying for the consequences of your misdeeds, my lord!" she flashed bitterly. "Through no fault of my own I find myself driven from my home and unemployable, and that after only one meeting with you. I shudder to think what would happen after a week in your company."

But that seemed to divert him, for abruptly he laughed. "Come, these accusations are getting us nowhere. Is marriage to me really so bad an alternative?" He frowned suddenly, and added, "Unless . . . Am I being a complete fool and there is someone else? If so, you needn't worry, for I will make all right with him. Good God, is that it? If so, why didn't you say so from the beginning?"

She was tempted to agree, merely to put an end to the argument, and could not help wondering as well what he could possibly hope to say to put everything right when he had been found kissing her in her bedchamber at two in the morning. But instead she said wearily, "There is no one else. Would that ease your conscience if there were?"

"Good God, woman, you would try the patience of a saint! You have made it plain you don't like me, but it is not a love match I am proposing. I am merely trying to save your reputation—lost, admittedly, through no fault of your own. I do you the credit to think you would scarcely wish, or credit, an undying pledge of affection from me under the circumstances, since we scarcely know each other. Or is it Lady Layton you object to? If so, I can assure you the affair is at an end after last night."

"Until the next one."

Then she was sorry to have revealed so much, and took an agitated turn around the room, trying to calm herself. At last she took a deep breath and turned back. "I'm sorry. I fear I'm behaving badly. Neither of us is to blame for last night's fiasco, and I am fully aware you can desire such a marriage less than I. It must seem incredible to you that I might refuse your . . . very obliging offer. But I do refuse. I believe I am indeed somewhat straitlaced, as I said, and I only know that between your notion of marriage and mine there can be no meeting, my lord. I am not sure I will ever marry, but if I do, I shall wish for something more in my husband than a . . . a handsome face and a charming manner. And I will want far more than a fashionable marriage between two people who seldom meet. If that sounds naive, as I have no doubt it must to you, there's no help for it.''

He smiled wryly. ''At least I can't accuse you of pulling your punches, can I? But I think you will prefer even my frivolous nature to total ruin. I am not such a coxcomb as to offer you material advantages in place of the marriage you desire, but at least I can promise you I will try to make you happy, and will do my best not to force myself upon you any more than necessary.''

She was bound to acknowledge that he was behaving far better than she would have believed, or indeed had any right to expect. He could not be accustomed to meeting with such dislike, and must certainly never have expected to have his offer thrown back in his teeth when he finally got around to dropping his handkerchief. But he had accepted her diatribes cheerfully, even gracefully, and gallantly refrained from pointing out to her that he, and not she, had most to complain of in so uneven a marriage.

Moreover, everything he said was true. If Mrs. Chudleigh withdrew her patronage, Nicola could find lodgings somewhere without the immediate need of supporting herself, but Kinross was right to say it would be a very lonely life. Worse, the thought of removing from Cornwall, or at least the sea, and being cooped up in some big city such as London was infinitely depressing to her.

But if she were more honest with herself, the thought of removing from Rosemullion was most depressing of all. It seemed particularly unfair that her whole life should be disrupted and she be forced from the place she loved because of the brief visit of one who would soon be gone again, no matter what happened.

Abruptly she came to a sudden decision. ''Very well! I

won't consent to marry you, my lord, for I am determined such a marriage would be disastrous. But I will agree to an engagement. It occurs to me that perhaps we are both taking too melancholy a view of the matter. My reputation will be protected by an engagement nearly as well as by a marriage, and in a few weeks you will be returning to London again. By that time the talk should have died down, and in a little while no one will be very surprised when our engagement comes to a natural end. In fact, I will take great pleasure in publicly jilting you, if you must know.''

He burst out laughing. ''Why do I get the feeling that you will? If nothing else, you should be good for my vanity, Miss Nicola Lacey, for you are fast deflating it. I'll agree to that, though I think you're being unnecessarily optimistic. Where scandal is concerned, the world has a long memory. But we'll worry about that later. At the moment, let's shake to seal the bargain.''

She regarded him mistrustfully, but then unwillingly put her hand in his. He laughed down at her for a moment, looking suddenly uncannily like his portrait, the sun from the windows behind him gilding his fair hair. But this time he did not kiss her hand as she had half-feared, but merely stood holding it in his warm clasp.

''To the strangest engagement that ever a man embarked on!'' he said ruefully. ''I won't say whether you are going to prove good or ill for me, my sweet Cousin Nicola, for I don't know that yet. But I suspect you are certainly going to prove unlike any other female of my acquaintance, and I must confess I had begun to believe all women were alike.''

She had to resist her betraying blush—as well as a faint disappointment when he released her hand again. Unpleasantly aware of it, she escaped quickly, vowing that for her own peace of mind, if not her resolution, she would do as well to spend as little time in Lord Kinross's company as possible.

For his part, Kinross watched her leave with a half-frown in his eyes, that was still there when the Honorable

Gideon Harewood next encountered him. "Hey! What's this? You look like you're on the way to someone's funeral," he exclaimed cheerfully. Then, remembering the mood of his recent breakfast companions, he added feelingly, "Which seems to be the general mood around here. Told you this house party was a mistake."

Kinross abruptly shook off his unaccustomed abstraction. "You've got the wrong sacrament. In fact I'm on the way to someone's wedding, not funeral. My own, if you must know."

Harewood's jaw dropped. "If that's a joke, it ain't funny," he said briefly. Then, as his suspicious nature stirred, he added in horror, "Good God! Is that what was eating Layton at breakfast?"

"I've no idea. And it's hardly a subject I'd joke about. But Judith Layton is not the bride, if that's what you fear. Despite what you think of me, I draw the line at becoming betrothed to another man's wife." He glanced around and added abruptly, "Here, come out with me for a stroll. The very walls around here seem to have ears, and too many people know about the affair already."

When he had regaled the aghast Mr. Harewood with the night's adventures, and their aftermath that morning, the latter was torn between incredulity and relief at the close call Kinross had had. But he said sarcastically, "Only you would go off to tryst with one female, find yourself in the wrong room, and linger to be caught by the first female's husband! But you're right, marriage is the only answer. Is she an antidote?"

His tone suggested it was a foregone conclusion, which caused Kinross to smile. "Not at all. In fact, she's remarkably striking—especially in dishabille, though she seems to affect a prim look in the daytime. I've a suspicion you'll approve of her."

"If you imagine I'm likely to approve of such a disgraceful affair, you're mistaken. But I should have known she'd be a beauty. If it had been me who found myself forced to marry a perfect stranger, she'd be a dried-up spinster at her last prayers. In fact, I'm beginning to suspect your aunt's right, and this poor relation engineered the whole. Mighty clever, if so, I might add.''

"Then I give her credit for being an excellent actress as well as clever. I told you you'd approve of her. She's made it plain enough the marriage is little more to her liking. In fact, she will consent to no more than an engagement, and means to jilt me as soon as the gossip dies down. Odd as it may seem, she desires something more in a husband than a . . . What were her exact words? Oh yes! A handsome face and charming manner.''

Mr. Harewood's jaw dropped for the second time. "If she said that, she's either dashed clever or one woman in a million," he said with conviction. He considered the matter for a moment, and added gloomily, "Probably dashed clever. She consented to the engagement, didn't she? Even if she means to break it off now, which is by no means probable, the weight of your money will soon enough dissuade her.''

"Good God, you're as flattering as she is! It plainly has not occurred to you that some woman might actually love me for myself." Then, as his friend looked appalled at his slip, Kinross laughed. "Never mind. I have given up on that hope. But really, Gideon, as my oldest friend you should have warned me my reputation had become so unsavory, for I had no notion of it.''

Harewood snorted. "The only reputation you have is for being far too easygoing for your own good.''

"So I had always thought. But it seems my aunt has a better network of spies than we ever seemed to manage during the war and has ferreted out all my misdeeds. Miss Lacey accused me to my face of having paid off Lady Jane Fox under just such circumstances.''

Harewood, who was one of the few who knew the truth, exploded. "If so, I hope you explained that you did no more than pay for her recuperation after she had made your life miserable for months, hounding you unmercifully, which is more than any other man would have done!''

Kinross shrugged. "What do I care what version gets

around? But I had no idea my activities were the interest of so many people. I may as well publish my every doing in the newspaper and be done with it.''

"Aye, just as well," agreed Mr. Harewood philosophically. "It's one of the drawbacks of being the richest prize on the Matrimonial Mart. But if this cousin really don't approve of you, which I'll admit would be a novelty, why not just buy her off as well? You can afford it, God knows."

Kinross's good-humored expression darkened slightly. "Yes, that's what she obviously expected me to do. But whatever my reputation, I'm not quite such a loose screw as that. She already thinks my money insulates me from the consequences of my actions. She may be right, but I have no intention of letting an innocent victim bear the brunt of my own sins."

Mr. Harewood looked skeptical. "Aye, but if she really dislikes you, it's better than being forced into marriage with a perfect stranger. Not that being disliked mustn't be a new experience for you."

Kinross frowned. "I assure you I don't expect to be liked by everyone I meet! Nor do I imagine I'm irresistible to the opposite sex. My God, what a coxcomb you must think me if so. Between you and Miss Lacey I'm even beginning to wonder myself."

10

Kinross next went to speak to his aunt, thinking ruefully he had seldom enjoyed a morning less. He told her bluntly what had happened, making no attempt to excuse himself, but while she was properly shocked, she was by no means reconciled to the necessity of his throwing himself away on so unequal a match.

"I don't mean to sound hard," she insisted ingenuously. "But I think even Nicola would agree she could scarcely have hoped for so brilliant a match. It's a great pity it ever happened—not that I mean to scold you, for I'm sure it's not my place. But aside from every other objection, I really think Nicola is far too serious for you. I would have said before this that she didn't even approve of you, for she is absurdly straitlaced, you know, and forever devoting herself to good works. I'm sure it's all very admirable, but I've always thought it would be most uncomfortable in a wife, particularly to one in your position, my dear Kinross. Not to mention being such a waste!"

"She doesn't approve of me," Kinross admitted ruefully. "It seems you have given her a most unflattering portrait of me, ma'am. How did you come to learn of it anyway?"

"I felt a little ill in the night and rang for my maid. She saw you coming out of Nicola's room and felt it necessary to inform me this morning."

"I'm obliged to her," he said a little grimly. "But I certainly didn't get the impression last night that Miss Lacey was absurdly straitlaced. In fact, I would have said she was more angry than shocked or embarrassed. But I confess I'm becoming more and more curious about her. She mentioned something last night about my father thinking hers a radical, and you said something almost the same just now. And now you tell me she is forever engaged in good works, which is unusual, to say the least, especially for a member of this family. Why did I never hear of them before now?"

"Oh, the connection is quite remote," his aunt assured him. "I forget how it goes, but it is through her mother, I do know that. Oddly enough, I think Nicholas Lacey was the one who never approved of the relationship—at least that's always the impression I got. But then, he was quite unconventional, you know. He was always writing radical tracts and stirring up the locals, so you can understand why there was some resentment against him from people like us. I don't know if he really was behind some of the riots of the last century, as some people have accused, but he certainly was involved, and even supported the miners in their demands."

"Was he a labor organizer?" he asked in surprise.

"Oh no, nothing so vulgar as that!" his aunt assured him hastily. "I don't mean to give you the wrong impression, for he was quite a charming man, and received by everyone. But he always made me feel vaguely guilty, as if the condition of the poor and all the injustices in the world were my fault, which of course is absurd. I'm sure I regret such things as much as anyone, but there is nothing we can do, after all."

Kinross looked skeptical. "It's no wonder he was unpopular. Are those the immoral principles his daughter has been raised on? That will make her unusual in London."

"Oh well, I didn't mean that, exactly. But it is true that her father maintained a friendship with some very questionable people, including that Mr. Bentham who writes all that republican nonsense, and some of it quite salacious as well, or so I understand. Naturally I have never read any of it."

"Naturally," agreed Kinross gravely. "Does Miss Lacey share these highly unconventional notions?"

"Oh I don't mean she's as bad as that. In fact, I'm quite

fond of her. But you must see what I mean that she will hardly make you a conventional wife. It would be different if she herself were ambitious in that direction, but until today I would have sworn she wasn't. I really didn't think she would ever marry, if you must know."

He thought cynically that his aunt had also been prepared to take advantage of that situation for her own ends, and had made no attempt to make sure she met any eligible males. But he said merely, "You begin to terrify me. Will she make me give away all my money to the poor, do you think?"

His aunt's shocked expression made it plain she did not find that funny, and reminded him that his father, as well, had never possessed much of a sense of humor. He dropped the subject, but went away with a good deal to think about. It was not difficult to see that his aunt was more than willing to sacrifice her companion's reputation for his own advantage, which surprised and annoyed him slightly. Like Nicola, she also seemed convinced that a temporary engagement would suffice. But unfortunately he lacked her confidence either in her ability to silence her maid, or in the belief that the public's memory was so conveniently short. But in the end he could do no more than extract a promise from her to apologize to her protégée and accept the engagement with at least the semblance of complaisance.

But then, he was unwillingly aware that his aunt was right, and a Puritan wife would indeed be an oddity in his world, where the fashionable were adept at averting their eyes from any troubling reminders of the real world outside their privileged existences. And when misfortune was thrust before their notice, they were always ready, like his aunt, to believe that such evils were inevitable, and so shrug aside any responsibility.

He was, in fairness, bound to admit that he was little better. And a wife devoted to good works was likely to soon grow wearisome, as his aunt had suggested. The few philanthropists he had known had all seemed to possess even less humor than his aunt, and took themselves far more seriously. And if Nicola Lacey were indeed a free thinker, like her father, she was unlikely either to fit in or to appreciate the shallowness of the *ton*, where women with any more serious idea in their heads besides what ball gown to wear that evening were apostrophized as bluestockings and were generally unpopular.

It was unfortunately a little late for such worries. If the story were all over the house by now, as seemed likely, both Nicola and his aunt were being naive to believe it still might be hushed up. Nor, despite what his aunt had just told him about his prospective bride, did he place any real reliance on Nicola's vow to jilt him in the end.

He was realistic enough not to blame her for such practicality, but could not help wondering if her philanthropy would long survive her transformation into exactly the rich and fashionable woman she professed to despise. At the very least, his coming marriage should prove interesting. He wondered how Miss Nicola Lacey would take to London, and even more amusing, how London would take to her.

His ensuing interview with Judith Layton was even more unpleasant, but at least allowed him to dismiss any lingering doubts he might have had about Nicola's complicity in the absurd tangle.

She was waiting for him when he came downstairs again, and pouted provocatively at sight of him. "Darling, there you are! I have been trying to speak with you all morning. Layton has told me everything, of course! He thought I'd be annoyed, but of course I guessed immediately what had happened. Was there ever so nonsensical a mix-up?"

He suddenly had no desire to discuss it with her, but said merely, " 'Nonsensical' is not the precise word I would have chosen, I'm afraid. I thought you said you could handle your fool of a husband?"

She came closer, so that he could smell her intoxicating perfume. "I can!" she said huskily. "He must have had too much to drink last night. You needn't fear it will happen again. I've made it plain the laughingstock he'll appear if he dares to divorce me. But you must admit it was better for him to have burst in on the scene he did, instead of the one he might have. I almost wish I had been there, for it must have been hilarious. I can imagine how shocked he was.''

He looked at her as if with new eyes, not much liking what he saw. ''You have a strange sense of humor, in that case,'' he said a trifle grimly. ''In fact, why did you change rooms with Miss Lacey at the last minute?''

Her eyes narrowed; then she shrugged and laughed. ''Oh well, I'll admit I suspected Layton meant to try to trap us. Don't be cross. You should in fact be grateful to me, for you would hardly relish being named in a divorce suit any more than I would. And I never expected you to be there, of course, for I wrote you a note telling you not to come.''

''And slid it under the door for anyone to find. In the meantime you saw no harm in allowing your husband to burst in on Miss Lacey—to teach him a lesson, is that it? It didn't occur to you that at the very least she would be frightened and embarrassed, and at the worst, Layton would find me there, as he did?''

She came to wind her white arms around his neck. ''Darling, what does it matter? She'll get over it. From what I hear, she's an old maid and can use the excitement. Of course I never expected you to be there anyway. Should I be jealous? She hardly seems your type.''

He unwound her arms. ''I am beginning to wonder what my type is. But I'm afraid the joke's on you, my dear. Thanks to your ill-timed sense of humor, I have had no choice but to ask Miss Lacey to marry me. Unlike you, she failed to see the humor of being caught with me in her bedchamber at two o'clock in the morning, and neither did my aunt when she came to learn of it.''

For a moment she was unable to disguise the fury in her beautiful eyes. Then she seemed to realize she had betrayed herself, and turned away to inspect her reflection in the mirror, to carelessly tweak a curl into place. ''Darling, don't be melodramatic. Nothing happened, after all—or at least I'm assuming nothing did. I can make sure Layton keeps his mouth shut, believe me. Buy this Miss Lacey off, if you're so worried. She's some penniless cousin, isn't she? God knows you can afford it.''.

When he merely stood regarding her, she had the grace to flush a little, then shrugged and turned back. "Oh, very well, marry the chit if you insist! I had no idea you were so gallant. I confess I might have been tempted to let Layton find us if I'd guessed you were so easily duped, my sweet. But in either case it need make no difference to us, surely?'' Again she tried to wind her arms around his neck, at her most flirtatious.

He adroitly stepped back. "I've always admired your single-mindedness, Judith. It's one of the things that first attracted me to you—aside from the obvious fact of your beauty,'' he said truthfully. "But I have no intention of risking a second visit in the middle of the night from your overzealous husband. I can hardly be forced into marrying both of you.''

His manner was quite pleasant, but not for the first time she found it impossible to penetrate his charming mask to discover what he was really thinking. When she had first succeeded in capturing his attention she had assumed, from his reputation, that he would be easy to manipulate. But instead she had found him unexpectedly and oddly elusive. He was an attentive lover, generous and charming, but she had never quite been able to convince herself she knew him any better now than at the beginning of their affair.

She had indeed come there with the notion of trying to force him into marrying her, for she had thought him conventional enough to feel constrained by his sense of honor if he were to be responsible for the breakup of her marriage. Only, at the last minute the night before, she had suddenly developed cold feet, recalling Percival's sneering comments and fearing that she would lose everything.

Well, it appeared Kinross was just such an honorable fool, but she had merely succeeded in engineering his marriage to some penniless little nobody instead. It was a bitter pill to swallow, but she was not the woman to admit defeat so readily. So she smiled and abruptly assumed the practicality she knew he admired in her on occasion. "As you wish! In fact, whether or not you are married means little to me. And my foolish husband seems ready enough at the moment to believe you came all this way to carry on an intrigue with your mousy little cousin. This engagement may provide the perfect blind for us. Have you thought of that?"

She smiled, convinced of her own allure, and wisely dropped the subject. The engagement was a nuisance, but no more, and might even prove convenient, as she'd said.

11

Nicola, in the meantime, was dreading being required to meet the rest of Kinross's guests. She was tempted to again plead the excuse of a headache to keep from going down for dinner, but wouldn't give Kinross the satisfaction of thinking her such a coward.

Unfortunately the headache was real enough after her sleepless night. Nor did a second and still more painful interview with Mrs. Chudleigh help any.

To his credit, Kinross had obviously kept his word and told his aunt the truth, but that worldly lady could hide from Nicola even less than from her nephew the fact that she was less than enthusiastic about the match. She was bitter in her animadversions against Lady Layton, however, whom she obviously blamed for the whole. She had been dreading housing her, and after this she was sure she would have trouble bringing herself even to be civil to the woman.

That her nephew was equally responsible for carrying on an affair with his mistress under her husband's very nose she conveniently managed to overlook, however. Nicola was half-amused by this willful deception, but chose to put an end to the pretense at once.

"Whatever Lord Kinross may have told you, ma'am, I have no intention of marrying your nephew. I have told him I will agree to no more than an engagement, just until any gossip there may be dies down. He didn't believe me, I suspect, but you may be very sure I meant it."

Mrs. Chudleigh could scarcely hide her relief, and any remaining constraint in her manner dropped away. "Oh, my dear, I'm so glad. I had no wish to offend you, but I can't think such a marriage would work. You are from two different worlds, after all, and worse, Kinross is used to being courted by the most *ravishing* beauties. I don't mean to be unkind, but it is always best to face facts. I fear you would only be made unhappy if he should grow bored with you, which would be bound to happen. I don't mean to suggest he would ever mistreat you or be deliberately unkind, for you must agree his manners are charming, and so unaffected! I sometimes think his wife will be the luckiest of creatures, for I'm sure there's not a sweeter-tempered man living. It's no wonder he is so sought-after. But . . . well, you are so much more serious than he is, aren't you, my dear, and know very little of his world, after all. And of course I would hate to lose you as well, for I flatter myself we get along so well. I hope you know how fond of you I have become."

Nicola was tempted to point out that if she married Kinross Mrs. Chudleigh would not be losing her, but on the contrary gaining a niece, but restrained the unkind impulse.

But Mrs. Chudleigh had already hurried on, "And you needn't worry, my dear. Naturally I have already threatened to dismiss Mary if she dares breathe a word of any scandal, and I'm sure Lord Layton will have no desire to publish what happened." She caught sight of the clock then and exclaimed, "Heavens, is that the time? I must go and change for dinner or I'll be late. Really, I can't help thinking if that creature had any decency she'd leave, but then , it's been obvious from the first that she hasn't any. Which reminds me, will you tell Poole to serve the best burgundy? My dear brother was always most particular about his wine, and I'm sure Alex is the same."

From which Nicola gathered wryly they were back on the same footing, Mrs. Chudleigh having dismissed any possibility that her companion and general dogsbody might one day become her nephew's wife.

But she obligingly went down to confer with Poole, who

assured her with dignity that he knew just what his lordship liked, before she herself went reluctantly up to change for dinner.

She had not many dinner dresses, for she had never had occasion to need them, and her mourning state limited her choice even further. In the end she chose one of her oldest and least becoming gowns in defiance of the occasion, knowing she could never compete with the voluptuous Judith Layton. Let Kinross make what he could of it. She had not discussed the subject with him, but cravenly hoped he meant to delay announcing their so-called engagement as long as possible. And certainly, from her unrelieved black, he could not flatter himself that night that despite her words, she was eager to take advantage of the situation.

Nor, if she had ever been tempted to abandon her scruples and accept Kinross's offer, did her reception among his chosen friends that evening encourage her to hope that she could ever be accepted in his world. She had seen the assembled guests only at a distance, and had found little to appeal to her, and they proved even more unlikable and unfriendly at close range.

Lady Layton was flirting with a tall, dissolute-looking gentleman as Nicola came in, and though she was facing the door, pretended deliberately not to see her. Nicola, who scorned being jealous of such a woman, nevertheless had no trouble in disliking her heartily. She thought she looked vain, immoral, and unexpectedly stupid, for all her success at achieving her ends. Her husband was standing a little apart, scowling at his wife's flirtation with another man; and though Nicola felt sorry for him, she liked him little better. He seemed unpleasant and ill-at-ease, as if despite his title he never quite fit in; and when he saw her he couldn't resist looking her over as if mentally undressing her, obviously trying to discover what so notable a connoisseur as Kinross could see in her.

She blushed hotly in resentment, but was fair enough to acknowledge that it would have been difficult for either of them to overlook the unfortunate circumstances of their first meeting.

The other young lady, Miss Siddings, was overdressed for the occasion, and seemed merely foolish, simpering at something a slightly portly, exquisitely dressed gentleman was saying to her. Nicola had seen him arrive with his lordship and knew him to be the Honorable Gideon Harewood, reputedly a close friend of Kinross's.

It became immediately apparent, when Mrs. Chudleigh performed the flustered introductions, that most of the assembled guests dismissed her at once as of no importance. She had seen that Lord Kinross was not yet in the room, a circumstance she was uncertain whether to be sorry or grateful for, but Lord Layton bowed coldly, Miss Siddings regarded her curiously and uncharitably and seemed disinclined toward friendliness, and the tall, unpleasant-looking man, who turned out to be Sir Guy Percival, looked Nicola over with his heavy eyes in a manner that seemed assessing and oddly unpleasant.

Nicola found herself also disliking him on sight, for no other reason than his unpleasantly drooping eyelids and faintly sneering expression. As for Lady Layton, beautiful in white and gold, with sparkling emeralds around her throat, she regarded Nicola mockingly, with a small condescending smile taking in her modest toilette and lack of jewels before turning away again without bothering even to acknowledge the introduction. She could hardly have said more plainly that she regarded her as no competition whatsoever.

Nicola was left standing alone, as effectively snubbed as she had ever been in her life. She was angry enough to want to turn and walk out without another word, but would not give them the satisfaction of being rid of her so easily.

It was left to Mr. Harewood, who evidently possessed a kinder heart than the rest, to hesitate, then walk over and engage her in rather stilted conversation. But even he seemed reserved and by no means friendly.

Fortunately—or perhaps unfortunately, as it turned

out—Kinross came in almost immediately, followed by Poole and two footmen. Nicola was thus given an excellent opportunity of observing the truth of Mrs. Chudleigh's belief that he had only to enter the room to dominate a party. It was as if they had all been colorless puppets only waiting for him to breathe life and vitality into them. He looked exceedingly handsome in evening dress and seemed to bring good humor and normality into the room with him. Certainly the ladies present, and Nicola was ashamed to say she was no exception, turned eagerly toward him, all boredom instantly evaporating. Even Mr. Harewood looked vaguely relieved to see him.

But a moment later Nicola had reason to regret his presence, for she saw that the footmen bore silver buckets of champagne, and Poole was importantly bearing a huge silver salver of champagne glasses.

She must have looked as appalled as she felt, for Kinross caught her eye and smiled reassuringly across the room at her before saying cheerfully to the room at large, "I'm sorry to be late, but I had to organize some champagne. This is something of a celebration, in fact. I want you all to drink with me."

He waited until Poole had passed out the glasses, while Miss Siddings made fatuous comments and Lady Layton looked suddenly furious. Nicola couldn't be sure, but she thought Mr. Harewood also stiffened beside her, and Mrs. Chudleigh looked torn.

The atmosphere could hardly have been less festive, but Kinross blithely raised his glass and exclaimed, "I wish you to drink to my future bride, Miss Nicola Lacey!"

Not very surprisingly, the evening deteriorated rapidly after that. Lady Layton flashed Nicola a look of sudden venom, and deliberately put down her glass and did not join in the toast. Sir Guy Percival looked both amused and unpleasantly speculative, and Mr. Harewood resigned. It was left to Miss Siddings to explain and comment foolishly, which seemed to be her alloted role in life.

Kinross could hardly have been unaware of the awk-wardness of the scene, and the lack of enthusiasm among his friends, but no one could have guessed from his demeanor that he was not embarking on a highly sought-after engagement. Nicola did not know whether to give him credit for his acting ability or to believe him wholly insensitive to atmosphere. But she feared he would have no desire to compliment her on her acting skill in return, for she knew she appeared wooden and wholly unconvincing as a blushing bride.

But Kinross seemed capable of coping even with that, for he easily parried Miss Siddings' foolish questions, maintained the semblance of a celebration until dinner was announced, and then insisted upon escorting his betrothed in to dinner himself, ignoring the superior claims of his aunt and Lady Layton for his arm.

As they went in together, he said in a low voice, "You will have to look happier than that, my dear Nicola, or everyone will indeed begin to suspect the engagement. You look as if you're going to a funeral, in fact."

"I would have said the same accusation could be made of most of your friends, my lord," she said bitterly. "It must have been obvious to you that no one in that room tonight approved of our so-called engagement."

"Good God, what does that matter? I'm not marrying to please them."

She regarded him in growing dislike. "I can't decide whether you can really be quite so frivolous or if this is a mask put on for my benefit. But you can't really expect me to believe you are wholly indifferent to what your friends think of so disastrous a marriage?"

"And I can't decide whether you really hold me in so much contempt, or merely believe me in need of a sharp set-down. But since we are now officially engaged, I wish you would call me Alex. Or if that seems too friendly, under the circumstances, at least drop my title. We are cousins, at the very least, and everyone knows I dislike formality. But with the exception of Harewood, of course, none of these people are particular friends of mine. Did you think they were? It's no wonder you hold me in such contempt.''

She regarded him in astonishment. "Are you telling me you held a house party for a group of people who are none of them your friends? For God's sake, why?''

"Harewood wondered the same. And I must confess I'm beginning to wish them all at Jericho," he said cheerfully. "But at any rate, none of them need bother you. If they become too unpleasant I'll get rid of them, and they are hardly representative of those you'll meet in London, believe me.''

She turned away in incredulity, both because he seemed to accept that she would be going to London with him, despite everything she had told him to the contrary, and because she couldn't believe even he could be so insouciant as to invite four people he disliked to come so far from London on an extended visit. Her contempt for him deepened, and she began to wonder if despite his noble demeanor he was nothing but a charming, weak fool. She certainly doubted he could get rid of his guests easily even if he wanted to, and began to question whether he would have the resolution to even try.

But it seemed his aunt was not the only one in his family capable of ignoring unpleasant reality at will. Kinross himself seemed to take nothing seriously, least of all the thought of marriage to a total stranger. It showed her just how unimportant marriage was to him, and should be a lesson to her if she were ever again tempted to abandon her scruples.

12

D inner was also strewn with minefields, as Nicola soon
discovered. After the first few she gave up trying to
avoid them, determined to show Kinross exactly what he
could expect if he were so foolish as to marry her. She did
not deliberately draw attention to herself, and held her
temper with what grace she could manage under his
friends' condescension, but she answered their snide
questions truthfully, refusing to prevaricate for their
benefit.

Judith Layton started it, pointedly fingering the
sparkling emeralds around her own throat and saying
provocatively, "But Miss Lacey wears no jewels, Kinross.
How remiss of you."

By Sir Guy Percival's expession of enjoyment and her
husband's sudden suspicion, Nicola had no trouble in
deducing that the emeralds about her own neck were a gift
from Kinross. She put down her knife and said pleasantly,
"No, I don't care for them."

"You have indeed found a paragon among women in
that case," remarked Percival with his faint sneer. "But
rather a waste for a man of your wealth, wouldn't you
say?"

"I would agree with you that I have indeed found a
paragon, but the answer is that I haven't yet had time to
buy her a betrothal gift," said Kinross easily. He studied
Nicola, appearing to consider the matter, and added, "I
think pearls, now that I consider the matter, don't you?
Sparkling stones are always slightly vulgar somehow."

At Judith Layton's sudden annoyance Nicola had to
hide an unworthy amusement. She had not expected Kin-

ross to protect her from the others' malice, nor was she certain from his bland manner whether his insult had been intended. But in either case it was now plain that he was indeed the source of the expensive emeralds around the other's white throat.

Lady Layton fingered them again and said drawlingly, "Thank you for the compliment, darling. But if emeralds and diamonds are vulgar, I don't in the least mind appearing common."

"Especially when they suit you so well," agreed Percival smoothly. This time there was no question about the underlying malice. "But I take it the . . . er . . . engagement is somewhat sudden if you haven't even had time to buy a betrothal present? This is indeed romantic. Almost a fairy story, in fact."

Again there was no difficulty in recognizing the sting behind the supposedly bland words. But Kinross said cheerfully, as if taking them only at face value, "Yes, isn't it? I'm sure you'll agree I've been luckier than I deserve."

"Someone has," drawled Lady Layton. "A fairy story is indeed a good name for it. You're Cornish, Miss Lacey?" Her tone implied her opinion of the fact.

Nicola decided to take her tone from Kinross, at least in the present circumstances, however much she might resent his laying her open to this. "Why, yes," she said sweetly. "Lord Kinross and I are distant cousins, in fact. Or had you forgotten he was born in Cornwall as well?"

Judith looked annoyed at her slip, but Kinross merely grinned. It was left to Mr. Harewood to unexpectedly come to Nicola's rescue. "In that case you can no doubt tell us waht we ought to see, Miss Lacey. Kinross is wholly unreliable about the local sights."

"What, do you mean to trot about playing tourist, Harewood?" demanded Percival with raised brows. "That should afford entertainment for the rest of us. I had no notion you were so energetic."

"If I'm in the district I may as well see something of it," retorted the other irritably. "Besides, there seems to be devilish little else to do."

"I would like to see you dashing about looking at dolmens and quoits, Gideon," Kinross agreed. "For once I must side with Percival."

Nicola glanced at Kinross sharply, again wondering if he were quite so simple as he seemed, or if his words indeed held a hidden sting. But again his handsome, cheerful face revealed little of what he was thinking.

"What's a dolmen?" inquired Miss Siddings curiously. "And a . . . What was it you said? Quirt?"

Nicola forgot her suspicions in renewed annoyance when Kinross said, "You'll have to get Miss Lacey to explain them to you. I'm afraid Harewood is right, and I'm shockingly uninformed on the land of my birth."

Nicola had no desire to be forced into explaining anything to a tableful of shallow people who had no real interest in the subject and could scarcely even trouble to hide their boredom, but was annoyed enough to assume a tour guide's manner and say brightly, "Quoits, not quirts. Both are Stone Age burial chambers, found extensively in Cornwall and Ireland, but very few other places. There are several excellent examples around here, if you would care to see them. They are really quite fascinating and estimated to be at least four thousand years old."

Miss Siddings shuddered dramatically and said frankly, "It sounds ghoulish to me. Were people really buried in them?"

"Oh yes. Some are quite famous, like the Nine Maidens near Lands End. Then there are the Merry Maidens, which are large stones, nearly fifteen feet high, said to be maidens petrified for dancing on the Sabbath. Close to them are two other menhirs, as they are called, known as the Pipers, allegedly two young men who played for them, and thus met the same fate."

"Really, they're quite disappointing, though," objected Mrs. Chudleigh, silent until now. "I thought them nothing but a tumbled pile of stones when I first saw them, certainly bearing no resemblance to maidens or anything else. And like Miss Siddings, I've always found the thought of them quite ghoulish."

"I remember seeing the Nine Maidens as a child," observed Kinross, looking slightly interested. "I'm sure I was too young to really appreciate them, but I didn't find them ghoulish at all. Were they burial chambers as well?"

Nicola was obliged to be grateful to him for his show of interest, whether feigned or not. "No, probably used for some sort of cremation. No one really knows, I think. Of course the legends that built up around them are mainly a Christian attempt to explain them." She had briefly forgotten herself in her own interest in the subject. " 'Maiden' is said to be a corruption of 'maedn' or 'maen,' Cornish for 'stone.' And the Hurlers, in Bodmin Moor, were said to be men turned into stone for profaning the Lord's day with hurling a ball. But there are other legends that grew up around such stones as well, for the Merry Maidens are on the site of the last great battle in the west, when the Saxons under Athelstan defeated King Howell and his Cornish forces. Under that legend the Pipers are said to be the rival kings, and about them lie the bodies of their slain."

"You sound very knowledgeable on the subject," remarked Kinross. "Do you speak Cornish as well, Nicola?"

"Cornish antiquities were a particular interest of my father. But no one speaks Cornish anymore, I'm afraid. The last woman to speak the Cornish tongue reputedly died in 1777."

Kinross looked rather startled. "That's a remarkably positive date. How can you be so sure?"

"Her name was Dolly Pentreath and she lived in Mousehole. My father once met her."

"Yes, but is the language dying out wholly bad, Miss Lacey?" Harewood asked curiously. "I would have thought that the sooner the county emerged into the nineteenth century and became indistinguishable from England, the better."

She glanced at Kinross, and was momentarily tempted to say no more, knowing it would be a waste of her breath.

Then abruptly she was ashamed of her cowardice, for she no longer cared what these shallow people thought of her, after all. "We are not indistinguishable from England, for we have little say in our government, and are generally considered by most Englishmen to be little better than barbarians," she said deliberately. "And our speaking of English was imposed from without, as a conquered people, not because of economic necessity. The language is lost completely now, for there were almost no written records of it, and whatever your politics, I think that must universally be considered a tragedy."

"Yes, but the Cornish people are almost unintelligible, even when supposedly speaking English," pointed out Mrs. Chudleigh foolishly. "I can't think what difference it can make."

"As far as I'm concerned, the Cornish *are* barbarians, or at least the peasants I've seen since we arrived," put in Lady Layton rudely. She added caressingly to Kinross, "In fact, it's obvious you can hardly be Cornish, darling, with your fair hair and blue eyes. Miss Lacey, now, looks far more typical of the Cornish people I've seen so far."

Nicola took great pleasure in saying, "Then I'm afraid looks are deceiving. The name Kinross is almost certainly of Celtic origin, I believe, while my own family is descended from one Gerald de Lacey, a Norman Frenchman and one of William's barons."

Kinross's blue eyes shone with appreciative laughter, again surprising Nicola, and he said readily, "Oh, I don't dispute it. From all I've been able to tell, my ancestors seem to have been a thoroughly rascally lot. The title was obtained by the first Alexander Kinross as a reward from Elizabeth for little better than piracy, however convenient she may have found it, and his successors seemed to have continually skirted the thin edge of the law. Certainly they did their share of smuggling over the years, and Rosemullion itself was built with plundered gold, or so the story goes."

"How thrilling!" gushed Miss Siddings. "Are there still pirates here?"

"The Royal Navy has pretty effectively put a stop to piracy these days," said Nicola dryly.

"But not to smuggling, or so I understand," offered Kinross curiously. "Even if my own family may have turned belatedly respectable."

She shrugged. "As long as there are heavy duties and poverty in Cornwall, there will be smuggling. The late war did much to encourage it, with the general starvation, the heavy duties on salt, and the dislocation of the usual Cornish markets. I can remember when the fishermen couldn't afford enough salt to cure their pilchards, unfortunately the mainstay of a great many local diets. Their seine nets were sometimes emptied directly on the fields for manure, for it was worth little more. But more often they would leave their hauls in the shallows until enough salt could be smuggled from France to cure them. I couldn't find it in me to blame them for that."

"Good God, no," agreed Kinross easily. "But usually their haul is less basic, isn't it? I can remember my father telling me most of the brandy drunk in the county was smuggled, and a good deal of the tea and gin."

"Yes. Most people wink at smuggling here, and it's difficult to get a conviction, even when smugglers are caught. There are reputed to be whole villages involved in the trade, for it sometimes takes several hundred men to transport the goods, once they're landed."

"I can remember when I was a girl there used to be pitched battles between rival gangs," put in Mrs. Chudleigh with a shiver. "I fear Lady Layton is right, and most Cornishmen are little better than barbarians, under the skin."

"But you're not above drinking run burgundy, ma'am, or buying French silks and velvets," pointed out Nicola wryly.

"Oh well! I'm sure I never approved of that horrible war anyway, and it was almost impossible to get any luxuries otherwise. I must say I have a sneaking sympathy for the smugglers, for the duties are iniquitous."

"Well, I have a sneaking sympathy for them as well, for

I must confess I always wanted to become a smuggler myself when I was a child," said Kinross. "It sounded far more romantic than the life laid out for me. I once tried to convince a boatman I knew then, and who I was convinced was among the brethren, to take me out with him. He refused, whether because he was wholly innocent or because he suspected I would be nothing but a liability to them, I'll never know. But I'm afraid we can't just flout the laws we don't like, Aunt. In fact, I hope we're not still drinking run burgundy here?"

"It would be impossible to tell," his aunt answered truthfully, "for your grandfather and even your father used to wink at any suspicious doings, and were not above buying a cask or two if offered. But as Nicola says, smuggling has never been taken very seriously here in Cornwall."

As Kinross looked rueful, Nicola said, "I said I can't blame the poor people for smuggling in necessities to survive, ma'am. But the ultimate answer is not to wink at the smuggling, but get the laws changed that impose such hardships on the people."

"A herculean task, I fear," said Kinross with cheerful indifference. "You might as well try to convince the locals to pay full price for their brandy. Both are impossible, I would say."

"I doubt you'll be as tolerant when it comes to Cornwall's other most frequently smuggled commodity," said Nicola dryly. "It's not only the royal treasury that's being robbed, for copper and tin ore are frequently smuggled out to trade for the brandy, gin, and perfume being smuggled in. Most mine managers find it impossible to stamp out the practice."

"Well, I for one don't care about smuggling," pronounced Miss Siddings, stifling a yawn. "Everyone does it, even in England. But what about the wrecking we've heard so much about? Is it really as dreadful as they say?"

Nicola stiffened, sorry now she had prolonged the discussion. "I'm sure any stories you may have heard have been exaggerated," she answered shortly.

"I do know that mine managers and owners certainly deplore the practice of wrecking," said Kinross, "and not necessarily on moral grounds. Frequently an entire mine will be emptied if there is a ship threatened off the coast. I can remember watching one foundering off the Manacles, which can be spotted from the headlands here. I'm afraid I was avidly curious to watch it go down, conscienceless little beast that I was. I don't remember if Trelowarren was emptied, but I do remember there were watchers all along the shore, following it like vultures."

Nicola had to swallow the sick bile rising up in her throat. "Fortunately there is a great deal less of it these days," she said quickly, trying to change the subject. "And it's not nearly so brutal as it once was."

"The wrecking laws encouraged the prevention of any sailor or passenger from reaching the shore alive," explained Kinross for his guests' benefit. "If there were any survivors it was not considered legally a wreck. It used to be a brutal business indeed, for the wreckers, frequently entire villages, I'm afraid, made sure that any survivors never reached shore. I don't think anyone ever actually lured ships in, as used to be rumored, by simulating a bobbing ship with a lamp tied to a cow's tail, or by bonfires on shore. But along these coasts, as I remember, there's usually no need. They're treacherous enough to be the graveyard of far too many ships as it is."

"What are the Manacles?" inquired Miss Siddings. "Is that what you called them?"

"Again, my cousin will have to correct me, but as I recall, they're a group of treacherous rocks just off Porthoustock, not too many miles from here. It's a reef, but all but one of the rocks are covered at high tide. Those with local knowledge can pass safely through the channel between the reef and the shore, but larger boats always give the Manacles a wide berth. If they're blown off course, they stand little chance of avoiding being broken up on the rocks. Thousands of men have lost their lives there over the years."

"Do you sail, my lord?" inquired Nicola in some surprise.

He grimaced ruefully. "I used to, as a boy. I haven't had much opportunity in recent years."

"Yes, but getting back to the wrecking," pursued Mr. Harewood, unexpectedly interested, "what made the difference, Miss Lacey? You said it's not nearly as bad as before."

Nicola was far from pleased to have the conversation returned to that particular subject, but she said, "I doubt anyone really knows. My father always maintained it was directly due to Mr. Wesley's influence."

As Miss Siddings looked curious, Kinross explained, "She means the Methodist preacher, I believe. I knew he was reputed to have spent a good deal of time in Cornwall, but I've never heard him credited with that particular virtue. He was certainly unpopular with the gentry, at least at first, for they thought he stirred up the populace unnecessarily."

"In point of fact, they should have been grateful to him, for he taught the poor to dwell on something besides their empty bellies," answered Nicola.

"Dear me, I do believe we have a Puritan among us," drawled Judith Layton unpleasantly, obviously deciding Nicola had dominated attention for far too long. "Are you a Methodist yourself, by any chance, Miss Lacey?"

"Not at all. I think the poor would have been far better served by concentrating on their hunger and doing something about it," she retorted bluntly.

Kinross burst out laughing. "I begin to think my fiancée is a radical, not a Methodist," he corrected. "But then, I was warned your father was a friend of Jeremy Bentham's."

Nicola flushed, which annoyed her. "If it's considered radical to think men should be paid a living wage and be able to support their families with dignity, then I'm unashamedly a radical," she uttered challengingly.

She was begininng to be familiar with his charming

ability to slide away from any confrontation, for he said lightly, "It's only radical for someone in your position to care, my dear. Most of the women—and men!—of my acquaintance are too busy planning their next dinner party or purchasing a new hunter to know or care what the lower classes are suffering. I honor you for it."

She was rather annoyed to find the wind thus adroitly taken out of her sails, however little she believed he meant what he said, but Percival said unpleasantly, "I must confess I can't resist the supreme jest of the richest man in England about to take a radical to wive. I applaud your tolerance, my dear Kinross, but I wonder if you've fully appreciated the irony yet. I also wonder how long Miss Lacey's admittedly admirable principles will survive after her marriage."

"I am tempted to show you," Nicola retorted, hating his sneering self-satisfaction.

Mrs. Chudleigh, who had been aghast at the direction the conversation had taken, and had several times tried to capture her protégés's eye, rushed hurriedly into speech. "Really, Nicola, the dinner table is hardly the place for such a discussion. I'm sure we all deplore the poverty in the world, but we are hardly going to solve it tonight."

Nicola's green eyes began to flash a little alarmingly. "And when would it be a good time to discuss it, ma'am?" she inquired with deceptive calm. "Are you afraid it might upset our appetites to realize children are starving not a mile from here?"

It was Kinross who looked a little startled. "Surely you exaggerate?"

She could not hide her contempt. "It is a long time since you were home, my lord," she reminded him. "You might be surprised at what you'll find."

He frowned again, but this time Mrs. Chudleigh firmly steered the conversation onto safer ground.

Nicola, convinced it was pointless to pursue the topic, said no more, and contributed very little to the rest of the dinner-table conversation. The remainder of the evening was dominated primarily by Lady Layton, who kept the conversation firmly on people and events that Nicola did not know, and peppered her conversation with appeals to Kinross to remember when Lady Dawlish gave that ball last spring where Bertie walked around the ballroom on his hands, or when dear Duncie lost a packet at the Derby last year and had to borrow coach fare home again.

Kinross's charm was such that it was impossible to tell whether he saw through this obvious ruse, but Nicola no longer much cared. She excused herself as soon as possible after the tea tray was brought in, and went up to bed, convinced that if nothing else, she had succeeded in demonstrating to Lord Kinross exactly how undesirable a marriage between them would be.

And since that had been her main purpose after all, she was at a loss to explain why the obvious truth of that statement should rankle so much.

13

If Nicola expected Kinross to ignore her or to immediately try to put an end to their absurd engagement,
she was to be disappointed. He sought her out shortly after
breakfast the next morning, as if nothing were in the least
wrong, and invited her to go on a picnic with his guests.

She was conferring with John Carhays, the architect in
charge of the structural renovations being carried out at
Rosemullion. He was a modest and likable young man who
had been educated in England but had chosen to return to
his native Cornwall despite the fact he could make a far
better living elsewhere. She honored him for that, and
usually they were on friendly terms, but for some reason he
appeared withdrawn and stiff that morning, which had
puzzled her a little.

She had decided to ignore it, and was discussing the
coping along the east end of the building with him, which
was dangerously loose, when Kinross came in with his
usual easy charm. Even to her biased eyes she was bound
to acknowledge he instantly made young Carhays appear
colorless and even stiffer by comparison, though the
architect was a personable enough young man.

"There you are," said Kinross. "Are you always such
an early riser, Nicola?" he teased. "I can see you will
indeed have to reform me."

She could not prevent her betraying flush, but stiltedly
made the necessary introductions. To her amazement,
young Carhays grew even more stiff if possible. If she
hadn't known him so well she would almost have said he
was sulking. Since she knew he was grateful for being given

the job of restoring Rosemullion, she was even more at a loss.

Fortunately his lordship seemed not to notice, but chatted pleasantly with him, complimenting him with flattering sincerity on his work and promising to take a tour around with him in the near future.

At least she was bound to acknowledge that Kinross did not seem to reserve his charm for only his social equals, nor did he condescend to the young architect. But Carhays responded only unwillingly, and soon made an excuse to leave them, their own earlier discussion unfinished.

Nicola watched him depart with furrowed brow, wondering what on earth could be the matter with him. She turned back only when Kinross echoed her own thought. "What's the matter with him? Or does he disapprove of me too?"

"I've no idea," she answered rather shortly. "Perhaps he has something on his mind."

Kinross's fair brows rose. "And I imagine I can guess what it is too," he said lightly. "I thought you assured me there was no one else?"

When she merely looked genuinely puzzled, he abruptly smiled down at her in a half-exasperated way. "Good God, I am beginning to think you really are a witch, my sweet cousin, for no real woman could be as unworldly and naive as you seem to be. Can it really be, with all your shrewdness, you haven't guessed that what's wrong with young Carhays is jealousy? He looked, in fact, as if he would have liked to shove my commission and my compliments down my throat, but was too well-bred to do so."

She stared at him aghast, not wanting to believe it, but unable to explain the architect's unlikely behavior that morning in any other way. She was even more annoyed that Kinross should have been so quick to see it when she herself seemed to have been willfully blind. It had not occurred to her to see Carhays in any other light than as a friend, but it was not impossible that he, lonely and educated above his fellows, and thus at ease in neither world, had mistaken her friendship for something much warmer. If so, she was deeply chagrined at her blindness. She was not so naive as Kinross suggested, nor so vain that she imagined every young man who was pleasant to her was in love with her. Certainly their conversations had seldom gone beyond business or their mutual concerns over Cornwall's future.

But she had no desire to hurt him, if Kinross's suspicions were correct. And if Carhays had indeed heard of their supposed engagement, she very much feared she had. Aside from every other consideration, he would no doubt feel she had sold out, for they had frequently discussed the problem of Cornwall's brightest children defecting to England, where opportunities were greater. He would think she had lost no time in choosing an advantageous marriage over her concern for the land of her birth.

Then, aware that Kinross was watching her with a look of understanding amusement on his handsome face, she said bitterly, "If so, my lord, it is but another thing I have to thank you for. He will no doubt believe, as everyone else will, that I lost no opportunity in securing an advantageous marriage, or worse, forced you into offering for me. Believe me, I find that far more objectionable than a ruined reputation."

He merely shrugged. "Well, I hope he won't throw up the job because of it. He looked to be a promising young man."

"Since you paid for his education, my lord, he should be," she said icily. "And this is a ridiculous conversation that I have no intention of continuing!"

"I agree. In fact I came, before we were distracted by young Carhays' devotion, to ask if you would come to my rescue. I've been constrained by the duties of a polite host to at least make some push to entertain my guests, and have suggested a picnic this afternoon. Since I am unfamiliar with the best locations, I was hoping you would take pity on me and join us."

She hardened her heart against his almost palpable charm and said coldly, "Either your aunt or Poole will be able to advise you. I'm afraid I teach a class at the mine on Sundays, so I won't be free to join you."

He frowned a little, as if unprepared for her refusal, as well he might be, but said lightly, "You'll have to do better than that, I fear. What kind of a class do you expect me to believe meets on Sundays?"

"One for children who must work in the mine all week long and can get their education no other way," she retorted. "I am sorry, but I consider it far more important than wasting my time with a group of people I care nothing about and who dislike me. It is a credit to the children that they choose to spend their one free day a week in a classroom in an effort to better themselves one day, and I won't disappoint them."

His golden brows drew together in a startled frown. "Are you saying children of school age work in the mine? I know they used to when I was a child, but I assumed we were far more enlightened now."

Her lips twisted a little. "You would think so indeed, in this enlightened age, but unfortunately it isn't true. The mine managers will tell you it's simple economics. Women and children under twelve, who are too young and weak to go down in the mines, wash ore on the surface to free ablebodied men for the heavier work. It certainly is simple economics for the workers, for they require the whole family to be employed merely to survive. But when children as young as seven or eight are already at work in the mines, I think you will see it doesn't leave much time for education."

"But that's one of the richest mines in the world," he protested. "Are you seriously telling me men can't make a living wage there?"

"That's exactly what I'm telling you. Miners haven't had a rise in wages in fifty years. The adventurers must be paid, after all. And even on a rich mine like the Trelowarren, the workers are pitted against themselves, bidding for the richest strikes. The lowest bid wins, but sometimes they don't even make a profit, depending on the difficulty of the pitch, and the amount of power required to bring it to the surface. And that's the tutworkers and tributers, the aristocracy of the miners. The bal maidens make five pence a day, and children four.''

"Good God! But how is it you know so much?"

"My father made improving the working conditions in the mines one of his lifelong ambitions. He succeeded in changing very little, unfortunately. Have you ever been down your own mine, my lord? You should try it sometime," she said bitterly. "It's an eye-opener, believe me. the place looks like some bleak desert, or hell on earth, and that's just on the surface. At the beginning of their core the miners descend the dripping shaft by slimy ladders, often with broken rungs, with the only light a smoky hempen candle stuck to their hats with a piece of clay. Then at the bottom, which may be as much as three hundred fathoms down, they must creep along a narrow pitch, far from any ventilation, and where temperatures are ninety degrees or higher. The air is frequently so stifling they have to employ a boy to fan the candles to keep them alight. And at that depth there is constant danger of fallen rock, mistimed explosions, or the engines failing and flooding the mine completely. Then at the end of their eight- or twelve-hour shift they climb a hundred or more fathoms back to the surface, dripping with sweat, frequently to find a freezing January evening they must walk home in, often as much as five miles or more."

There was still a vague frown between his brows, and his eyes were narrowed on her, as if he had never seen her before. "Don't tell me you've actually been down one yourself?"

"Of course I have!" she answered shortly. "Did you really believe I would make such statements without seeing for myself what it was like? In fact, it should be something every so-called Christian is required to experience at least once. It would give them a whole new perspective, believe me. I'm ashamed to say I found it so horrible I could endure it only a short while before having to escape to the surface again. Just the thought of being obliged to remain down there for eight to twelve hours at a stretch, day after day, fills me with creeping horror.''

"Yes, but they must be used to it, surely? And I suppose there's no other way to get the ore up,'' he countered reasonably, in the argument so-called responsible people always used.

She could not quite hide her contempt. "There is a difference between necessity and closing your eyes to any notion of improvement because of it. People have died for years because of smallpox, but that's no reason not to vaccinate against it, now that we know how. I think it's revealing that you were forbidden to go to the mine at all as a boy. Most owners and adventurers take good care not to inquire too closely into the source of their wealth, for they would be appalled by the conditions themselves. It's much easier to stay away, telling themselves things have always been done that way, and anyway, the hapless miner knows no better. And it's all made much worse because Cornwall has long been plagued by absentee owners like you and your father before you, who believe the only possible civilization is to be found in London. You leave everything to your managers, who have no incentive to change anything, because that would mean a drop in profits. You don't even have enough concern to assure yourselves your managers are honest.''

"Are you telling me my manager is unreliable?'' he demanded.

"So far as I know, he is wholly reliable. I am merely telling you Trelowarren is run no differently from any other mine in Cornwall, which is to say deplorably.''

He looked a little rueful. "You do hold me in contempt, don't you? But at the risk of merely increasing your low opinion of me, what do you expect I can do about it? I regret I know nothing about mining, nor am I the only stockholder.''

"Nevertheless you are the largest. But I don't expect you to do anything about it, any more than any of the others have. I expect you to return to London in a few weeks and

conveniently forget you owe your heritage and wealth to
Cornwall. That's what you've been doing all your life.''

He flushed a little at her open disdain, but shrugged.
"At the very least I'm not going to solve the problem
today, and my guests are waiting. Who pays for your
school, by the way?''

She had expected nothing else, so tried not to reveal her
bitter disappointment. "You do, to a certain extent. Mr.
Trevethy, your manager, kindly allows us to use one of the
mine offices, and my services are naturally free. Or
perhaps in fairness I should say that your supporting me
enables me to volunteer my services. Supplies and books
are the main problem, but my own old headmistress, who
is a friend of mine, gives us what she can, and we make
do.''

"What you need is a real schoolmaster," he said
positively. "Particularly after we are married, you will be
unable to keep it up as you like. That at least is something I
might be able to do something about.''

"What we need is for children not to have to work to
help support their families," she retorted bitterly. "But
you need not point out to me again that I'm naive. I'm
aware it's not only in the mines that children are forced to
go out to work at six or seven. And I have been trying to
decide ever since I met you whether you can really be as
shallow and unconcerned as you appear, my lord! It must
be more than painfully obvious to you by now that we have
not a thought in common. As a wife I would be nothing
but an embarrassment to you, and I have no desire to fit in
among your friends. I have consented to a sham engagement only, but even that is becoming absurd.''

"My friends might surprise you," he said pleasantly,
but with a hint of steel beneath his voice. "But I have no
intention of arguing my worth to you. Only, if you are as
committed to your ideals as you say, hasn't it occurred to
you that marrying me would give you the means of achieving a great many of them? Wealth has its advantages as
well as its disadvantages, don't forget.''

"I'm not yet that desperate!" she snapped.

But that seemed to restore his good humor, for he merely laughed. "At the very least you are good for my vanity, for I fear it had become more insufferable than I knew. In fact, Gideon approves of you, which I knew he would. But I regret I really must go. We will have to finish this fascinating discussion later, I'm afraid."

But at the door he turned back to say lightly, "Only take care you don't go too far, sweet Cousin. I must confess it is rather galling to be dismissed as quite so frippery a fellow, when I had always thought myself a reasonable enough man. I might even be tempted to try to prove you wrong one day."

She was left to frown after him, uncertain of his meaning, and a little troubled by the vague threat in his words. But since she was unable to believe him likely to take anything she had said seriously, any more than he took their supposed engagement, she angrily dismissed the subject, more troubled by John Carhays.

In the end, she was obliged to dismiss that subject as well. There was nothing she could do about it if Kinross's suspicions were correct, and she had no desire to encourage the architect any further, if he were really falling in love with her. She was fond enough of him, but had never looked at him in the light of a possible suitor, perhaps because he was very little older than she was herself, and of a gentler nature. She could only hope his resentment would blow over and they could be friends again, once this absurd engagement was at an end. And as far as she was concerned, that couldn't happen soon enough for her.

14

The picnic seemed to have been a success without her, if conversation at dinner that evening were to be believed. The only thing that seemed to have occurred to mar the afternoon was that Kinross had run across an old acquaintance. Nicola judged by Lady Layton's and Miss Siddings' expressions that he had been less than genteel, but it seemed Kinross had prevailed upon his old friend to take the party out sailing the next afternoon.

Even Mr. Harewood looked a little glum at the prospect, and Miss Siddings couldn't prevent herself from saying with grating playfulness, "I only hope we won't be in danger of our lives, my lord. I must confess I've seldom met a man who looked more dangerous. Wherever did you meet him?"

"I've known him since I was a boy. In fact, he's the one I once suspected of being a smuggler, and tried to convince him to take me out with him. At any rate, he's wholly trustworthy, and one of the finest sailors in Cornwall, which is the same as saying in the world. He taught me what little I know. His boat is also surprisingly sleek, which is one of the reasons I suspected him so long ago, so you won't have to worry about being uncomfortable. In fact, if the weather remains this beautiful we're in for a pleasant day. It's hard to believe we left autumn behind in England isn't it?"

Nicola excused herself early that night as well, and took good care to remain busy in the back reaches of the house the next day, having no desire to be roped into the proposed sailing party. Even so, as she coped with any number of minor emergencies and then settled herself to doing household accounts, she couldn't help noticing with a certain wistfulness that it was indeed a beautiful day for sailing.

She was still engaged in the last boring task when the sailors at last returned, windblown and healthy-looking from their day out in the open. She caught a glimpse of them from the window, and couldn't help noticing that this time the outing did not seem to have been an unqualified success. Lady Layton was looking a little green, as if she were not a good sailor, and was clinging picturesquely to Sir Guy Percival's arm, while Miss Siddings hovered attentively, her own complexion unfashionably and rather painfully reddened by the sun.

Sir Guy was looking sardonic, which seemed to be his normal expression, and Mr. Harewood bored. There was no sign of Lord Layton, who appeared to have absented himself from the party, but Kinross looked disgustingly cheerful and vital in a coat that matched his blue eyes and with his golden hair ruffled attractively by the breeze.

He at least had enjoyed himself, for Nicola could hear him talking to Mr. Harewood in the hall after the others had gone on uptairs. She had evidently not closed the door completely, for she could hear Mr. Harewood say bitterly, "I might have known the divine Judith would get seasick."

Kinross laughed, but said more sympathetically, "Seasickness is no laughing matter, believe me. My father used to invariably suffer from it, and he was never ill otherwise a day in his life that I can remember. But he had only to step on a boat to be prostrate within ten minutes."

"Well, it ain't my favorite form of transportation if we're being honest," retorted Mr. Harewood bluntly. "But I'd have felt more sympathetic if she hadn't suffered quite so artistically. Which reminds me, you're not seriously thinking of buying the boat that strange friend of yours was telling us about, are you?"

"If Tom Trengrouse recommends her, you can depend upon its being an excellent deal," answered his lordship positively. "In fact, Tom's taking me in the morning to inspect her. If I can get as good a price as he thinks, I must confess I'm seriously considering it."

"But what in heaven's name for?" exclaimed the exasperated Mr. Harewood. "It's too small to be comfortable, from what he was telling us, and what the devil do you want with a boat in London? You can scarcely sail it up the Thames."

Kinross laughed. "No, but I can berth it at Southampton. Or more likely leave her here, and use her when I come down. At any rate, I've no use for a yacht. Something small enough to handle myself is what I want."

"Aye, that's exactly what I'm afraid of. What about these rocks you were so obliging as to tell us about the other night? It seems to me these are hardly the waters to be playing about in. In fact, to listen to that dashed sailor friend of yours—which I didn't, because for one thing it was clear it amused him to try to frighten us, and for another, I wasn't much more enthusiastic than Judith Layton, and to be told when you're tossing about in a dashed cockleshell that these are the most treacherous waters in the world is hardly conducive to a comfortable ride—I'm sure they're not, for the place seems littered with the wrecks of ships and the bones of drowned sailors, every one of them far more experienced than you. Not that I expect that to deter you from spending a fortune on a boat you'll never set foot on again once you leave here."

"Well, at least if I do, I won't expect you to go out with me. But I'd forgotten how much I used to like sailing. It's odd, isn't it? I remember very little of my early life here, but it seems strangely pleasant and appealing to me now."

"That won't last once you begin to get bored," said Mr. Harewood, echoing Nicola's own thought. "But I'd best go up and change for dinner. I feel the need for a sustaining period of solitude after this afternoon."

She heard the sound of someone going up the stairs. She thought both had gone until she heard Kinross's voice next conferring with Poole, far enough away that she could no longer understand the words.

She was certainly unprepared to have the door to the library where she was working swing open the next moment and Kinross himself stroll in. "Hiding from me, Cousin Nicola?" he inquired pleasantly. "I looked for you this afternoon, as you no doubt well know."

"You flatter yourself, my lord," she said bluntly. "I had work to do today."

"I can only say you seem to be remarkably busy, unlike those of us who have nothing better to do than play. But I can't help thinking you are violating the spirit, if not the letter, of our agreement," he complained mildly. "It hasn't escaped my notice—or anyone else's, for that matter, I imagine—that you spend as little time as possible in my company. That's hardly conducive to convincing people of the depth of our mutual attachment."

"I fear you vastly overrate my acting ability, my lord!" she retorted tartly. When he merely laughed, she added curiously, "And hasn't it occurred to you that none of your friends seems to believe in our so-called engagement? It seems to me we might have saved ourselves the trouble."

"You can hardly expect them to when you can scarcely bear to be in the same room with me, my sweet Cousin," he answered lightly, idly playing with a letter opener on her desk.

She flushed, and abruptly changed the subject. "Which reminds me that I couldn't help overhearing you and Mr. Harewood in the hall just now. If you are indeed meaning to buy a boat, my lord, I beg you to hire a local seaman to sail it for you. This is not the place for inexperienced sailors."

He looked up, a little surprised by her vehemence. "I begin to think you would prefer it if I drowned myself at sea," he joked. "Shall I leave you Rosemullion in my will, since you love it so much?"

"That is a cruel and unfunny jest, my lord!" she cried angrily. "Perhaps you're not aware my father was killed in a boating accident."

Instantly the mockery died from his handsome face, and he put down the letter opener. "I'm sorry, I didn't know. It is indeed an unfunny jest and I apologize for it. And it was an even greater tragedy, for your father seems to have been a most remarkable man. I'm sorry I never knew him.''

As usual she was disarmed by praise of her father, and had to blink back sudden foolish tears. "He was indeed a remarkable man, and I doubt I will ever cease to miss him. But perhaps you will understand why I don't find jokes on . . . that particular subject amusing. More, I fear I have a great contempt for anyone without a healthy respect for the sea. I have lived beside it all my life, and know how treacherous it can be."

"Was he caught in bad weather?" he asked sympathetically.

She shook her head to drive away the painful memories. "No, he was attempting to rescue a fool who had underestimated his own inexperience, and ventured too near the rocks. They were both killed, unfortunately. But I don't wish to talk of it, if you don't mind."

"Well, I give you my word I don't mean to take any foolish chances, for I have a very healthy respect for the sea. Nor is it at all certain I'll even buy the boat."

His eyes had been resting idly on the papers spread before her, and now as he took in their significance he frowned and added abruptly, "But I begin to think I've been remarkably blind! While you are up early and seem to be busy all day, it hasn't failed to strike my attention that my aunt rises late, lounges around her room until noon, and then frequently spends the afternoon napping or doing desultory needlework. In fact, I'm beginning to be more and more curious about this remarkable industry of yours. It's you, not my aunt, who have been responsible for the transformation of Rosemullion, isn't it? Don't bother trying to deny it. I should have suspected at once when I saw how efficiently everything was being handled. Whatever her virtues, and I'm sure she has many, my aunt doesn't strike me as being either particularly energetic or capable."

Nicola flushed once more, and was angry with herself for the betraying warmth that invaded her cheeks. "What does it matter who does it, my lord, so long as everyone is satisfied? At any rate, I like to keep busy."

"So I've noticed," he retorted with unexpected grimness. "But it makes me feel a complete fool. I have everywhere been extolling my aunt's virtues—even to you, as I recall—while all the time you have been responsible for the transformation I see around me."

She was a little surprised by his vehemence, but said pacifically, "I've enjoyed the challenge. Anyway, after my father died, I needed something to keep me busy. If you are pleased with the results, that's reward enough."

He shrugged. "I am more than pleased with the results, as you well know. But at the very least I should have been paying you a salary all these months. You seem to combine the duties of housekeeper, architectural adviser, bookkeeper and majordomo, from all I've been able to tell. It seems you would be a bargain at any price."

This time she could not hide the spurt of anger she felt. "I'm grateful for the compliment. But since I've been your unwitting pensioner for nearly a year, I'd say we were more than equal. I should no doubt be paying you room and board if we are to keep strict accounts, for not only did you never invite me to become a permanent resident, it was obvious you had forgotten my very existence until you arrived here three days ago."

Abruptly he laughed, the odd moment gone. "I should have known I'd only succeed in insulting you again, but that wasn't my intention, believe me. I meant only to try to make it clear that I am very much in your debt. I remember Rosemullion as an uncomfortable and unpleasant place I had no particular desire to return to. You've somehow made it into a home," he said simply.

She was once more disarmed, and a little ashamed of her quick temper. "I . . . thank you," she said unwillingly. "But I didn't do it for you, if you must know. I'll confess I've coveted Rosemullion since the first time I saw it. I've even been a little jealous of you, if you must know, especially when you seemed to appreciate it so little. Even Mrs. Chudleigh seems to regard it as more of an inconvenience than anything else, and would far prefer to live in a row house in town. If I was insulted it was perhaps because I have come to regard Rosemullion—however insensibly—as a little bit my own by right of affection, if nothing else. To see it begin to look as it should again is repayment enough.''

He gave his heart-stopping smile, so attractive because it always seemed to be so genuine, and one she was discovering she was having to steel herself against more and more. "If you love it, you have more right than anyone else to it, for it has certainly not been appreciated in my lifetime, I fear. My stepmother hated the place, and my father was little better, and I have few happy memories myself, though more than I had realized. And at least if you love my home that's something, I suppose," he added ruefully. "I'll have to remember to use it to my advantage, for I seem to have few others in your eyes, God knows."

She stiffened immediately, annoyed that she had once more allowed his charm to undermine her resolve. In his quick sympathy about her father, and his discussion of the home she loved, she had forgotten that he was a practiced flirt, and was no doubt so used to having women fall at his feet that he couldn't help turning on the charm to every female he met. Certainly there could be no other reason for his rueful words, for she knew that he could desire a marriage between them even less than she did, whatever he pretended.

She must remember that and be on guard for it in the future, for she must never be in danger of letting herself forget that it meant nothing to him, and that he made love to women as easily as he breathed.

So she answered coolly, pointedly returning to her accounts. "I hadn't realized you required my approval, my lord. I would have thought the devotion of Lady Layton and Miss Siddings and your aunt would be enough to hold even you, at least until you return to London. Now, if you will excuse me, I at least have work to do and must get this finished before tonight."

Fortunately she did not look up to see the quick flash of

anger in his very blue eyes. But when he had left without another word, for some reason she found herself quite unable to return to her accounts, despite having pleaded the urgency of her task.

In the end, disgusted with herself, she closed her books and fled outside, needing the solace of the wind and the sea.

15

Nicola may not have seen that betraying flash of anger in Kinross's eyes, but in the next few days the suspicion that he was deliberately trying to make her fall in love with him took increasing possession of her mind.

If so, she did not need to be told it was prompted by nothing but pique. He was obviously not used to finding anyone immune to his famous charm, and meant to punish her by demonstrating just how irresistible he could be. She was aware that such practices were common in his world, where gentlemen frequently made wagers on who would succeed in thawing a particularly frozen beauty, or boasted of their ignoble conquests, but it merely increased her contempt for him.

Not that he was in the least blatant in his intentions. He was far too experienced a flirt for that. He continued to call her by amusing names, and idly defended her from the worst of his guests' neglect, but he never made the mistake of stepping over the line she had obviously drawn, or again betraying his anger. He also seemed to be wholly content with his engagement, despite his mistress's growing resentment and his friends' dismay.

She was obliged to admit that he was undoubtedly a past master at a game she knew less than nothing about. Certainly to remain teasingly aloof was far more effective than to rant and rave or try to force himself on her, and so skillfully did he mask his intent behind the required public facade of their supposed engagement that she could never quite be certain she hadn't imagined the whole.

She was even obliged to admit that she was not as immune to his undoubted charm as she would have liked to believe—or have wished him to know. He was no doubt shallow and vain and interested in little but his own pleasure, but he was charming, amusing, and never above his company, nor did he say cutting things, as Sir Guy Percival did, or betray any consciousness of his wealth and position. In fact, she began to understand the encomiums his aunt so frequently received, for he must indeed be a paragon among the spoilt and conceited fashionable London throng.

Nor was he a complete rake, as she had expected, at least away from London. He drank sparingly at dinner, seldom consented to sit up late with his guests playing cards, as she gathered Percival was eager to do, and frequently rose at dawn for an early-morning ride. To Percival's sneers and Lady Layton's complaints that she seldom saw him, he said cheerfully he was on a repairing lease. If so, Nicola was obliged to admit he looked disgustingly healthy, his face taking on a becoming tan and his eyes clear and bright.

Nor was he out of place in Rosemullion, as she had also anticipated. She had expected a spoilt, vain fop, soon bored to distraction in the country and sneering at the undoubted inconveniences of Rosemullion, despite its improved state. But although Lady Layton made no secret of the fact that she found the isolated setting impossible and the soft-voiced Cornish servants backward, Kinross soon had them slavishly adoring him, as Nicola had rueful reason to know, and even when a piece of damaged coping from the roof nearly fell on him one day, he merely laughed it off.

She was mortified, for she had meant to set the workmen onto that as she and John Carhays had discussed, but had forgotten in her recent emotional turmoil. But he would only say in jest, "I hope you don't dislike me so much you have decided to be rid of me. If so, you are certainly not to be blamed. The house has been falling down for fifty years or more, I fear. I must really meet with your Mr. Carhays and put some more sweeping structural repairs in train."

"Why?" she could not prevent asking bluntly. "You know you will never live here again, my lord."

But he only smiled and looked inscrutable, which was a trick she discovered he had whenever a topic he didn't want to discuss came up. He was, in fact, a past master at avoiding unpleasantness, for he coped with Judith Layton's thinly disguised complaints and her husband's suspicions with charming tact, turned aside Percival's sneering unpleasantness when Nicola herself was tempted to slap his face, and managed to make so impossible a house party seem normal, at least on the surface.

He even was tolerant of his aunt's devotion, though it obviously occasionally startled him, and charmingly endured Poole and his wife's tearful reminiscences. It was painfully obvious that he had not given them a thought in the intervening years, but he managed to hide the fact well, recalling under prompting the treats Mrs. Poole had used to make for him, and the time Poole himself had rescued him from some boyish misdeed.

Nicola herself stumbled upon one of these sessions, surprised to find Kinross in the kitchen, to the giggling scullery maid's embarrassment, being regaled with ale and pasties fresh out of the oven by an attentive Mrs. Poole.

"Aye, you was a rare handful, you was," said Mrs. Poole fondly, urging another pasty on him. "I well remember the times his lordship decreed you was to be locked in your bedchamber without any supper."

"And I well remember that I seldom went without any," retorted Kinross, rewarding her with his dazzling smile. "You usually managed to rescue me." He caught sight of Nicola then and his eyes began to twinkle at her, but he said merely, "But I hope you don't mean to regale Miss Lacey with all my youthful misdeeds. She disapproves of me too much already."

Nicola had discovered that Poole and his wife were among the few who actually approved of the supposed engagement, hoping, no doubt, that it would mean his lordship might return to Rosemullion more often. Mrs. Poole sighed now and said fondly, "That I can't believe, my lord. Such a handsome man as you've grown to be, and far more approachable than your father, even if I do say so.''

"No, my father was not very approachable," agreed Kinross ruefully. "But I mustn't get in your way any longer. I never hoped to be rescued for foolishly having missed lunch, and only came in this way to avoid tracking mud and sand all over the house. I'm afraid we landed at a dashed inconvenient spot—the result of my poor piloting, no doubt.''

He had indeed bought the boat he had gone to see, despite Mr. Harewood's advice, and frequently went out with the old seaman Trengrouse as guide and teacher. The latter had proved to be a wizened old fisherman, more than likely involved in smuggling, by the looks of him, who had once or twice come up to the house to meet him, much to Mrs. Chudleigh's disapproval.

Mrs. Poole beamed and brushed aside any suggestion that she might object to any amount of mud and sand tracked across her polished floors, or that his lordship could ever be unwelcome in his own kitchens. But Nicola was obliged once more to acknowledge what good manners he possessed, despite his many other faults. He need not take time to be kind to such old servants, after all. It gained nothing for him, and in a few more weeks he would once more have forgotten them all completely again.

It was all the more surprising when she considered that he must have been petted and cosseted from the hour of his birth, not so much because of his name as because of his great personal charm. He should have been spoilt, but oddly that was the one accusation she found harder and harder to make stick, whatever else she might think of him.

She dared not withdraw so pointedly at sight of him, but pleaded a need to consult with Mrs. Poole, which was indeed why she had come, to escape leaving with him. It was at moments like these that she liked him the most, and stood in constant need of reminding herself that it would be fatal to fall victim to his undoubted charm. If he were carelessly kind to the Pooles, he had a very real reason for the half-teasing smiles he directed at her, and his careless flirtation.

But unfortunately she was not so successful in avoiding him the next afternoon.

She had needed a break from herself, and had stolen away for an hour's sketching on the cliffs. She was as usual so engrossed in her work that she didn't hear anyone approaching, and started violently when Kinross's amused voice said, "Not playing truant, are you, Nicola? I had given up hope of luring you away from your duties. I had no idea I was such a hard taskmaster."

She flushed and glanced around, not wishing for a *tête-à-tête*, but seeing no way to avoid it. "I am not nearly the martyr you obviously imagine me, my lord. I get away frequently, and often take whole days on my own. But you needn't wrap it up in clean linen. I have no doubt I must appear boring to you and your friends."

He laughed. "What you mean is we appear entirely frivolous to you." Then he spied her sketchbook and his fair brows rose. "What's this? Have you yet another talent I haven't discovered? You are indeed a paragon."

She had no desire for him to see her work, but would not stoop by engaging in a tussle with him over her sketching block. She merely shrugged and resumed her study of the horizon when he took it from her.

He was silent for a long moment, eyeing the rough sketch she was working on, then once more surprised her. "This is good. You're obviously no simpering female trying to look interesting, but a serious artist. I'm impressed."

She flushed, embarrassed by this unexpected praise. "You flatter me, I fear. I sketch only for my own enjoyment and have no illusions about my talent."

"I won't patronize you by saying anything more, for my opinion is worth very little, I'll admit, but I think it very good."

Before she could guess his intention, he had begun to thumb back through her sketchbook. She made a brief helpless gesture, then subsided in resignation, knowing what was to come. She could tell immediately by his face when he had reached the sketch of himself she had done.

It was a cruel caricature, done in a weak moment, showing him as a Greek god, with a laurel wreath around his brow. His extreme good looks were accentuated to the point of effeminacy, and she had made him look spoilt and weak, which was uncalled for.

He studied it for a long moment, faint amusement in his eyes, then looked up. "Is this what you really think of me? If so, it's no wonder you don't want to marry me."

She was suddenly uncomfortable, but too honest to take refuge in an easy answer. "No," she admitted. "I'm sorry you saw that, in fact, for it was done in a resentful moment, and is wholly mean-spirited."

He smiled at her unexpected apology. "Oh, I don't know. It's quite clever, as a matter of fact. Yet another profession you could follow if you ever needed to, for this rivals Cruikshank at his most lethal. I'd like to keep it, in fact. May I?"

She shrugged helplessly, unprepared for this request, or so mild a reaction. But she could not resist saying challengingly, "Will you be honest with me for once in return, my lord? You have no more desire for such a marriage than I have, admit it. Oh, perhaps your motives were chivalrous at first, to save my reputation, but now it is only your pride that makes you persist in so obvious a misalliance. It amuses you to tease me, obviously, and make me a laughingstock before your friends, but in truth you are secretly a little piqued that I could dare to resist your famous charm, when you might have far more beautiful and fascinating women for the lifting of a little finger. But I find your pursuit far from amusing, believe me. In fact, I suspect you of having determined to make me fall in love with you, to punish me."

He stood regarding her quite steadily. For a moment she thought even that had failed to get through to him, but then saw from his eyes that he was quite dangerously angry. She knew a little thrill that she could rouse at least that emotion in him, but then began to regret her rash words. She was not afraid of him, of course, but he looked unfamiliar suddenly, as if his pleasant mask had been stripped away to reveal a very different man.

Then it was back firmly in place, so that she was no longer sure she hadn't imagined that revealing moment. He came toward her, saying lightly, "If I meant to make you fall in love with me, my sweet Cousin Nicola, I would go more directly about it, believe me."

She refused to give him the satisfaction of showing she was a little afraid of him, and said defiantly, "If I had fallen all over you, as most women no doubt do, you wouldn't have looked twice at me. Admit it!"

"Oh, readily. But you're too modest, which is one of your chief charms, I must confess. Any man must always have looked twice at you, my charming Celtic witch, especially as I first saw you."

She threw up her hands, as always disliking this side of him the most. "And that is precisely the charming, meaningless answer I would expect you to make. Can't you be honest at all?"

"Oh, I'm being painfully honest at this moment. You are far more beautiful—and desirable—than you have any notion, my dear. You should not look quite so much as if you are daring a man to kiss you, in fact, for few men can resist that particular challenge."

She knew he was only playing with her, but could not repress a faint thrill of fear. "Another typical answer!" she said in contempt. "If a woman is unwilling, men are always quick to accuse her of being coy, or a tease. It salves your vanities, no doubt, instead of being obliged to admit you are not irresistible, as you all seem to believe."

He looked genuinely amused for a moment, and before she could prevent him, he had captured her hand. He studied it, "I am far from imagining myself irresistible, little though you may credit it."

"You don't have to," she said bitterly, incurably honest. "You have had women falling all over you since you were a child, no doubt."

He burst out laughing. "I won't bother to dispute that, for you have obviously imagined me some remarkable Casanova. I fear the truth would lower your flattering portrait of me more than I can bear." He glanced again at her and added, "Which reminds me, I have yet to keep my promise to buy you a betrothal present. I still think pearls, for you have remarkably white skin, did you know, and beautiful shoulders."

Her gown was more than modest, she knew, and she had a shawl around her shoulders to keep out the chill wind. She tried to prevent the betraying blush his intimate words invoked, but feared she didn't succeed, especially when he reached out and put a light finger to the delicate bones at the base of her throat.

He ignored the jump of her pulse, which she feared he could feel through his finger. "I wish I shared your artistic skill, in fact," he added whimsically, "for I'd like to paint you as I first saw you, with your hair wild about your shoulders and your white skin glowing in the lamplight. Or perhaps I would paint you against the cliff, which seems your more natural setting, in a filmy gown, your shoulders bare and your green eyes glaring at me, as they're doing now."

She cursed her own lack of sophistication, for she was more disturbed by his touch and the picture he conjured up than she liked to admit. She tried to break his spell by saying stiffly, "I have never disputed your experience at making yourself agreeable, my lord. You no doubt know just how to make foolish women fall in love with you."

"But not you, I take it? And do you know, I have an odd ambition to hear my name on your lips, at least once."

"All right then, Alex! And if this is an experiment, it's gone far enough. I am ready to return to the house."

"If it's an experiment, it's a most enjoyable one, I must confess. I am demonstrating what I would do if I were really bent on making you fall in love with me, my sweet Nicola. You should be grateful to me, for I am betraying all my secrets. But I think it's more than time you came out of your ivory tower, however briefly. And I think you will be the first to agree that few are more qualified than I to corrupt you, if only just a little.''

She tried to pull her hand away, no longer caring how she betrayed herself. ''This has gone far enough, my lord!'' she cried sharply.

''On the contrary, it hasn't gone nearly far enough.'' His eyes held hers, and then abruptly, and quite deliberately, he placed his lips on her wrist, where her pulsebeat and the blue line of her vein were visible.

She gasped and jerked back, hardly knowing what she was doing, foolishly unaware of how near the edge she stood.

The next moment his hand had shot out to cruelly grasp her wrist and pull her back from the edge.

''You little fool!'' he exclaimed furiously, his face far from charming for once. ''Would you really go over the cliff rather than have me touch you?''

She was oddly weak-kneed, now that she was safe, and had to resist the impulse to cling foolishly to him. A glance over the edge showed her the fate she would have experienced on the rocks below if he hadn't been standing there to rescue her, and made her feel faintly sick. ''I'm sorry,'' she managed breathlessly. ''I don't know what came over me.''

He shrugged and released her, making her suddenly sorry for his lack of support. ''It seems all too obvious to me. Do you really hate me so much?''

''I . . . don't hate you at all,'' she said inadequately. ''Why should I?''

He shrugged, looking oddly forlorn on the edge of the cliff for one moment, his hands shoved in his breeches pockets and his golden hair blown in the wind. ''I must confess I had not thought myself such a demon,'' he said wryly. ''But you have finally made your point, sweetheart. I won't trouble you again.''

Without another word he turned and walked away, leaving her strangely unelated by her hollow victory. Then she shook her head and made herself dismiss the absurd impression that the rich, handsome Lord Kinross could ever be deserving of her pity.

16

True to his word, after that Kinross stayed strictly away from Nicola. He was pleasant when they met, and maintained the polite fiction of their engagement before the others, no doubt in compliance with their original agreement, but made no further attempt to seek her out nor subject her to his dangerous charm.

Nicola tried hard not to be disappointed, at the same time disgusted with the weakness of human nature. She had desired nothing but to be left alone, but now that she had gotten her wish, her vanity was more than a little piqued. Nor could she help wondering if Kinross had resumed his relations with his beautiful mistress, as seemed probable if her smug expression and her husband's renewed jealousy were anything to go by.

As for the rest of them, they scarcely maintained the pretense of being polite to Nicola unless Kinross was in the room. Only Mr. Harewood seemed in the least kind, but even he maintained toward her a faint reserve not untouched by pity. She was grateful to him, but soon warmed to him for quite a different reason. It became quickly apparent that he disliked his fellow guests almost as much as she did, and tolerated them only out of loyalty toward his friend. He could scarcely bring himself to be polite to Percival, seemed merely to tolerate Lord Layton and Miss Siddings, and seemed completely immune to Lady Layton's undoubted charms. Nicola soon began to suspect he sought her out after dinner as much for his own sake as hers, and thus began to relax a little in his company.

That he was wholly exasperated by his friend's continued flirtation with Judith Layton under her husband's nose, only thinly camouflaged by his supposed engagement to Nicola, she had reason to learn, for she once accidentally overheard them arguing about it. That the conversation was equally unflattering to her merely added to her discomfort and humiliation, and made her wish she had never been placed in the position of being forced to eavesdrop.

She was behind one of the perpendicular shelves in the ornate and old-fashioned library, idly looking for the illustrated Malory Kinross had referred to on that first, disastrous night, when they wandered in, evidently in the midst of a heated discussion. She started to disclose her presence at once, but hesitated for a fatal moment, not wishing to betray her vanity by letting Kinross know what she was looking for.

Then Mr. Harewood's next words froze her where she stood, ridding her of all desire to call attention to herself.

"I never thought you'd be such a fool," Mr. Harewood said with the bluntness of a very old friend. "All I can say is, take care you ain't forced into the position of marrying two females, which I'd imagine might try even your famous address."

Her face began to burn, and she drew back further behind the bookshelf, having no wish to hear any more, but no choice but to remain until they left. But she might have known that not even so old a friend could provoke the annoying Kinross into a real argument. He merely sounded rueful when he answered, "I imagine it might. Don't worry, one engagement at a time is more than enough for me."

"It's one too many, if you ask me," said Mr. Harewood with disastrous frankness. "Not that I don't prefer Miss Lacey to that she-viper Judith Layton. At least she seems harmless enough, if a thought unconventional. Never did like reforming females, myself, for I suspect they'd be dashed uncomfortable to live with, but then, I'm not the marrying kind. All I know is Layton ain't as deceived by this supposed engagement of yours as you think. Nor is Percival—though he has his own reasons for pretending to be so, probably unpalatable. In fact, I told you this was going to be a hell of a house party. It only needs for you to be found in Miss Siddings' bedchamber next to put the final seal on it.''

Nicola, her ears and cheeks burning, abruptly thrust her hands over her ears, having no desire to hear any more of so humiliating a conversation. She wondered angrily if there were anyone in the house who didn't know the real reason behind her engagement, for it was apparent Mr. Harewood had been treated to the full story. It was no wonder she was treated with thinly veiled condescension by all of them, for they must know the engagement was a sham, and she herself not worth troubling over.

When she at last dared to pull her hands away, the two men were gone, and she lost no time in taking herself off, her book forgotten. She was ashamed and humiliated, and longed to put an end to the whole charade. Only her pride prevented her from withdrawing completely and refusing to come down anymore even for dinner. But since that was what most of them patently wanted, she refused to give them the satisfaction.

Kinross, at least, was making an attempt at maintaining the fiction of their engagement, though he no longer sought her out privately or bothered to invite her to join them on daytime outings. But when Lady Layton and Miss Siddings prevailed upon him to convey them into Falmouth for a ball at the new assembly hall one evening, he seemed to assume she would make one of the party.

Nicola took great pleasure in declining, pleading her mourning. Lady Layton looked momentarily pleased, but Kinross's handsome face tightened, and for a moment he looked as if he were going to make some comment. But after a moment he shrugged and said no more.

Nicola was perversely piqued, but spent the evening grateful for the solitude, and went early to bed.

At dinner the next evening it soon became apparent that the ball in Falmouth had been so successful it had inspired

Lady Layton with the notion of giving a grand ball at Rosemullion while they were there. Mrs. Chudleigh seemed equally enthusiastic, and kept recalling the days of her youth when they regularly gave balls in the famous long gallery, half of the county coming to stay and the festivities lasting for days. She quite happily joined Lady Layton, with whom she had been on far from easy terms until now, in discussing possible dates and whom they should invite, and how many beds would be needed for overnight guests, her previous hostility temporarily forgotten.

Nicola thought Kinross a complete fool where his mistress was concerned, for he agreed to everything and made no objection to spending what quickly became apparent would be a small fortune, given the lavishness of their combined plans and the shortness of the notice. Well aware who would bear the brunt of the work and concrete planning in the end, Nicola took no part in the discussion, having every intention of absenting herself from that event as well.

Nor did Kinross ignore his male guests' entertainment. He took the gentlemen out riding or, on several occasions, into Falmouth, and once, at Lord Layton's insistence, even to try out his coverts, though he promised them very little actual sport. Nicola, who overheard the conversation, could have told them that there was unlikely to be any sport, but thought better of it. She was well aware that local poachers kept the game on Rosemullion severely depleted merely to feed their families, and that the ancient gamekeeper, who was retired now, had blinked at it for years, since no one hunted there anymore. But she had no desire to cause old Nanfan, the gamekeeper, any trouble, nor to get into any further arguments herself, and so said nothing.

She herself was out walking the afternoon they chose, for she caught sight of the hunting party briefly in the long wood on the bluff above the house. It was a perfect autumn day, and she had taken a stray dog she had rescued and installed in the stables, to the ancient head groom's patent disgust, out with her.

Seeing the hunters, she feared the dog would be frightened by the sound of their guns, for she had long ago learned he was a consummate coward. But the animal, whom she had christened Macduff, seemed oblivious of the occasional firing, and lalloped along after her, his ears alert, joyously sniffing out game of his own, and dashing off from the main path to pursue any particularly intriguing smell.

He was headed toward the cliffs, for his favorite pastime was chasing sticks along the beach, a game he never tired of. She had rescued him from drowning as a puppy, but he obviously retained little recollection of his unpleasant ordeal, for he showed no fear of the water. He quite happily splashed in after sticks, returning with his prize to shake salt water all over her and invite her to throw it again.

She knew what he wanted, of course, but hardened her heart against his mute appeal. It was an unseasonably warm day for the brisk climb required down to the sea, and she had an appointment with the stonemasons that afternoon. They were out of sight of the hunting party now, but from time to time she could still hear the sound of firing. Certainly she had no premonition of danger, for no experienced hunter would ever make the mistake of firing into the open. If Kinross and his guests did not know it, they had Nanfan with them, who was wholly reliable. In fact, the ancient gamekeeper had been touchingly delighted to be pressed into service again, and had brought his grandson along with him, hoping to obtain a post for him in light of his lordship's supposed engagement, and presumably changed plans.

Nicola, knowing how the engagement was looked upon by most of the servants, found herself in a wholly untenable position, in fact. Like Nanfan, most hoped his coming marriage to a local woman meant his lordship might return to Rosemullion more often, and restore it to its rightful place as a nobleman's principal seat. Nicola, knowing that was unlikely ever to happen, and that their engagement, which had never been more than a polite fiction, was no longer given even lip service by most of his lordship's guests, felt guilty for rousing hopes destined to be dashed.

There were a few, of course, like young Carhays, who plainly believed she had wasted little time in selling out to the highest bidder, and made their bitterness plain. But though the accusation rankled, and her previous excellent relationship with the architect had become stiff and strained, she could hardly excuse herself without even more embarrassing revelations she had no intention of making, and so refused to consider the problem. If she had wished for a warmer relationship with Carhays, it would have been different, of course. But as it was, she had no choice but to shrug it off, and be sorry if she had really hurt him.

Shaking off those gloomy thoughts, she momentarily weakened, longing for a walk along the shore herself. Then, catching a glimpse of the oppressive sky, which promised rain later, she resisted, and firmly called the dog to heel.

He came tearing back, his tongue lolling, and regarded her hopefully. She laughed and said firmly, "Sorry, not today, my lad! You'd best not wander too near the woods, either, for you don't want to be mistaken for a woodcock. In fact, it's time we headed back."

He hung back, disappointed, but she deliberately turned away, calling him to heel once more. She had gone perhaps a hundred feet when there was a shot, sounding nearer than the rest, followed immediately by a heartrending yelp.

As she turned in horror, she saw the dog lying motionless in the path where she had left him.

She had no thought for her own safety. There was no room in her mind for anything else but horror and rage at the criminal fool who could have done such a thing. Unhesitatingly she began running back along the path, shouting in her fear and rage, "Damn you! Don't you know any better than to fire into the open? Oh God, Macduff!"

Then there came a second shot, almost on top of the first, and she herself went sprawling in the path.

17

Kinross, in the meantime, was regretting having offered an afternoon's sport, for they were having no luck. Old Nanfan, evidently feeling it as a personal failing, kept repeating glumly that he feared the coverts hadn't been looked after properly in years, and the predators not kept in check as they should have been. He had warned his late lordship what would happen, but no one had hunted there in more than twenty years, after all.

That certainly seemed true, for the paths were so overgrown they were sometimes impenetrable. Lord Layton, who had somewhat unpredictably proven a dedicated hunter, muttered something unkind under his breath, but Kinross said cheerfully as he pushed back a branch threatening to slap him in the face, "I can believe that. The place feels like an enchanted forest, in fact. I expect to meet a pixie around every bend."

Nanfan smiled taciturnly. "Aye, there's strange enough things happen in Cornwall, my lord, I'll grant ye! But the only thing ye're likely to meet here is poachers, I regret, for it would take more'n me, at my age, to keep 'em out. Most are prompted by hunger, howsoever, so in the lack of other instructions, I'll confess I've no' 'ad the heart to lay traps, as some in these parts do."

"Good God, no!" answered Kinross. "They're welcome to whatever game they can get. But I begin to think we're wasting our time and may as well go back."

Layton said ill-temperedly, "It's no wonder, if poachers have been allowed to roam here at will. I begin to think you and your fiancée are well-suited, my lord, for I've never heard such a novel argument. By your theory, one might as well open up one's doors to thieves, on the grounds their needs are undoubtedly greater than your own."

Kinross held on to his temper with an effort. "At any rate, it seems we'll find no game today. I suggest we head back."

Harewood, who had joined the expedition only unwillingly, hailed the suggestion with apparent relief, but Percival said with his usual sneer, "Surely you won't force Layton here to return without killing something, Kinross? It's obvious he's been longing to shed blood of some kind for days now. Slaughtering a few defenseless birds is usually the recourse of well-bred Englishmen too civilized to give in to their more savage tendencies, isn't it?"

Layton made no answer, but merely scowled and stalked off, but young Nanfan couldn't quite hide his amusement at the gibe. He was a cheerful young man who had proven willing and intelligent, clearing the way for them as much as possible, and surreptitiously supporting his grandfather over the worst of the ground. He was respectful enough, and youthfully embarrassed by his grandsire's frequent admonitions to him, but seemed to find the strangers from London a source of innocent entertainment. Layton's peevishness and Percival's snide tongue were clearly out of his experience, and Mr. Harewood's lack of enthusiasm for the outing amused him, as if they were all creatures from another planet.

Kinross, less entertained by the vagaries of his guests, was beginning to think of ways to bring the house party to an end. He could not do so before the ball, of course, but Layton's bad temper and Percival's unpleasant humor were beginning to wear on even his cheerful nature.

In fact, not for the first time he wondered why Percival had joined such a party, particularly since he was obliged to observe his emeralds every night around Judith Layton's beautiful white throat, a circumstance that must have been galling.

He was abruptly brought out of his thoughts by Nanfan saying sharply, and with strong indignation, "Here! Don't fire into the open, my lord! Begging your pardon, but you should know that's one of the first rules of hunting."

Kinross looked around quickly, to discover that Layton had wandered a little way off and was indeed aimlessly pointing his gun down and out of the woods, toward the open cliffs.

Layton, naturally looking furious at this reprimand from an underling, did not move, but snapped over his shoulder, "There's nothing there but a few gulls, and at least I might get a shot or two in. It's clear we'll get no sport otherwise!"

Kinross disliked the man, and found the thought of potshotting at harmless sea gulls distasteful, but supposed he was merely being squeamish. Still, Nanfan had every justification for his objection, and he supported him instantly. "Nanfan's right, Layton," he said warningly. "The house is in that direction, and you never know who might be out on the cliffs. I'm sorry for the lack of sport, but I think we'd better pack it in for the day."

Layton paid no attention to either of them, and deliberately let off one of his barrels at a free-wheeling sea gull they could see through the trees just below them.

The next instant there was a piercing yelp, and then a woman's voice, shouting in fear and anger, "Oh God! Don't shoot! Oh, *damn* you, don't shoot! Don't you know any better than to fire into the open?"

Kinross's heart froze as he recognized Nicola's voice. He swore and abruptly thrust his gun into the startled hands of Harewood, who was nearest him, and snapped, "Take that piece away from that fool Layton!" before racing for the edge of the woods.

The going was rough, and more than once he was slapped in the face by low-hanging branches, his hat knocked off and his jacket torn. When he reached the edge of the woods he caught a glimpse of Nicola running along the edge of the cliff down below, frantically waving her arms to ward off any further shots. A few yards before her on the path lay an ominous black heap that seemed to be some animal or other.

He started down toward her, noticing that she seemed to have no thought for her own safety, which was typical. If some madman were shooting erratically up above her, the last thing she should be doing was running into the line of fire, of course, but that thought seemed not to have occurred to her. He started to shout to her, but trusted that Layton would by now have realized what he had done, and be sorry for his reckless burst of ill temper.

Even as the thought crossed his mind, though, there was a second shot almost directly behind him, and something went singing past his ear, so close he could almost feel the air of its passing. Almost at the same moment Nicola herself went sprawling full length on the path.

For one heart-stopping moment of horror he thought she'd been hit too, and froze, seemingly unable to make his brain or his limbs function. Then, miraculously, the sprawled figure moved, and Nicola struggled up to her knees, sitll shouting and cursing. Kinross's heart bounded up in a dizzying relief as intense as his earlier rage had been, and he began to run toward her again, slipping and sliding down the grass. He had no thought for how near the ball had passed by his own head, but was intent only on reaching her.

At the same time, he could hear Harewood shouting testily behind him, "Put up! Put up, you damned fool! Good God, have you gone mad?" and someone else blundering heavily through the undergrowth after him. Even as he watched, Nicola had gained her feet again, as intent on reaching the still shape in the path as he was her.

He was close enough now to recognize a large dog, lying ominously still. She reached it almost at the same moment, and a new fear struck him. He feared the animal must be dead, or at best gravely wounded, to judge from its inactivity, but if not, she might be badly bitten.

He covered the last few yards in an undignified scramble, ignoring the damage to his expensive clothes, shouting to her not to touch it. But she gave no sign of having heard him, and collapsed on her knees by the animal, desperately going over it for wounds.

When he succeeded in reaching her at last, he was badly winded and had to restrain himself from pulling her away out of danger. She had dragged the creature's head into her lap, and turned a passionate, tearstained face up to him. As she recognized him she cried brokenly, "Damn you! Must you destroy everything you touch?"

He was unprepared for the wave of guilt and pity that swept over him. She had always been so cool in his presence, but now her face and gown were filthy from her fall, and her hair tumbling down untidily, her beautiful black-fringed eyes the drowned green of the sea in a summer squall. She seemed wholly oblivious of her appearance, however, or of the tears streaming unashamedly down her cheeks.

He ignored her accusing words to crouch down beside her, gently running his hands expertly over the dog. The animal was unconscious, but still breathing. There was an ugly gash along the top of its head where the shot had obviously plowed, but fortunately he could find no sign of any other wound.

He said very gently, "He's not dead, or even dying. In fact, I suspect he's suffering from no more than what would be a concussion in humans, for the wound doesn't look that serious. It's lucky we were only using birdshot."

She had allowed his inspection, obviously recognizing he knew what he was doing, but she cried bitterly now, "Yes, isn't it? Otherwise you might have killed us both!"

He had already begun to clean the wound with his handkerchief, his hands sure and unexpectedly knowledge-able. But he glanced up at that to say a little grimly, "I thought you had been hit as well. Good God, you little fool, don't you know any better than to run straight into the path of gunfire?"

"And don't you know any better than to fire into the open?" she countered furiously, fast returning to normal. "Damn you, I should have known nothing would be safe as long as you and your friends were here!" Abruptly she scrubbed angrily at her tearstained face, as if belatedly ashamed of her betraying weakness, unaware she only succeeded in making matters worse. "Oh, why is he so still?"

She still held the dog's large head in her lap, unmindful of the blood, or that she was crouching in the dirt, her face streaked by dust and tears. Kinross, used to women like Judith Layton, who seldom made a gesture without calculating its effect, and devoted their entire lifetime to their appearance, felt a little as if he had been struck in the stomach by a large fist, and found himself staring foolishly at her, almost as if he had never seen a woman before. And certainly he had never seen one like her before, who was genuinely unashamed of her emotions, and was far more concerned with the fate of a mixed-breed dog than her appearance, or what he might think of her.

Only when she frowned and grew impatient at his slowness did he remember his task and finish binding up the wound with his handkerchief. "I'm no surgeon, of course," he said reassuringly, "but the wound is shallow, and doesn't seem to have done much damage. He ought to be all right, but we should get him back to the house as quickly as possible."

She started up immediately and unselfconsciously held out her arms to receive him. "Yes, oh yes! If you could just lift him up to me—"

He grimaced, and said a little roughly, "You can't carry him—he's far too heavy, and a deadweight at the moment!"

"Of course I can!" she insisted stubbornly. "He's little more than a puppy. Oh, don't stand there arguing, but give him to me. Anyway, there's no time to send for someone from the house."

In that one speech she could not have more clearly conveyed her opinion of him. It obviously did not occur to her that he might carry the dog, and he flushed, more wounded than he cared to admit. "I assure you I am not quite so much a park saunterer as to leave you in the lurch with a wounded dog," he said tightly. Then he recognized Harewood's winded figure hurrying toward them, and added more lightly, "But never mind. Here's Gideon, thank God!"

Her face showed she was far from being as appreciative of this fact, for she obviously considered the natty Mr. Harewood even more unlikely to carry a dirty and wounded dog nearly a mile in his arms. But though Kinross was a little amused, despite himself, he turned to greet his old friend with relief. "Thank God you've come. Did someone unarm that fool Layton?"

Harewood was breathing heavily, and was dangerously red in the face, but that seemed to be caused as much by temper as overexertion. "Aye, Nanfan did!" he answered briefly. "Layton claims his second barrel discharged by accident, but I don't believe him."

"No, he's a fool! But it was stupidity, no more."

Harewood said grimly, "Criminal stupidity, in that case! I saw how close he came to hitting you."

Kinross looked briefly amused again. "Even so, he wouldn't have done much harm with birdshot. Not that I remembered that myself when I saw Nicola fall. And this is hardly the time to discuss it. Will you go ahead and warn Trotter I'll be needing him? He'll know what to do for this fellow."

Mr. Harewood started to say something more, then seemed to recall Nicola's presence and thought better of it. But he looked skeptically at his friend's burden. "Good God, you can't carry the animal all the way back, Alex! Better send for a litter. Which reminds me, I should have asked before. Are you sure you're all right, Miss Lacey? Damned fool thing to have done, running out like that in the line of fire, but damme if I've ever seen anything braver."

"For heaven's sake, don't encourage her, Gideon," complained his lordship. "She obviously already feels the dog's danger is excuse enough for what she did. I only know I lost ten years off my life when I saw her go down after the second shot."

Young Nanfan rushed up then, followed closely by his

hobbling and highly apologetic grandsire. They assured him that Lord Layton had been disarmed, and none too tactfully, judging by young Nanfan's kindling expression. He added darkly, too angry to be discreet, "Begging your pardon, my lord, but Granfer took his gun hisself. Lord or no, he should've known better than to fire into the open that way! Is the dog badly hurt?"

"No, but Miss Lacey might have been," responded Kinross shortly. "You may be sure Lord Layton will not take a gun out on my property again. But we'll discuss that later. Run on ahead, if you will, and warn my groom Trotter that I require his assistance. You should find him in the stables at this hour."

Young Nanfan regarded the spectacle of his elegant master carrying a bloodstained mongrel dog and seemed to share the others' opinion, for he said doubtfully, "Happen I should take the animal instead, my lord! He's bound to be dirty an a'."

"If it comes to that, I'm quite dirty myself by now," said his lordship ruefully, tiring of the argument. "I seem to have slid ignominiously down most of that hill. Now, do as I say!"

Young Nanfan shrugged and ran obediently off, leaving his grandfather to continue the ridiculous argument. Despite his years, he was stubbornly determined to carry the dog back himself, and only when Kinross, taking a belated look at Nicola and noting the waxiness of her complexion, abruptly ended the discussion by starting off toward the house, did he give up and trot along behind.

Kinross, thinking Nicola looked as if she could stand little more, was cursing himself belatedly for having sent young Nanfan on ahead. He was, in fact, regretting his insistence on carrying the dog, for she looked as if a sudden strong wind would blow her over, her skin colorless and moist, and her eyes strained. He had a sudden absurd urge to thrust the dog into Harewood's arms and pick her up instead, but resisted, knowing both would resent it. Instead he had to content himself with saying abruptly, "Perhaps I should have let the boy take the dog, for you don't look much better yourself, Nicola. At least let Gideon take your arm. I know better by now than to insult you by asking if you carry any smelling salts, but to be frank, you look as if you could use them."

She brushed aside this rather unflattering aspersion on her appearance and merely wrinkled her brow. "I wonder if smelling salts would be any use for a dog?" she inquired anxiously. "I confess I don't like this long unconsciousness."

Kinross shrugged and gave it up, realizing that at the moment her concentration was all on the dog.

18

Nicola was reluctantly persuaded to leave the dog under Kinross's groom's capable care, who assured her he would be right as new in a few days.

Once they had escorted her back to the house and she had gone up to wash and change, Harewood remarked thoughtfully, "Strange girl! You'd have thought she was carrying on over her nearest relation instead of a mongrel dog. I said once she was either damned clever or one in a million, and now I'm beginning to wonder if I wasn't being even more astute than usual."

When Kinross merely shrugged and turned away, he added bluntly, "But that's neither here nor there. Between you and me, I don't believe that second shot was any accident this afternoon!"

"Don't be a fool! If he'd hit me, the most I'd have suffered would have been some damage to my dignity," answered Kinross rather impatiently. "Which admittedly may have been his object. But in either case, I'd appreciate it if you wouldn't go about repeating that. This house party is unpleasant enough without that."

Harewood looked surprised, but agreed sarcastically, "Aye, I'm likely to go about repeating such a tale! But if you take my advice, I'd take care not to give him another opportunity if I were you. And I'll admit if it'd been Percival I could more readily suspect it. What's he up to, by the way? I never thought he'd stay in a place where the greatest entertainment is a picnic or a day's sailing and there are no high-rollers or all-night whist parties at the very least. More than that, he's putting himself to the trouble to be at least tolerable, which is unlike him. I can't help thinking he's up to something."

But this time Kinross merely laughed. "He's probably merely enjoying living at someone else's expense," he said carelessly. "He's the least of my worries at the moment. But I'll admit once this damned ball is done, I mean to be rid of the lot of them!"

Harewood looked astonished. "Rid . . . ? Does that mean you're staying?"

"Yes, there's a great deal of work to be done here. I didn't realize how much until I came. It seems foolish not to see to it while I'm here."

Mr. Harewood, no fool, said slowly, "Miss Lacey doesn't have anything to do with that decision, does she? I've no wish to insult you, dear boy, but I like Miss Lacey. I'd hate to see her hurt."

Kinross laughed savagely. "Thank you! Between the two of you, my vanity has taken a severe beating lately, I must confess. *She* obviously believes me so insignificant that I could be more concerned with my clothes and my guests than rescuing a wounded animal! And you obviously believe me capable of seducing an innocent girl for my own amusement. It should no doubt be a lesson to me."

"Then you *are* serious?" said Mr. Harewood blankly. "I must confess I'd begun to wonder. Knew you was making a dead set at her, of course, but at first I wasn't sure it wasn't only pique. Not in your usual style, after all. Only this afternoon, I began to think perhaps I was mistaken."

Kinross grimaced. "Yes, this afternoon was a revelation to me, as well. She didn't give a damn about me, or what I thought of her, much less my money or position. I begin to think she's the first genuine woman I've ever known—with the possible exception of my mother, and I scarcely remember her, of course. But you were right, damn you! I *was* pursuing her out of pique initially. In fact, she accused me of trying to make her fall in love with me, and I'm

ashamed to say she was nearer than she knew to the truth.
I'm not quite such a coxcomb, for I always intended to go
through with the marriage, but I'll admit her indifference
stung. Especially when you have been lecturing me on the
same subject so recently. She once nearly went over a cliff
to escape me, did you know that? I hadn't realized I'd
begun to believe quite so much in my popularity, for that
was a facer, I can tell you."

"Good God!" said Mr. Harewood. "What do you
intend to do? No wish to be rude, but I can't say she's
exactly bowled over by your famous charm."

Kinross shrugged. "I mean to marry her if I have to
abduct her to do it. Regardless of any other consideration,
I have no intention of allowing her to pay the price of my
own folly. After that, it's up to her. I won't force myself
upon her, if that's what you fear. She loves Rosemullion,
so she may well choose to remain here."

Harewood frowned, finding such words doubly ironic
from the usually irresponsible Kinross, who had never had
to pursue a woman. From one or two hints he had
received, he was by no means as certain that Miss Lacey
was as indifferent to Kinross as she wished to appear, but
he wisely saw no reason to point that out.

His lordship's groom was able to give Nicola a comfortable report on Macduff's recovery the next morning,
and so she was free to turn her attention to preparations
for the ball.

She had already endured a trying interview with Mrs.
Chudleigh over it, for that lady refused to agree that
Nicola might absent herself on the excuse of her state of
mourning, as she had done when they attended the
assembly in Falmouth. Mrs. Chudleigh said frankly, and
with unexpected resolve, that since she had become
engaged during that period, she could hardly plead the
excuse of her black gloves. If she did, it would only give
rise to exactly the sort of speculation they most wished to
avoid.

"At any rate," she added, as if to clinch the matter,

"Kinross has already charged me most straitly not to let you back out. Not that I meant to anyway, for I tell you frankly I have no desire to see That Woman lording it over the rest of us, as she did in Falmouth, and hanging on to Kinross's arm, even if you do!"

Nicola might know that she could provide no competition to Lady Layton, but wisely carried her arguments straight to the source, refusing to permit Lord Kinross to dictate to her.

She found him at last in the long gallery at the back of the house, where Poole had warned her he had gone. He was standing in shirtsleeves and stocking feet, and lightly testing the strength of a foil between his hands, the sunlight from the mullioned windows gilding his hair. He looked unexpectedly striking, like one of his more swashbuckling ancestors, and she had to steel her heart against his undoubted appeal.

He looked up and saw her then, smiling for a moment in genuine pleasure, in a way that made her oddly breathless.

"I didn't realize you fenced," she said foolishly.

He pulled on his coat, once more becoming the familiar leader of fashion. "Only indifferently," he conceded. "Were you looking for me? That must be a novelty. I was waiting for Gideon, but he seems to have forgotten our appointment. I fear I am growing sadly out of shape from all of the inactivity here."

She raised her brows. "Surely you have less chance for exercise in London, my lord. I thought all Londoners spent their days in endless balls and routs and social calls."

His face tightened for a moment; then he recovered himself. "Oh, I'm really not quite so useless as you clearly believe. When I'm in London I box and fence, during the fall I hunt almost every day, and in between I get what exercise I can. I am aware that none of that can compare in importance with running this great house or teaching children of miners how to read, but I am not quite the sybarite you so obviously think me. But I'm sure you didn't seek me out to discuss my exercise or lack of it. In fact, it is so rare an occurrence I should mark it down in my calendar, for usually you avoid me whenever possible.''

Then, when she flushed, he added more kindly, ''I am at least relieved to see you looking better this morning. Trotter assures me Macduff will be as good as new, and will scarcely remember his ordeal in another couple of days, by the way. I must confess I wasn't so sure I could say the same about me when I saw you go down yesterday. I lost half a year off my life at least, I know. Incidentally, Lord Layton has been brought to the realization he should apologize to you. Nor will he be allowed out with a gun on my property again, you may be sure.''

She had no desire to be forced to receive such an unwilling apology, but said stiffly, ''Thank you, but it's hardly necessary. Nor is it why I came. I wish to make it plain that I have no intention whatsoever of attending this ball you are giving.''

''Why?'' he demanded bluntly.

''I would have thought that was clear. On top of everything else, my father has not been dead a year yet. It would be most improper for me to attend.''

''On the contrary, your father's death has nothing to do with it, and we both know it,'' he countered coolly. ''I know you dislike me, but can't you stand even to be present in the same ballroom with me?''

''As usual, my lord, your vanity betrays you,'' she retorted hotly, for once unable to hold her tongue. ''Has it never occurred to you that I might merely object to making a laughingstock of myself before my neighbors?''

Then she was sorry to have said so much when he frowned abruptly and took her up on that. ''A laughingstock? My vanity must indeed be considerable, for I had not believed that to appear in public as my fiancée is to be made a laughingstock. That is what you meant, I assume?''

She blushed, and then was angry at her folly. ''If I have offended you, I apologize, my lord,'' she answered. ''But it must be more than obvious that this so-called engagement of ours is fooling no one. I think it is more than time we put an end to so ridiculous a farce.''

"So now it is a farce to be engaged to me!" he exclaimed. "No, don't bother looking so meek and innocent, for I'm no longer deceived. Since I came you have missed few opportunities to deflate my no doubt overweening vanity. But as for our so-called engagement, you gave me your word it would stand, at least until I returned to London, and I intend to hold you to it.''

"Why, my lord?" she inquired as bluntly as he had. "Because you find it a convenient protection? Lord Layton can hardly accuse you of stealing his wife if you're supposedly engaged to me, is that it?''

He held on to his temper with extreme effort. "Whatever my reasons, I am holding you to your word," he said shortly. "The engagement stands—at least until I return to London."

She was surprised at his unexpected vehemence, but then shrugged, admitting defeat on the matter of the ball, at least. "Very well, my lord. But that's not the only reason I sought you out this morning. Poole has asked me to confer with you on the matter of champagne for the ball. I suppose there must be some, of course, but except for a glass toasting our engagement, I've never tasted it, and Poole is by no means as sharp as he once was. It would perhaps be as well for you to order it from Falmouth yourself.''

His expression lightened into incredulity. "What, you've never drunk champagne? What a benighted life you've led, my child. Don't you know champagne is one of life's most rewarding pleasures, and certainly the oil that makes most social events bearable? I shall have to increase your experience, I can tell.''

"You have done that already, my lord, believe me," she countered dryly.

He laughed, but this time refused to take up the gauntlet. "But I will certainly see to the champagne. And I mean also to make you admit there is pleasure to be had in so frivolous a pastime as dancing. Your education has been sorely lacking until now.''

Thus committed to attending the ball, however unwillingly, when Mrs. Chudleigh was inspired to offer a length of green silk she had ordered and never used, Nicola had no choice but to accept it. She was a creative needlewoman, and since her purpose in attending was to quiet gossip, not attract attention, she didn't doubt she could make something satisfactory, if unlikely to rival Lady Layton's expensive French creations.

She would have preferred something in a less brilliant shade, but had no time to be picky. Nor could she deny, as Mrs. Chudleigh smugly pointed out, that the beautiful fabric was oddly becoming, bringing out the mysterious depths of her eyes and contrasting strikingly with her black hair and white skin.

Only much later did it occur to her to wonder if she had been once again manipulated by Lord Kinross—whether it was he, not Mrs. Chudleigh, behind the offer of the expensive green silk. But by then the gown was half-finished, and proving even more successful than she had dared hope, and so she cravenly dismissed the matter from her thoughts.

19

Kinross, in the meantime, was finding his previously comfortable life remarkably unsatisfying. His relationship with Judith Layton had become merely an annoyance to him, for she refused to believe it was at an end; his guests he found more and more of a nuisance, and he was engaged to a woman who openly despised him. The worst of it was he was beginning to wonder if he could really be the pompous, spoilt fool that Nicola obviously thought him.

As if to disprove at least one of her unpleasant accusations, he found himself riding to the mine on the afternoon of the ball while the ladies rested. He'd had one or two interviews with his mine manager since he had been back, but they were always carried out at his convenience, and in the comfort of Rosemullion, and Nicola's uncomfortable references to dreadful conditions and the convenient consciences of absentee owners rankled more than he cared to admit.

It was true enough that he had seldom been allowed near the mine as a boy, and could not remember the last time he had been there. Like everyone else, he had accepted what he had considered the unpleasant necessities of the industry, but as he approached the mine, he saw it as if through her eyes, and was more than a little horrified by what he saw. Trelowarren might be one of the richest mines in the world, but it was situated in a bleak desert wholly unlike the lush surrounding countryside. The ground, devoid of vegetation, was blackened with coal and oil, and everywhere were ugly piles of ore, dwarfing the humans nearby.

Far worse, the air for nearly a mile around was rendered noxious by an overhanging pall of coal and warm coppery vapor. He had begun to smell it while still some distance from the mine, and at the source it was difficult to breathe. He was used to the dreadful conditions in London caused by the inhabitants heating and cooking exclusively with coal, but this was far worse. The draining engines loomed over all like foreboding towers, rising nearly one hundred feet into the air, creaking and booming with every stroke, while their chimneys belched flame and smoke, to add to the hell-like atmosphere. He was obliged to admit that Nicola had not exaggerated the aesthetic horrors, at least.

Nor did the few humans he could see look much better. There were several woeful figures in tattered garments in view as he approached, pickaxes on their shoulders as they crawled out of a dark fissure in the earth, as if indeed out of the bowels of hell. He knew enough to recognize a mine shaft, and that the place was undoubtedly littered with them, the openings unmarked or protected in any way, and distinguished only by ladders leading down into the depths of the earth. It was one of the reasons he had been forbidden to go there as a child, for anyone taking a careless step, particularly in the dark, risked tumbling into a shaft and never being heard from again.

The ore, on a belt of some sort, was being pulled out of the shafts by mules, which were being flogged without mercy by a number of dirty children of about six or seven. He frowned, then saw other, slightly older children, along with women, resignedly washing and sorting through the ore without looking up, as if so deadened by the monotony of their task that they had forgotten all else.

Then one of the urchins glanced up and saw him. His jaw dropped as if he were suddenly confronted by a being from another planet, as indeed Kinross ruefully acknowledged he must appear, and nudged the boy beside him. Soon all were staring at him and his immaculate clothes, without visible resentment or even curiosity, as if he were so far out of their ken as not to be real to them.

Kinross found a burst of anger surging through him,

mingled with horror and pity, but inquired of the nearest urchin where Mr. Trevethy, his manager, could be found.

The child merely gaped at him, but one of the women abruptly jerked her thumb in the direction of a building off to one side that looked cleaner and more civilized than the rest. Kinross thanked her and started toward it, obliged to pick his way carefully over the ground, uneven and treacherous with rocks and pebbles. He was aware they all stared after him with that same nearly sullen regard.

He had almost reached the office when his manager came out. He too looked as if he couldn't trust his eyes, but then started forward, exclaiming in astonishment, "My Lord Kinross! Is anything wrong?"

"No, nothing," said Kinross pleasantly, shaking his startled manager's hand. "I merely thought it past time I had a look at the source of my wealth. I must admit it's hardly a prepossessing sight, however."

Trevethy was a fleshy, not unattractive man in his late thirties or early forties who had been hired by Kinross's father some ten years before. He looked even more startled, as well he might, but said merely, "No, no! It's hard to draw copper out of the earth in a pleasing manner, I fear. In fact, anyone not obliged to work in a mine should stay away, for they're damned unpleasant places. Believe me, I would myself if it weren't my job. You can't really be serious about wanting a tour, my lord? You said nothing of it when we met last week."

"No, it was rather an impulsive decision. My guests are resting in preparation for this evening's ball, and I found myself at rather a loose end, so I thought I'd come and get some idea of how a mine works. I confess I'm woefully ignorant on the subject. Which reminds me that I hope we'll be seeing you this evening? My aunt tells me I may look forward to that pleasure."

"Yes—oh yes!" said the other a little hastily. "I must thank you for inviting me, my lord, for I'm greatly looking forward to it. I must confess we get few such entertainments this far from civilization." He added, as if belatedly, "I understand, in fact, that congratulations are in order, my lord, and that the ball is in some part an engagement party? If so, I hope you will accept my sincere felicitations, and that your marriage will mean we may hope to see you in Cornwall more often."

They were conventional enough words, but Kinross wondered from whom he had learned of the engagement, and looked at his manager with new interest. He had given very little thought to him before, tossing aside his periodic reports half the time without reading them, leaving it to his business adviser to pore through the boring detail. He had always seemed capable enough, but there was some stiffness in his tone that made Kinross curious now. As if aware of it, Trevethy added, "You must know Miss Lacey and I are . . . old acquaintances."

Kinross wondered *how* old, or if, like young Carhays, Trevethy had nursed fond hopes in that direction. Nothing would surprise him about Nicola at this point. "Yes, of course, you know her through her school, don't you?" he asked. "I've been meaning to speak to you about that, as a matter of fact."

"Yes, I understand she will naturally be obliged to give it up," agreed the other.

"I am by no means as certain," confessed Kinross a little ruefully. "But in either case, a real teacher should be found. I will of course pay his salary myself. I would like to leave the choice up to you, if I may, for you will know the requirements better than I. Miss Lacey also tells me she is using one of the mine buildings, but I think a proper school should be built. I would suggest you consult young Carhays on that, since he is involved in work at Rosemullion, but you may have someone better in mind yourself."

"Certainly, my lord!" agreed his manager, but with a slight frown. "But while it's not my place to say so, of course, isn't that a rather extravagant expenditure for a class held once a week, if that? And you can hardly hope to find a qualified teacher willing to come all the way from Falmouth for one day a week. I applaud your motives, but I think you have allowed Miss Lacey's . . . er . . . undoubted enthusiasm to weigh too heavily with you. Most of these children will only end up in the mines eventually, you know.''

Kinross smiled. "That may be so, but it won't be for a lack of an education at least. And I fear I haven't made myself quite clear. I mean the school to be full-time, for I see no reason why children should be employed in the mine at the age I see them. I didn't believe, when Miss Lacey first told me about it, that in this enlightened age we could still be using child labor, and now that I have seen it, I don't mean to be a part of it. I want a stop put to it at once.''

20

Trevethy looked astonished, as well he might, since Kinross had never before interfered in the running of the mine. He said with a faint condescension in his voice, "I applaud your humanity, my lord, but you will forgive me if I think you have not thought out the situation thoroughly. Not only are all mines run this way, I assure you, but the locals won't thank you for your interference, however enlightened it may seem to you. In fact most families rely heavily on their children's wages to survive, just as their labor is necessary to keep most mines profitable. They, like the women, free the more experienced men for the heavier work below."

"Then I would suggest we pay the men—and women, if we must employ them—a decent wage in the first place," retorted his lordship. "Perhaps you can explain to me why one of the richest mines in the country can't afford to pay its workers a living wage? I will admit I am woefully ignorant about the whole process—something else it is perhaps time was changed—but I'll confess I can't understand it."

Trevethy had to hide a smile, and his tone became even more condescending. "I assure you I would be equally at sea at Almack's, say, or if I suddenly found myself in the queen's drawing room, my lord, places where you are unquestionably at home. No one expects a man in your position to concern himself with every little detail of the workings of so vast an enterprise. But you would be concerned, I believe, and with some reason, if Trelowarren or any other mine suddenly stopped paying its adventurers a reasonable profit. Nor would that serve the interests of the people you profess to want to help. You have not lived in Cornwall for a number of years, my lord, but I think even you can remember the hard times and subsequent riots we suffered in the last century. Now that the mines have begun to be profitable again, thank God, you may be sure the workers are grateful for steady employment, for they remember those times even better than you do. You won't earn their gratitude by risking their current prosperity with some newfangled London notions, believe me."

Kinross found himself unexpectedly disliking his mine manager, though he had always found him competent and pleasant enough before. But he said equally enough, "Well, it does no good to argue at this point, for as I've said, I know very little about the subject. It is something I hope to remedy, starting today. What brought the turn-around in profitability, by the way? The invention of the new engine by Watt?"

Trevethy relaxed too, evidently grateful for the neutral subject. "Yes, but not immediately, and of course the war helped, making the country more dependent upon local metals. And Watt was by no means the inventor of the first engines. That was done by Newcomen, nearly seventy-five years ago. Unfortunately they were inefficient, and expensive to run. Before that, of course, the only method of draining the mines, which in this country is the chief problem, was by adits—horizontal draining tunnels," he painstakingly explained.

"I do at least know that much," answered Kinross, beginning to be reluctantly amused at being lectured as if he were a schoolboy. "I am not completely ignorant on the process. I remember being taken to see the Great County Adit when I was a child. What did it do, extend something like forty miles underground and link more than one mine near Redruth and Chacewater?"

"Yes, thirty at last count, my lord. It once was possible to descend a shaft by the east end of Redruth bypass and walk all the way underground almost to Bessoe. But of course, as you may know, most of the tin deposits have long since been depleted, and copper is unfortunately found only at much lower levels, making adits impractical. Nor were Newcomen's engines much more successful. A great many famous mines were flooded and closed down completely, we once thought forever. Then Watt's new engine changed all that. One of Watt's engines easily drained the water two of the old Newcomen engines had failed to do, and used only a quarter of the fuel to do it. But such miracles seldom come cheap. They were for many years prohibitively expensive, and Watt demanded a royalty on each of his engines equivalent to a third of the value of the coal saved, which most mine owners couldn't afford."

"Yes, I can vaguely remember hearing talk of that," said his lordship. "Wasn't there some other problem as well—a cheaper, vast new source of copper discovered somewhere else? I know my father almost sold his shares in the mine, thinking they were now worthless."

"I'm sure you don't need me to tell you it's fortunate he didn't, my lord," said Trevethy with heavy irony. "But those were hard times. My father was manager at Poldice during that time, and it and half of all Cornish mines were forced to close down, even the largest like Dolcoath. Thousands of miners were thrown out to starve. That's the major reason why you won't find many miners complaining about conditions today, for they know how well off they are by comparison. I realize Miss Lacey, following her father's example, is impatient of such practicalities, but you won't find many local people to agree with her—mine owners or workers. I don't wish to offend you, my lord, but Nicholas Lacey was generally considered an impractical dreamer locally, one who was unprepared to accept reality. I admire Miss Lacey very much, but if you'll forgive my saying so, it would be a mistake to base your decisions solely on her highly idealistic view of the world and her desire to keep out what she sees as undesirable English influence."

"I don't intend to make any decisions until I have looked into it for myself," retorted his lordship with slightly diminished patience. "What happened to make the difference? To make the mines profitable again, I mean.''

"Two things, actually. Watt's patent ran out in 1800, leaving others free to copy and improve on his engine, and the Parys mine in Anglesey eventually became exhausted. The war also stimulated both invention and demand for copper and tin, as I said, so that at a time we were finally able to go deeper and deeper there was suddenly a market for the copper we produced. With the help of the newest engines we're able to go deeper than anyone ever imagined even twenty-five years ago. Under your feet, little though you may realize it, are some shafts running as deep as three hundred fathoms. Some people might argue that you are standing on one of the richest square miles of ground in the world, despite its unprepossessing appearance.''

He sounded very knowledgeable, and Kinross forced himself to mitigate his growing antagonism. He said merely, ''I'd like to go down one, if I may. I'd like to see for myself what it's like.''

If he had asked to be lowered into the deepest pit in hell, it was doubtful if Trevethy could have looked more astonished. "Surely you're not serious, my lord? For one thing, you're not dressed for it, and for another . . . well, I tell you frankly it's not a particularly enjoyable experience. I go down as seldom as possible myself. Nor will you learn anything more below than you can at the surface, for the conditions are hardly conducive to a leisurely study.''

"Nevertheless, I'd like to go down," insisted his lordship, still pleasantly. "If you don't care to risk your own clothes, someone else may as easily take me. One of the miners, perhaps.''

Trevethy frowned, but seeing the other was determined, smoothed out his face and said heartily, if insincerely, "No, no! I'll be happy to take you. Let me just get some smocks, though I fear they will do little enough to protect your clothes, and tell my clerk where I'm going.''

He returned with two smocks, and a hat for his lordship, since as he explained, the only light below was provided by hempen candles stuck to the miners' hats with a bit of clay, to keep their hands free for climbing. He doubted his lord-ship would wish to risk his expensive beaver. Kinross, feeling foolish, changed his hat for the other, and put on the smock, aware as he did so that the women and children, still covertly watching them, were gaping in astonishment. Like Trevethy, they evidently felt that any-one not required by necessity to go down into the mines must be crazy.

Kinross shrugged and followed his manager to the nearest ladder. The climb down was unexpectedly treacherous, for the ladders were by no means solid, and a contraption Trevethy explained as a kibble raced up and down on ropes beside them. They contained ore being brought to the surface, but since far too frequently lumps of ore seemed to spill out, threatening to carry the climber down with them if one weren't extremely careful, it required more skill than he had expected merely to descend into the bowels of the earth.

Worse, Nicola's likening it to descending into hell was forcibly brought back to him, for the temperature started rising almost immediately, and soon became stifling. The light provided by the candles on their hats was uncertain at best, and soon began to seem as if it would go out alto-gether in the thinning atmosphere, and the nightmare of being plunged into complete darkness in this inferno was not one he liked to contemplate. He could only be horrified that Nicola had actually descended into that hell when he himself had to fight the urge to break for the surface and the comparatively clean, cool air above.

As if reading his thoughts, Trevethy, some feet below him, paused at the next pitch and asked, as if casually, "Seen enough, my lord? I assure you it only gets worse from here, and you've done more than most owners ever do by descending this far."

Kinross could see the ladder extending on below them, seemingly to infinity, until it was wholly swallowed up in darkness. The heat was already intense, and he had no doubt that he had seen enough already to convince him of every horror of mining Nicola had tried to point out to him. But the thought of her daring what he shrank from made him gesture impatiently downward, saving his breath for the climb.

Certainly he had always believed himself in reasonably good condition, but the notion of the miners making that climb every day, working a full, backbreaking shift, and then faced with the climb back to the surface and probably a mile or more walk home, soon filled him with awe. The few he saw below looked unhealthy and taciturn, their backs bent seemingly permanently from crouching in the narrow tunnels, and their faces black from soot and smoke. Most eyed him with blank stares, a few with resentment, but then, Kinross had no doubt his own face was black as well, and his eyes were red-rimmed and burning from the noxious fumes. His lungs felt ready to burst, filled with the thin, burning air that seemed inadequate to long sustain human life. It must have been ninety degrees at least down there, and he was covered in sweat, so that he soon wanted to tear off his clothes or to loosen his cravat at least. He didn't know how men stood it day after day, for he feared he would soon go stark, raving mad if forced to spend eight hours down there.

By the time they returned to the surface at last, he wa beyond words, grateful merely to haul great gasps of comparatively cool, clean air into his lungs. His legs felt like jelly, his lungs on fire, and he knew the other must be silently enjoying the spectacle of his once-immaculate employer reduced to such a state, especially after having insisted upon his own fate.

If so, Trevethy took care not to reveal it, but invited his lordship to come to his office to clean up. Kinross was grateful to accept the offer, and once alone, abruptly stripped off his coat and shirt, needing to scrub away the memory of that hellhole completely.

Once restored to some semblance of respectability, though he feared his top boots would have to be discarded, and his buckskins might never be the same again, he exclaimed incredulously, when he rejoined his manager, "Far from changing my mind, Trevethy, I am beginning to think we should have to pay a man twice—three times!—what we do to make him go down there. Good God, I have never doubted my own courage, but I must confess I couldn't face it day after day.''

Trevethy smiled tightly. "Nor could I, my lord, but it's different for the miners. You might say they have been bred to it, for most are third- or even fourth-generation miners. By the same token, you or I would scarcely care to muck out our own stables or black our boots, but there is never a shortage of workers eager to take on such tasks. A free market has always been the backbone of our economy, and at the root of England's greatness, I think you will agree. I don't mean to sound pompous, my lord, or insensitive, but such workers don't consider it demeaning, or even as unpleasant as you or I might. They know little better, after all, and must be grateful to get work of any kind.''

Kinross began to understand what Nicola and her father had been struggling against all their lives, and why she was so bitter, but he saw no reason to prolong an obviously futile argument, at least for the moment. "Thank you for a . . . most enlightening afternoon," he said merely, unwonted dryness in his tone. "I won't soon forget it, believe me.''

Trevethy smiled more naturally, evidently believing he had succeeded in making his own point. "I will admit it is an experience, my lord, and one perhaps more mine owners should share. But I fear it does no good to get carried away with sympathy, for all business is founded on hardheaded principles, where, hopefully, all parties benefit. Which reminds me. Will you be returning to London soon, my lord? I understand you usually hunt with the Quorn during the fall. I envy you that, I must confess, for I understand there is no other country like it.''

His meaning could not have been more clear. Kinross might have surprised him by his unusual demands, but Trevethy expected him, like most other gentlemen shareholders, to quickly place his own interests above the horrors he had seen that day and continue the polite pretense that such conditions might be reprehensible, but inevitable in an imperfect world.

Kinross found himself once more sympathizing with Nicola, who had undoubtedly faced such willful self-interest before. But he realized as well the temptation to abandon a battle he felt himself woefully unequal to. He might have been horrified by what he had seen that day, but Trevethy was right to be condescending, for he had shown no interest before, and had undoubtedly benefited from such practices for years. Worse, he knew too little about the financial end of the business to even argue with him intelligently.

With that in mind, he gave his charming, lighthearted smile and answered unrevealingly, "Not just immediately. But I won't take up any more of your valuable time at the moment. And I'll look forward to seeing you tonight. Which reminds me. While I'm here, I'd like to take the books home to study. Probably I can't make head or tail out of them, but at the risk of increasing your poor opinion of me, I'm afraid I have no notion what the mine actually brings in in the way of revenues. I am the largest shareholder, I believe? And as such, entitled to inspect the books whenever I care to."

Trevethy's faintly satisfied smile was wiped clean, and he stiffened visibly, but after a moment said smoothly, "Of course, my lord. But since we have not wound up today's business, perhaps I may have them dropped off to you tomorrow?"

"No, no, there's no need to go to so much trouble," said his lordship carelessly. "At any rate, I will be tied up most of tomorrow with my guests. But I won't require them very long. In fact, you could pick them up tonight if you're in a hurry."

Trevethy hesitated, but in the face of the other's bland assurance had no choice but to bow and give in. "If your lordship has the slightest question about my competency," he added stiffly, "you have only to say so. I believe you will find everything in order, however."

"Good Lord, no!" answered Kinross easily, with convincing charm. "If you must know, I am trying to impress Miss Lacey. She believes me wholly frivolous, you know, and I am trying to prove even I can gain a slight grasp of business. She's bound to be impressed to find me poring over the books as if I knew what I was doing, don't you think?"

Trevethy laughed, and abruptly relaxed, turning over the books without further question. He even ventured a slightly ribald jest about female foibles and insisted upon escorting Kinross to his waiting horse, unable to hide the faint contempt in his eyes.

21

In the meantime, last-minute preparations kept Nicola running all day. A number of invited guests lived too far to make it convenient for them to drive home in the early hours of the morning, and so rooms had had to be prepared, arriving guests settled, and a thousand and one emergencies arising from giving a sit-down dinner for some fifty of the area's most prominent people, and a formal ball for three times that number, dealt with. Nicola, dreading the evening's festivities, was glad to be kept busy, and would even more gladly have remained in the background, forgoing the dinner party beforehand entirely, and slipping into the long gallery, where the ball was being held, unnoticed after most of the guests had arrived.

Instead she barely had time to scramble into her new gown, dress her hair, and hurry breathlessly down just as dinner was announced by a self-important Poole. Kinross, of course, as host, had to escort the most prominent female guest in to dinner, who happened to be Lady Boscowyn, a gaunt dowager wearing an ancient parure made up of large and extremely dirty diamonds. But he managed to catch her eye as she slipped in, and smiled at her in a warm, intimate way that made her far more breathless than the hurry down the stairs had.

Then she made herself call her traitorous pulse to order, very aware that however unexpectedly becoming the green silk had turned out, there were at least half a dozen celebrated beauties present in the room that evening with far more beautiful gowns, and all with a greater claim on Kinross's attention. She could not hope to compete, and so was angry with herself for allowing the fact of possessing an attractive new gown, and attending her first ball, to so quickly drive all common sense out of her head.

As a result she deliberately kept her eyes off Kinross all during dinner, and made herself listen with every evidence of fascination to her own partner, a middle-aged and slightly deaf landowner from near Gweek. But she was aware that Kinross, seated with Lady Boscowyn on one side and a ravishing blond on the other, was evidently charming both of them, for from time to time she heard Lady Boscowyn's bray of a laugh, and the blond's admiring giggle.

Fortunately her own partner didn't realize who she was, or else had never heard of her supposed engagement, for he asked her no awkward questions. She listened with half an ear to his complaints about the iniquitous state of postwar taxes and the dangers to all upper-class Englishmen if the so-called reform movement weren't put down at once, by force if necessary, and heard so little of what he was saying that she was able only to nod and smile, no doubt convincing him she agreed with every word.

She was grateful when dinner was over and she could make the excuse of checking on the champagne and last-minute preparations for the ball to escape before the rest of the guests arrived.

When she returned to the long gallery some half-hour later, it was to find the ball already well in progress and Kinross dancing with the blond from dinner. As she watched, the dance ended, and he next led out another one of the local beauties, a Miss Grenville, daughter of one of the richest and oldest families in Cornwall. They made an exceptionally attractive couple, she vivacious and pretty, he looking distinguished and unfairly handsome with his gold hair gleaming in the candlelight, laughing down at something his lively partner was saying.

Nicola suppressed an unworthy wave of envy and went to find Mrs. Chudleigh to see if she needed anything.

She found Mrs. Chudleigh settled in for a delightful gossip with one of her oldest acquaintances, with no thought for her responsibilities as hostess, so Nicola was able to endure that dowager's rather pointed questions and felicitations stoically and escape as quickly as possible.

By then another set was forming, and Kinross was nowhere to be seen. She herself received a few bows, and even more curious and not always friendly glances, but she scarcely registered them. Then at last she caught sight of Kinross again, standing talking to Trevethy, his mine manager.

Kinross looked as pleasant as usual, but to her surprise, there was a dark flush on Trevethy's face, and he was gesturing rather forcefully. After a moment Kinross shrugged, his handsome face closing up slightly; and the next moment his attention had been demanded by a peremptory matron in a bronze silk dress and a turban. He said something more to his manager, then turned away to speak to the matron. But Nicola was surprised to see Trevethy stare after him with something very like malevolence in his fixed stare.

Kinross danced next with a plump schoolgirl, the daughter of the matron in the turban, then a triumphant Judith Layton, daring in heavy gold silk, her emeralds blazing in the light from a hundred candles. Nicola slipped into one of the deep embrasures the room was fortunately generously supplied with, and sank into a padded window seat, grateful for the hiding place.

She was pleased that a number of the guests who passed by her hiding place remarked on the changes in Rosemullion, and not a few were struck by the beauty of the long gallery, one of the last and most elaborate of that type built in either England or Cornwall, and thus a historical curiosity. Less to her taste, she also heard more than a few unguarded remarks about her supposed engagement to Kinross, none of them at all flattering to her.

Once she saw John Carhays go by, looking unfamiliar in evening dress, but was relieved he didn't see her. He might have felt compelled to ask her to dance, and since they had never regained their former friendliness after that day, it would have been awkward for both of them. Then she saw Kinross dance by with a strange redhead, and promptly and uncharitably forgot the architect completely.

She was beginning to think she should go again and check on the champagne, and was wondering whom Kinross would dance with next, when her embrasure was abruptly invaded by an unwelcome pair. "Devil take it, Alex, what's this your man's been telling my man?" said a well-known voice. "Staine says you were almost blown up in the village this afternoon by some local Jacobite. I thought you said Cornwall was civilized by now."

Nicola paled, and lost all desire to identify herself. Their backs were toward her, Kinross's head gilded by the candlelight, and she saw him shrug rather impatiently. "Damn Fletcher anyway! I told him to keep his mouth shut. It amounted to nothing, and was hardly a local Jacobite, I assure you. Just some poor half-mad devil with a grudge against the world. For God's sake, keep it to yourself, Gideon. I don't want to be forced to answer any awkward questions tonight."

Mr. Harewood's voice was ironic. "From the state of your coat, according to Fletcher, you're lucky to be able to answer anything. If your poor half-mad devil had been a little less mad, and had had access to more blasting powder, you might not have been with us tonight. They caught him, I hope? I don't want to appear overanxious, or offend you with my vulgar curiosity, but I can't help thinking that if he has such a grudge against the world, he might very well try again, with better luck next time."

"Good God, I told you he was scarcely sane! And from what I saw at the mine this afternoon, I don't know that I wholly blame him for bearing a grudge against me. I gather he used to work at Trelowarren, but had lately been dismissed for some reason or another. In this place that seems to be tantamount to seeing your family starve, for there's little enough other employment, God knows. They caught him, and questioned him, which is why I was so late, but I don't know that I mean to press charges. He has a wife and four children, and precious little hope of supporting them—especially if he's transported, as I suppose he would be. At any rate, as I said, working in the mines is enough to make anyone go crazy.''

He sounded unexpectedly angry, and Mr. Harewood glanced shrewdly at him and remarked more mildly, ''I admire your tolerance, dear boy, but this is carrying things a little too far, don't you think? Since Staine assures me the accident was serious enough to ruin your coat and inflict not a few superficial cuts, and I can tell for myself that you have been favoring your right arm all evening, however much you try to hide it, I find my own tolerance rapidly diminishing, despite the existence of a wife and four children.''

''Oh, leave it, Gideon!'' said Kinross a little wearily. ''I've already endured one unpleasant scene tonight. You seem to be seeing threats behind every tree these days. Tell me instead, since you seem so observant tonight, what the devil has happened to Nicola? She was certainly at dinner, being monopolized by Sir William Trelawney, but I haven't seen her since.''

There was an unmistakable note of possession in his voice, and Harewood looked at him rather frowningly, but shrugged. ''I haven't seen her either. Perhaps she had some emergency to attend to.''

''More likely she has taken the opportunity to slip off,'' Kinross retorted. ''I—''

Some betraying sound must have alerted him then, for abruptly he broke off and turned, catching sight of her lurking in the shadowy recess. His eyes narrowed on her pale face, as if wondering how much she had heard, but then he smiled and held out his hand to her with a definitely possessive gesture. ''So there you are! I was beginning to fear you had—''

''Turned coward at the last,'' supplied Nicola dryly, trying to resist the appeal of that smile. She had no doubt that every recipient of it that night had believed it meant only for her, but somehow it didn't help as much as it should. ''I'm merely hiding.''

''Yes, you do have a habit of hiding your light under a

bushel," he said, an uncomfortably intimate warmth in the glance he turned on her. "And usually without cause. Tonight you look . . . especially ravishing."

She rose, abandoning her hiding place with only a weak qualm, but remarked truthfully, "And that shows just how practiced a flirt you are, my lord. I look what I am in this glittering and expensive world—and that's sadly out of place."

"If you had not cravenly hidden here, my sweet Nicola, you would have discovered exactly how wrong you are. But I'm glad you did. I had certain duty dances to get behind me, and in the meantime someone else would have taught you the magic of a ball—young Carhays, for instance—which would have been a shame. I have reserved the privilege for myself of showing you what it can be like when just the right person is in your arms, and the candle-light and music and champagne all combine to make the night seem too short, and you two the only couple in the room."

She knew he had probably said much the same to a dozen—a hundred—other girls in similar circumstances. She also couldn't forget that he had not so long ago been trying to make her fall in love with him, out of wounded vanity. She could not trust a word he said, and would be a fool to allow her head to be turned by the flattery of being the object of that charm, whatever the reason.

But tonight, for some reason, she was tired of being calm and sensible. Perhaps it was the seduction of knowing she looked different in the vivid green silk. Perhaps it was no more than the wine she had drunk at dinner, when she had eaten very little else all day, or the relief of being merry again after a year of grief. But suddenly she wanted to know what it was like to have a handsome man make charming love to her, to feel beautiful and cherished, to give in to his own charming brand of irresponsibility. She only knew that her usual cautious practicality held as little appeal for her tonight as it undoubtedly did for Kinross.

As if sensing her weakening, he grasped her wrist and laughed down at her, his handsome face vivid in the flattering light, as if the portrait she knew so well had indeed come to life. "Go and get us some champagne, Gideon," he said over his shoulder. "Champagne is definitely what the evening calls for. And I promised to corrupt Nicola's high ideals to that extent at least, if I remember."

She started, and some sanity returned to her, for she had forgotten Mr. Harewood completely. But he had already faded into the throng, and she discovered it was as Kinross had said, the room seemed to hold no one but the two of them. When a waiter miraculously appeared, sent by Mr. Harewood, no doubt, and Kinross put a flute of champagne into her hand, she accepted it and sipped experimentally at the heady beverage.

"Well?" he inquired, watching her, laughter warming his voice. "Is it as bad as you obviously expected?"

She savored the taste, finding it not unpleasant, and oddly biting on the back of her tongue, and took another swallow. "No, it's quite pleasant, in fact. It tastes a little like moonbeams would, if you drank them." Then she blushed, wondering if she could already be drunk, for that was a singularly foolish thing to have said.

But he merely laughed indulgently again and drained his own glass before taking hers gently from her and setting both aside. "Very apt! But I don't want you tipsy tonight, despite what I said. At least on champagne. Let's dance."

She recognized that a waltz was playing, and wanted to tell him that she had never danced the waltz, except with other girls at school, but he gave her no opportunity. He grasped her wrist again in that quick, possessive way and pulled her onto the floor. Nicola had always enjoyed dancing, but romping with schoolgirls was a very different thing, she was quick to discover. She had no particular trouble following his steps, but his hand at her waist and the other clasping her own so warmly made her oddly flushed and breathless. He whirled her around and around, and if people stared at them with surprise or censure, she had forgotten to notice.

When he smiled down at her, clearly enjoying her own

enjoyment, she couldn't help laughing back, determinedly giving herself over wholly to the moment. She might regret it in the morning, but somehow she didn't think so. At any rate she might never have this chance again, and she meant to make the most of it.

He danced her around and around until she was breathless, then, when she thought her heart must burst, took pity on her and abruptly whirled her into another embrasure, even shadowier than the one he had first found her in. "This is an even better place to hide," he said in a low voice. "Do you know, I have never seen you look so carefree. It becomes you, sweet Nicola. You should laugh more often."

She was not so far gone, on champagne or waltzing, that that didn't bring her up a little short. Despite her momentary weakness, and the magic of the moment, she knew instinctively that she could never be what he wanted her to be, nor he what she wanted. They were as different as night and day—moonbeams and practical sunlight. Champagne and candlelight might seduce her momentarily, but she was too practical and realistic to imagine she could live forever for pleasure, or that it would be enough in the end.

Still she protested a little weakly, "I fear you are carefree enough for both of us, my lord. I am too hardheaded."

"On the contrary, I am beginning to think you are indeed a witch, for you bewitched me from the first moment I saw you, and tonight, in that green dress the color of your eyes, or the sea, you look as beautiful and mysterious as any enchantress."

"Witches are neither beautiful nor mysterious, my lord," she managed foolishly. "And I should never drink champagne again, if this is the effect it has on me. Tell me instead: is what I heard Mr. Harewood say true? Someone tried to kill you in the village this afternoon?"

He looked momentarily impatient again. "Gideon talks too much!" Abruptly he raised her chin with one hand, smiling down at her. She had begun to wonder if he were as drunk as she felt, but his blue eyes were surprisingly sober and intent as he bent his head toward her.

She knew suddenly that he was going to kiss her, but she seemed incapable of protest, even rational thought. This, indeed, she would regret in the morning, but at the moment her heart pounded in her breast as if she had been running, and she was so light-headed she instinctively put out a hand to steady herself, finding only the hard wall of his dark coat to hold on to.

For a moment longer the magical moment held, his golden head so close above her own black one, his eyes amused and unexpectedly tender. "I hadn't meant to teach you this, as well, sweet Nicola," he murmured. "At least tonight. But I can't resist, however much you may hate me in the morning." Then he took her mouth in a sweet, aching kiss, and she forgot sanity, everything but feel and sensation, the vital, heady sound of her own blood singing in her ears until she feared she must faint with it.

Then he lifted his lips an inch or two, and fastened something around her throat. "I have another promise to keep to you," he whispered. "More moonbeams, if you like, but of a more material form."

She was too drugged with sensation for a moment to pull her wits together, feeling only something cool and heavy around her neck. She knew her eyes must betray her, for they felt heavy and languorous, and full of questions and all the wrong answers. Shakily she put up a hand, only to feel the round, smooth shape of pearls.

Still for a moment she didn't make the connection to the betrothal gift he had publicly promised her. Then, as she did, and stiffened, the moment was unexpectedly shattered by a shrill scream.

"My emeralds!" shrieked a voice she recognized well. "My emeralds are gone!"

22

After that the ball, with its sweet, dangerous moments, was definitely at an end. Nicola didn't know whether she was relieved or sorry, but knew that for once she ought to be grateful to Lady Layton.

The ensuing scene was appalling. Kinross did what he could to smooth over the unfortunate incident, but it was difficult with Lady Layton in hysterics and wildly accusing one of the servants of having stolen her necklace. Mrs. Chudleigh was almost beside herself, and kept saying weakly that such a thing had never happened before, and the other guests were plainly embarrassed and ill-at-ease.

To his credit, Kinross insisted the clasp must have come undone and fallen while Lady Layton was dancing. But a search of the room produced no glittering emeralds, and even he was beginning to look a little grim by the time a shaken Poole had questioned all the servants and made sure none of them had found the necklace and put it aside for safekeeping.

But as Mr. Harewood, plainly annoyed, muttered within Nicola's hearing, all the servants must be aware of who the blasted thing belonged to anyway, since she had been flaunting it all over the house ever since she'd arrived.

The same thought had occurred to Nicola, and had driven out her own problems, at least for the moment. She did not believe any of the servants could be guilty, nor would they be foolish enough to steal so distinctive a piece, which must be hard to dispose of for anything like the value of the jewels.

At least locally, she was forced to acknowledge. Smuggling was still prevalent enough to make it not impossible that the emeralds could be smuggled into France and disposed of for a tidy profit, and with no risk of recognition or repercussions.

As if unwillingly thinking the same thing, Kinross, an artfully weeping Judith Layton collapsed against his white waistcoat, managed to place her firmly into the arms of her waiting husband, and came across to Nicola, standing forgotten on the edge of the colorful throng. "Whew!" he said, mopping his brow. "I apologize for this. It certainly wasn't the ending I had pictured for your first ball. And I have a strong urge to strangle Judith, I must confess. I don't like to ask, but are you and my aunt absolutely certain all the servants are honest?"

Nicola deliberately dismissed her own earlier doubts on the subject. "Most of the servants have been here for several years, and I believe Poole can vouch for all of them. I won't believe that any of them would be so bold—or so foolish—as to steal so noticeable a necklace in a room filled with over a hundred people, especially when it was bound to be missed almost immediately."

"Well, someone has, by the looks of it. Damn the thing! It's been nothing but trouble from the beginning. I almost—" Abruptly he broke off, his fair brows frowning a little, as if with a sudden rather startling thought. But after a moment he went on, "Never mind. I'm beginning to think we will have to send for the authorities, much as I hate to."

"You don't have to send for them, my lord," she answered, completing her transformation from breathless fool to the efficient Miss Lacey. "Sir Jonathan Trelissick, the local justice of the peace, is here tonight. He's the stout gentleman with the orders on his chest."

"Is he? Well, then I suppose I'd better go and speak with him. Don't—" Again he broke off, then shrugged as if recognizing the futility of what he'd been about to say. "Again, never mind. There's no need for you to stay any longer, for the ball is clearly at an end. What follows will probably be unpleasant, if I know Judith. I'll see you in the morning."

She was about to gratefully follow his suggestion when Percival, who had been standing behind Judith Layton observing the histrionics with his usual appreciative amusement, unfortunately spied the pearls about her own neck. She had completely forgotten them in the excitement of the moment, but his unpleasant eyes narrowed and he remarked facetiously, "I see Miss Lacey has finally abandoned her scruples against jewels. An odd coincidence, wouldn't you say, Kinross? Lady Layton loses a valuable emerald necklace the same night Miss Lacey acquires a no doubt equally valuable one."

Judith Layton's furious eyes darted to the pearls about Nicola's throat, and her mouth tightened spitefully, but Kinross, his usual good nature for once totally absent, said merely, "I will agree there are a number of odd coincidences about this affair, Percival, but this is hardly the moment to discuss them."

Nicola waited for no more. For once she was delighted to leave the unpleasantness for someone else to deal with.

But it was long before she slept. Tonight had at last forced her to come to grips with the depth of her own folly, for she could no longer deny to herself that she was any more immune to Lord Kinross's charm than any of the other weak women who had fallen in love with his handsome face and noble form.

In fact, she was worse than those she had professed to pity, for she knew now that she had been halfway to being in love with him long before she met him. She might have told herself she despised his shallow irresponsibility, but his portrait had become something of an obsession with her. When he had proven even more charming and fascinating in the flesh than his portrait had led her to believe, she had quickly succumbed to his pull like any lovesick fool, despite her fundamental disapproval of everything he stood for.

Well, he was the same man she had believed him to be, despite what her heart told her. However charming he might be, he was a man who lived on the surface, obviously incapable of taking anything very seriously. And however much she might have longed tonight to abandon painful reality, she knew instinctively she could never be happy trying to fit into his world. She was too dark and serious and cared too passionately ever to be at home there. And no amount of champagne or candlelight would ever change that.

That painful fact at last accepted, the thought of seeing him again filled her with panic. He was too experienced not to have recognized how complete was his victory over her tonight. And both her pride and her sense of self-preservation shrank from having him know how very little different she was, in the long run, from the rest of her foolish sex.

She was once more tempted to run away, in fact, but her pride and common sense belatedly prevented her from giving in to so melodramatic a gesture. She told herself that once she had acknowledged the danger she could be armed against it. But it was less that argument than the far more lowering suspicion that now that Kinross was sure of her he was unlikely to continue to pursue her that in the end convinced her to stay.

As for the pearls and the green silk dress, the one would go back to Kinross first thing tomorrow, and the other would be packed away as too painful a memory of her own folly. It was a pity the loss of her pride couldn't as easily be dealt with.

She rose late the next morning, suffering from a slight headache she had no doubt had been brought on by last night's unaccustomed indulgences.

Nor were her spirits much higher. She wasted no time in dispatching the pearl necklace back to his lordship with no note attached, then hurried downstairs, meaning to escape for an hour's walk on the cliffs before she must face the day's disasters.

Unfortunately they were waiting for her, for she met Poole the moment she came downstairs. He was for once looking every year of his age, and almost tearfully assured her that he could vouch for every one of the servants. He wished her to put in a word with his lordship, and she wearily promised to do so. She hadn't the heart to point out to the ancient butler that she feared she had very little influence with Kinross.

But it seemed plain the emerald necklace had not been found. By the time she had endured a second tearful interview with Mrs. Chudleigh, who irrationally seemed to blame Lady Layton for the whole incident on the grounds she shouldn't have worn such an expensive bauble in the country and had, in fact, been flaunting it in their faces for days in a most vulgar fashion, Nicola's headache had become acute. She said even more wearily, "Never mind, ma'am. I have no doubt Lord Kinross will buy her another one, since he seems to have been the source of the first. Now, if you will excuse me, I have a slight headache, the product no doubt of all the excitement. I am going out for an hour."

She left that lady staring after her in mingled fury at the source of the necklace and slight surprise at Nicola's unaccustomed curtness. But Nicola was beyond caring, and unashamedly fled outdoors.

The dog Macduff was completely healed now, and she took him with her for company, needing some simple animal comfort. She had seen nothing of Kinross, who according to Poole had been closeted with the authorities all morning, along with Lord and Lady Layton. She did not envy him, but could only be grateful to be spared a meeting with him again so soon after her betraying folly of last night.

She had been walking for nearly half an hour, having to continuously call the adventurous Macduff back, when she heard a shot at a not very great distance. It was near enough, and so unpleasantly reminiscent of the last time she had been out walking with Macduff, that she jumped, and glanced instinctively to make sure he was all right.

The dog had been sniffing at a promising rabbit hole, but he too stilled, his great head lifted suspiciously in the direction of the shot. Then, before she could guess his intention or prevent him, he gave a growl and abruptly bounded off in the direction the shot had come from.

She was instantly alarmed, if for no other reason than that it was not so very many days since he had recovered from his wound, and if she lost him now it might be some time before he found his way home again. But when she called him urgently back, he ignored her, streaking away across the cliff, his ears back and his legs a blur. She hesitated, then unwillingly picked up her skirts and ran after him.

She soon realized she had no hope of catching him, of course, but something kept her going long after she had a stitch in her side, and her concern was rapidly giving way to annoyance. The memory of the last episode was too fresh in her mind for her to feel at ease, and so she ran on, calling with increasing irritation.

She rounded a bluff to see that Macduff had stopped and was staring down the cliff, his hackles raised, and growling. She stopped too, a little frightened in spite of herself, and called to him.

At sight of her he gave a loud bark, then whined and started down, only to find it too steep and pull back. He paced restively, continuing to whine, then again started down, once more to withdraw in frustration and pace some more, appealing to her to do something.

She feared some animal must be wounded down there and covered the last few yards in an undignified scramble. She had no notion what she could do, and mistrusted her resolution even, but she put a reassuring hand on Macduff's head for her own comfort as well as his and said soothingly, "It's all right, boy. What is it? What did you find?"

He barked again encouragingly, and she looked a little fearfully over the edge, trying to see what had attracted his attention.

For a moment she could see nothing. Then to her horror she saw a body wedged precariously on a narrow ledge some twelve to fifteen feet below the path, and recognized Kinross's bright head, his face dusty and dreadfully still, his eyes closed. Below him another hundred feet were deadly rocks and the restless sea, ready to claim him if he stirred.

23

For a moment she could only stare down in horror and disbelief, unable to understand how he could have fallen. Then as she remembered the shot she had heard, and saw a spreading crimson stain on the right sleeve of his dusty blue coat, she reeled, suddenly so faint that if she hadn't instinctively staggered back she would have pitched over the cliff after him.

Panic and a blinding nausea swept over her, so that she could only stand helplessly, fighting to keep from retching. Blackness swirled around her and for a moment she was a child again, and it was not broad daylight but a misty, moonless night. The horror and the reek of blood were all around her and she could hear the dreadful sounds, see those grotesque figures outlined against the burning wreckage on the beach again, men and women both, inhuman in their drunken, murderous glee.

She backed again, making some animal cry, so caught up in the old nightmare that she had forgotten Kinross completely. Then Macduff whined and nudged her, obviously wondering what she was waiting for, and she came to with a start. She was weak and trembling, the sick bile still threatening to rise up in her throat, but she felt a new, dizzying relief as well, as if her old and shameful weakness had lost some of its hold on her. Kinross needed her, and there was no time for any other thought.

Still she had to steel herself to approach the cliff's edge again, fearful of finding him gone from the ledge and dead on the treacherous rocks below, or of being again overcome by the sight of blood. But this time when she looked, his blue eyes were open, if a trifle vague, and seemed to focus on her after a second.

"Nicola?" he said on a faint question. "I thought I must be dreaming for a moment." Then his eyes grew more alert, as if his mind were slowly beginning to function again, and he said more sharply, "What are you doing here? I . . . must have blacked out for a moment."

She had to close her eyes briefly as tears of relief and weakness pricked at her lids, then dropped to her knees, both because her legs threatened no longer to support her and because it made her dizzy to look over the edge at him. "I heard the shot, but it was Macduff who found you. Are you . . . badly hurt?"

"No." His voice was strained, but sounded oddly normal, considering the circumstances. "It seems I must be grateful to Macduff. The wound is only a scratch, but I'll confess I must have hit my head when I fell, for it hurts like the devil. The worst of it is I can't seem to think very clearly, and I suspect I need to. You say you heard the shot? You—or the dog—didn't hear or see anything else?"

"No. It must have been a poacher, for Nanfan has been complaining of them for years. He must have run away when he saw what he had done and feared he'd killed you." She was having increasing difficulty controlling her voice and shivered at a vision of him smashed on the rocks below. "But that doesn't matter at the moment. Are you in any pain?"

He couldn't help smiling, in a weak attempt at his old humor. "Not much, aside from a faint feel of absurdity. The ball seems only to have grazed my arm. But I almost undoubtedly owe you and Macduff my life. Remind me to be properly grateful when I get up from here."

She brushed that aside, too shaken to wonder at his words, but Macduff, hearing his name, barked loudly and tried again to find a way down the cliff. She pulled him back sharply, terrified he would go over the cliff and dislodge Kinross from his precarious perch, and said shakily, "Don't try to move. I must go and get some help."

"No!" He seemed aroused for the first time.

She was equally afraid to leave him, but said shakily, trying to convince herself as much as him, "The ledge looks stable enough. If you lie perfectly still you should be safe until I can get back. It won't take me much more than half an hour at the longest."

He smiled ruefully up at her. "I'm sorry! I didn't mean to frighten you, and the ledge is surprisingly comfortable, and obviously isn't going anywhere. But I think I can get up by myself. Just give me a moment to gather my strength."

She stared down at him, too terrified to voice her own fears. The ledge he was lying on seemed appallingly narrow, and the twelve to fifteen feet of rock to the top of the cliff agonizingly sheer. A man in top condition might conceivably manage it, though from where she stood there seemed little enough to cling to on that sheer rock face. But one dazed, and with his right arm hurt, stood little chance at all.

But something about his attitude, and his first sharp refusal to let her leave, at least got through to her, and she began to tremble all over again with renewed horror. Macduff, apart from his first growls, had shown no further aggression, and seemed to detect no one else nearby, but she couldn't prevent herself from looking nervously over her shoulder, half-fearful of finding some menacing figure behind her.

There was no one there, of course, but in any event one thing was settled. She had no idea how she was to get Kinross up off that ledge, but she knew she couldn't leave him there alone, helpless and wounded, while she went back for help.

Nor was there any time to think of her own safety. Kinross miraculously didn't seem badly hurt, but he must be got medical help quickly, before he weakened any further from concussion and loss of blood. Nor did she dare think what would happen if the ledge gave way beneath him.

But like the dog, she recognized in frustration that there

was no way to get down to him. As if reading her thoughts, Kinross said sharply, "For God's sake, don't try to do anything heroic, you little fool! All you'll succeed in doing is getting both of us killed. I'm admittedly not in the best shape for climbing, but I think I can make it, given enough time."

She was by no means so sure. Only the fact that she was unsure what anyone else could do if she went for help, for no one else could reach him either, steadied her and allowed her to prod her frozen brain into considering the problem rationally instead of with numbing horror.

She needed a rope, of course. She had dropped to her stomach on the grass by that time, but she knew even if she could manage to pull him up she could never reach him. She had never cursed her frail woman's strength more, and looked desperately behind her for some inspiration.

The nearest tree was some six feet from the edge, and might give her the vital leverage she needed, but without a rope it did her little good. She must think. Think!

Abruptly she pushed back from the edge and rose, frantically pulling off her petticoat and beginning to rip it into long strips. Tied together they might not be long enough, but she had to try. If they weren't, her skirt would have to go next, for she was beyond considerations of modesty.

When she inched back to the edge and dangled her makeshift rope toward him, he had managed to make it unsteadily to his feet, and was leaning weakly against the cliff face. She suppressed her instinctive cry of alarm and made herself say as calmly as possible, "Here, see if you can grab on to this."

He looked up, his dusty face only some six feet below her now. She could see more clearly how pale he was, and there was a bruise and a trickle of blood along one cheek. But now that he was on his feet he seemed to be more himself, for he regarded her makeshift rope with some amusement. "What in the world . . . ?"

"My petticoat," she answered bluntly. "And you'd better hope it's long enough, for if not, my skirt will have to go next."

"My ever-practical Nicola!" he said lightly. "But even if it were long enough, you could never hope to pull me up to safety. I appreciate the thought, but it won't work."

"I know that!" she said desperately. "But there's a tree here I think I can reach to tie it to, which will at least give you something to climb! You can't make it up on your own."

He looked more interested. "Let us by all means hope your petticoat is long enough, then," he joked.

Luckily, it was. When she had it tied as tightly as she could manage, she returned and inched forward to the edge, by this time completely impervious to the dirt she was accumulating. "All right. It's as secure as I can make it."

She had forgotten all about a possible assassin still lurking in the trees behind them by that time. Her heart was in her mouth as Kinross grinned, evidently appreciating her nervous cavil, and tested its strength with one hand. It seemed to hold, so he hesitated only a moment longer before gripping it with his good arm and attempting to pull himself up.

Despite his assurance that the wound was only a scratch, she saw now that his right arm seemed almost completely useless. The crimson stain was growing as well, but she refused to think of it, or what it meant.

She also tried not to think of what the climb must be costing him. She could see his face more clearly now, and it was gray and streaked with blood and sweat. But he himself seemed oblivious of the dangerous drop below him as he inched his way up the steep rock face, through sheer force of will as nearly as she could tell, joking and encouraging her as he came. In that moment she wondered why she had ever thought him weak and soft, for she thought she had never seen anyone display so much real courage.

It seemed to take hours, and her breath caught in horror every time he lost a few precious inches or his booted foot lost its hold and his whole weight hung momentarily suspended on her frail rope and his one good arm. But miraculously the knots held, and he somehow always regained his no doubt frail balance. More than once she was tempted to call it off and insist on going for help, but something—his determination, no doubt, coupled with some creeping feeling at the back of her neck—prevented her.

But once he was within reach, she ignored his prohibitions and scrambled at his coat, adding her own weight to his rapidly flagging strength so that he was able to at last get a leg over the edge. She then pulled frantically at him, hardly caring any longer if she risked going over with him.

By the the time he lay safe and spent, facedown in the cool grass, she was unashamedly crying. She was not even aware of it as she turned him partially to see to his wound, fearing what she would find. By this time she had been through so much she didn't even flinch as she unhesitatingly ripped his torn sleeve further to see how bad it was.

She suspected he had lost a good deal of blood, but she saw with relief that it was only a flesh wound, and the ball had passed cleanly through. It was deep and nasty-looking, and bleeding copiously again, but she at least knew enough to know it was hardly fatal.

She pressed her handkerchief tightly to it, and rapidly removed his cravat to use as a bandage, having no time to waste untying her petticoat.

She saw then that his eyes were open and regarding her as he said weakly, "First your petticoat, now my cravat. I dread to think what we must both look like by now. Certainly my reputation as a dandy will be forever spoiled in your eyes, I fear. But then, yours is also lost, for I will never again believe you the practical Miss Lacey."

When she frowned and went on with her work, he reached up and wiped away a tear on her face. "At least I'm glad to see I rate as many tears as a dog," he said humorously. "I don't think I've actually been cried over since I was a little boy. I find it . . . oddly touching, I must confess."

Only then did she realize she was crying, and scrubbed her face impatiently, unmindful of how she betrayed herself at the moment. "Never mind that. Where did you hit your head?"

He laughed, then groaned as the movement jarred him. "At the back. I must confess that that, at the moment, is giving me the most trouble. In fact, I should have sent you away long ago, which shows how muddled my head is."

She ignored that to make a gentle inspection of the back of his head. There was indeed a large lump behind his ear, and her hand came away damp with blood, but by this time she didn't even glance at it.

"Ummm, that feels good," he said, his eyes closed again in exhaustion. "You're indeed a witch, my sweet Nicola, for your hands are cool and gentle and seem to magically soothe away the pain. My mother used to do that as well. I'd forgotten how soothing a woman's touch could be."

She suspected he was no longer quite rational, and said urgently, "My lord! We've got to get you back. Do you think you can stand with my help?"

He seemed incapable of being serious, even at this moment, for he opened his blue eyes and said, an unmistakable laugh in his voice, "You've called me Alex at least once, and managed it very well, as I recall. Don't you think we're past formality by now?"

"Very well, then—Alex! Oh, for God's sake, must you flirt even in such a moment as this?" she cried in exasperation. "Try to get up."

He obediently made the effort, but though he managed to get to his feet, she was forced to take most of his weight. That seemed to sober him, for he frowned and exclaimed, "Hell and the devil confound it! I must be weaker than I thought. Hold on until I clear my head."

He shook it, as if by sheer force of will he could recover the strength in his limbs, and after a moment straightened, but nothing seemed able to conquer his irrepressible spirit. The normally impeccable Lord Kinross was dirty, dizzily sick from the blow on his head, and scarcely able to stand, but he smiled cheerfully at her. "That's better. Let's just hope my stomach behaves, for at the moment it's feeling decidedly unreliable. And I've a feeling I've betrayed myself enough in your presence for one day."

24

H is stomach didn't behave, and before they reached the house she was obliged to hold his head while he was shockingly ill over a bush. When he had recovered he said gamely, if a trifle grimly, "I'm sorry. There seems no end to my folly in your presence. I wouldn't blame you if you abandoned me to my fate."

She tenderly cleaned off his streaked face with a scrap of her petticoat, retrieved from her makeshift rope, and didn't even bother to answer. It would have done no good to tell him that in his present state he was far more human to her, and thus more likable, than when at his charming best.

By the time they reached the house he was almost completely spent, and was leaning heavily on her, however hard he tried to keep himself upright. He insisted, nevertheless, upon making it to his room without summoning help.

Nicola for once didn't argue, remembering the fear that had pursued her all the way back, as if she expected at any minute to hear another shot ring out. Instead she girded herself for the stairs, almost as anxious as he to reach the safety of his room without being discovered.

Once finally there, she lowered him onto his bed, an enormous affair hung in crimson silk. She gazed around at the magnificence of heavily carved paneling and the massive bed, one that for some reason she had never entered before, and couldn't help exclaiming involuntarily, "Good heavens!"

She had thought him only half-conscious, but he opened one eye at that to say breathlessly, "My father's doing, not mine, I assure you. Or were you enjoying envisioning all this splendor designed as the backdrop for my many orgies?"

She flushed, but anxiously felt his forehead. It was burning to the touch, but whether because he was becoming feverish, or merely from exertion, she had no way of knowing. "You should see a doctor, my lord," she said firmly, anticipating his answer. "That wound needs to be cleaned and dressed, and I'm worried about possible concussion."

"Nonsense." His eyes were weakly closed. "The wound is the merest scratch, and I will be all right once I've rested a little. The man I need is Gideon. Do you suppose you could find him for me?"

"Mr. Harewood?" she repeated in some surprise. She would have thought him the last man to be of any use in a medical emergency, but on second thought, knew him to be a sensible man and hoped he might be able to talk some sense into Kinross, and so readily agreed.

Kinross seemed to have slipped into a half-doze, so she had hopes he didn't hear her turn the key softly in the door behind her and take it with her as she left, effectively locking him in.

Fearing that her own appearance must be scarcely better than Kinross's by this time, she made herself hurry to her own bedchamber first, and quickly changed her dress and washed her face and hands. Seeing herself in the mirror, she could only be grateful she had taken the time, for she had no deisre to alert the whole household to what had happened. Nor, at that hour, could she rely upon finding Mr. Harewood alone.

But she was once more lucky, for she saw him strolling indolently across the hall as soon as she hurried down the stairs.

He looked up when she hailed him, and remarked somewhat bitterly, "You were wise to escape the endless discussion and recriminations at breakfast this morning, Miss Lacey. Judith Layton in full form is too much for me at any hour, but especially before noon. I am in the act of making good my escape right now."

She ignored that, and said rather breathlessly, "Never mind that! May I speak with you? Upstairs, if you please?"

His brows rose, but he obediently followed her up the stairs. When she led him to Kinross's room, and then produced a key from her pocket and unlocked the door, she saw he was regarding her with sudden acuteness, but she had no time to waste on false concerns of modesty, and ushered him into the room.

When he saw Kinross he exclaimed sharply, "Good God, what happened? Not another hunting accident?"

She had thought Kinross fallen into an exhausted sleep, but he opened his eyes at that. "You warned me this trip would be uncomfortable, Gideon, and you were right," he conceded with a weak grin.

Harewood went quickly across to the bed and gripped his old friend's good hand rather tightly. "Yes, but I never expected anything like this. You damn fool! What happened?" he repeated roughly. "Are you badly hurt?"

He looked questioningly across at Nicola as he spoke, and it was she who answered bluntly, "His lordship has been shot. The wound does not seem to be overly serious, but he has lost a considerable amount of blood, and also suffered a blow to his head as he fell. A doctor should certainly be sent for, but his lordship has refused to allow me to do so. I am hoping you may be able to persuade him to see sense."

"Good God, no one ever was able to make him see sense," exploded Mr. Harewood. "But this is beyond everything! First you are almost shot in a hunting accident, then some fool tries to blow you up, then that damn . . . that wretched necklace is stolen," he amended, as if only belatedly remembering Nicola's presence, "and now this! I thought you assured me Cornwall was civilized now."

Then he encountered Kinross's gaze, and evidently read a distinct message there, for he frowned, then coughed and added rather unconvincingly, "Oh well! Best leave him to me, Miss Lacey. If he won't have a doctor, he deserves my inept nursing."

"His lordship is in a fever and has no idea what he needs. If you are both, in your clumsy way, trying to get rid of me because the shooting was no accident, I am not a fool. I've already realized that," she retorted angrily, "Nor do I intend to leave here until I see his lordship's wounds tended to."

Kinross burst out laughing, then winced as the movement jarred his injured arm. "My sweet Nicola, you are a jewel among women, but I am not in a fever. I am merely trying to be practical, which you should admire. Much as I might prefer your ministrations over Gideon's, and however much I am aware that you saved my life today, I don't want you mixed up in this."

"It seems to me I am already mixed up in it," she retorted stubbornly. She had already begun to light the kindling laid ready in the fireplace. "And if you're worried about my reputation, I will remind you that it was ruined from the first moment I met you. At any rate, this absurd engagement must be worth something. My position as your fiancée must excuse my presence adequately, surely?"

He grinned again. "But then, you yourself have claimed that no one believes in our engagement."

She shrugged and went on with her preparations, but Mr. Harewood, who had been frowning, unexpectedly entered the lists. "That at least is no longer true after last night!" he observed critically. As Nicola annoyed herself by blushing, he added practically, "At any rate, it seems she already is involved, as she says, and she at least seems to have a cool head, which is more than I can say for you, you fool! I vote she stays."

Nicola cast him a grateful look, but had already taken matters into her own capable hands. "Help me off with his coat and waistcoat. Take care not to jar him too much, though, for I should warn you that despite his flippant attitude, he is by no means feeling as well as he pretends."

Kinross lay back against his pillows and grinned appreciatively at this sally. "I fear I cast up my accounts as we were getting here," he informed Mr. Harewood. "I knew she would never be able to forgive me for that, if everything else."

"On the contrary, I suspect it was one of the few times in your life you were rendered at a loss for words, my lord," she countered, and grimly set to work.

He grimaced, and submitted himself to having his coat and waistcoat rather clumsily removed, though he complained about his old friend's ham-handedness. He also observed Nicola calmly tearing up several of his shirts to make bandages, and remarked politely, the gleam of amusement in the back of his blue eyes, "Pray don't hesitate to take what you need, my sweet Nicola, and pay no attention to what Fletcher will say. After all, you gave up your petticoat on my behalf, so the least I can do is sacrifice a few shirts."

Mr. Harewood looked rather astonished, so while Nicola ignored them both and dealt with his wound, he regaled his friend with a highly colorful version of his rescue. That he played down his own role, and made himself appear more ridiculous than heroic, came as a considerable surprise to Nicola, for deprecating humor did not fit in with her image of him. But he made her appear heroic enough to make up for it, so that she was soon acutely embarrassed, until she simply stopped listening and tended to her grisly task.

She had feared she might disgrace herself again, but the afternoon's shock seemed to have combined to make her thankfully numb, so that she was able to discard his stained shirt and bandages and clean his wound without feeling her old panic or more than a touch of faintness. She thought she was hiding her emotions very well, but once she caught Kinross's concerned and rather puzzled eye on her. She flushed and bent her head further over her work.

Over her head he frowned, and said with unexpected bitterness, "Hell and the devil confound it!"

She glanced up, in control of herself once more, and inquired calmly, "Did I hurt you, my lord?"

"No, of course not. Only this is ceasing to be amusing."

"Only you would find it amusing in the first place," observed Mr. Harewood bitterly. "I warned you not to let them release that fool from the village. One attempt on your life may be overlooked, but if you ask me, two seem to go beyond what is allowable, even in Cornwall."

Nicola looked up from where she was gratefully tying the last of her bandage. "Did you have that man released, my lord?" she asked in surprise.

"Yes, but I don't think he—" Then he broke off and shrugged rather impatiently. "But my opinion is as worthless as anyone else's at the moment, for I have damnably little to go on. It might well have been an accident."

"I know I said it must be poachers, but I've been thinking, and no local man would be poaching during the daytime, my lord," she said grimly, "particularly when you are widely known to be in residence. But I don't think it's the man from the village either."

Kinross looked at her curiously, but Mr. Harewood insisted, "Then who, Miss Lacey? Blast it, this is supposed to be a civilized country, but the things that have been happening here lately seem straight out of the pages of some lurid romance."

"I suspect wherever Lord Kinross goes, his life more closely resembles a work of romantic fiction than a normal existence," put in Nicola tartly. "But I will remind you that the number of people in the immediate vicinity who might have reason to wish him dead seems excessive to one of my limited imagination."

"Aye, that's true enough," conceded Mr. Harewood unwillingly. "You'll never convince me that affair with Layton the other afternoon was an accident, for instance. But that's not to say he meant to kill him, as you are suggesting, Miss Lacey."

"I am suggesting nothing. Merely that the area seems littered with possible suspects, as near as I can tell." She was efficiently shaking up Kinross's pillows and now slipped one under his head. He smiled at her gratefully, in an oddly intimate way that made her heart jump betrayingly for a moment in her breast, but made no attempt to interrupt the conversation being carried on over his head.

"Well, I confess I don't like Layton, but . . . confound it, a fellow don't go about trying to put holes in his host! But I will agree that this absurd engagement don't seem to have pulled the wool over his eyes, for he obviously hates Kinross."

She was tidying up the room now to remove all traces of her recent grim task. "If so, he's not the only one. I have no wish to make wild accusations, but if you ask me, Sir Guy Percival, whatever face he may choose to show the world, is very much his enemy as well."

"By Jove!" exclaimed Mr. Harewood, evidently much struck. "You're right. Can't stand the fellow myself, in fact." Then sanity evidently returned, and he added grudgingly, "But again I'm bound to point out my dislike don't make him a murderer. But I must confess I've wondered what the devil he's doing here."

"So have I. It's certainly not fondness for his fellow guests," said Nicola dryly.

Kinross had been lying with his eyes closed, but now he observed with a certain weary amusement, "I thank you both for your flattering appraisal of me! But if you are both finished tearing my character to shreds, I will remind you this is all nothing but the most useless speculation at this point. But if it will make you feel any better, I've at least a suspicion what Percival is doing here. It don't make him a murderer, as Harewood says, but it at least gives him a motive for possibly wishing to remove me. I have a strong suspicion that the emeralds that have caused so much trouble were stolen, and if linked to Percival could almost certainly send him to the gallows."

"Good God," said Mr. Harewood faintly. "Are you sure? I knew I never liked the fellow, but this goes beyond all bounds of decency."

"No, of course I'm not sure. I'm only guessing, as you both are, and finding it a damned frustrating experience. But you yourself warned me Percival was on the brink of ruin. You also commented how strange it was he was carrying such a bauble about with him. But even when he tried to buy it back from me I confess I didn't suspect anything."

"He tried to buy it back from you? That's damned suspicious, for he had not a feather to fly with the night before," insisted Mr. Harewood. "I'm beginning to think you're right."

"But I'm beginning to think I'm completely wrong, for unless I miss my guess, he managed to get them back last night. That was no doubt his reason for attending this admittedly unlikely house party. So you see, we're back where we started. In fact, the only thing that seems clear is that Nicola is right, as usual, and I have more enemies than I ever suspected."

He had closed his eyes wearily again, and added, "But at the moment I confess I'm too weary to care much who is trying to rid the world of me. Come and hold my hand, sweet Nicola. I feel sure you're right after all, and I'm in danger of succumbing to a high fever."

When she went anxiously to feel his brow again, he smiled sweetly at her and drifted off to sleep, to the extreme frustration of at least one of his companions.

25

They were left staring at each other in silence. Mr. Harewood was the first to break it. "Devil take him!" he exploded feelingly. "That's all very well, but what are we to do in the meantime?"

It said much for Nicola's frightened and weary state that she wasn't even tempted to smile at his obvious frustration. "Hold his hand, I gather."

"Yes, but what did he mean he has more enemies than he ever suspected? Is he trying to suggest there's yet someone else trying to kill him?"

"You've known him longer than I have, sir," she answered rather bitterly. "But Lord Kinross seems incapable of taking anything seriously, even this. He seems to have developed his faculty for avoiding unpleasantness to such a high art that very likely he will have convinced himself that he was never wounded at all by the time he awakens."

"Oh well, it's not as bad as that," insisted Mr. Harewood rather weakly.

She was in no mood for pretense. "Isn't it? You will forgive me, but since I met him, Lord Kinross has treated everything as a huge jest, from jealous husbands to a forced marriage with a perfect stranger to more than one attempt on his life. He seems to rely on jokes and other people to rescue him from the consequences of his own irresponsibility. But someday he may finally face a situation where neither his fortune nor his undoubted charm is enough. I only hope I won't be around to see it."

Mr. Harewood looked both troubled and vaguely uncomfortable at this unexpected tirade from one usually so cool and self-contained. "Good Lord, I'm the first to admit he can be irritating," he conceded. "Nor am I making excuses for him. But he's not quite so frivolous as he seems. And in his defense, both his fortune and his charm have frequently proven to be a mixed blessing."

When she looked skeptical, he added frankly, "Both make some people envious or jealous, and others, like you, disapproving. And he can never feel he's really being judged for himself, you know. As for the size of his fortune, I suspect he must frequently wish it at Jericho, though he seldom says anything. Just consider all the people who must want something from him, from charitable organizations to friends who see no reason why with his fortune he couldn't invest in their favorite schemes or lend them a little something just to tide them over. When he does, it's never enough, or they see no reason to repay him because he has so much. And even in social situations it's a pain, for if he plays for high stakes and wins, people resent it, and if he loses they accuse him of being patronizing. No, having lived around him for so long, I must confess I don't envy him his fortune at all."

She was staring at him in astonishment. "I . . . I confess I'd never really considered it," she admitted weakly. "I can—reluctantly—see that so large a fortune might be a burden."

"Aye, and it's made worse, of course, because Alex is so easygoing," continued Mr. Harewood bitterly. "It's frequently gotten him into trouble, I can tell you. But I've always suspected at base he still considers himself the penniless outcast he was when I first knew him."

Then as she frankly gaped at him, he shrugged. "Did you imagine he was born the way he is now, wealthy and assured and charming? Far from it. He was sixteen when his family's mine finally struck its first rich vein. Before then he was the poorest boy at Eton, and generally bullied for his excessive good looks and Cornish birth."

Abruptly she sank into a chair, her legs no longer able to support her. All her childish preconceptions were coming back to haunt her and she was ashamed at how easily she had been misled by his looks into believing he must be exactly what he appeared. "Are you serious?"

"It's hardly something I'd joke about! But believe me, he's far from having led the charmed life most people imagine. Why do you suppose I've remained friends with him all these years? And even I don't know everything, of course, because he's too proud, and too charming, to let anyone guess what he's suffered. I do know that even before then his home life was far from idyllic. His mother died when he was very young, as you may know, and I gather his stepmother was never particularly fond of him. She may have been jealous, since she never had any children of her own. He's never talked much of it, of course, but with a stern and distant father and a cold stepmother, he seems to have been glad enough to go away to school. I've certainly always gathered that he had very few happy memories of his home, and little enough reason to want to return."

"Then, of course," he went on matter-of-factly, ignoring her shamed silence, "his looks and shabby clothes and Cornish origins hardly assured him of instant success at school. I think you know yourself what that can mean, especially among a group of English schoolboys. They bullied him unmercifully the first year or two, I remember. Unfortunately even by then he'd already developed his present technique of simply melting away from trouble. No doubt he'd had good reason in his life. I only know it was disastrous under those circumstances, for of course they thought him merely a coward, and it only made things worse. Again I don't mean to defend him, for no one knows better than I do how exasperating he can be on occasion, but, to be fair, he genuinely does dislike unpleasantness, and goes out of his way to avoid it. I suppose it comes from being so annoyingly good-tempered himself all the time."

She had almost forgotten to breathe, everything else for the moment forgotten. "What happened?" she managed, having no trouble in picturing the little boy he was describing—or losing her heart to him in pity.

"One day he'd had enough, and single-handedly tried to take on a whole crowd of the worst bullies," he said bluntly. "He almost succeeded, too, for he's never lacked courage. Sometimes I think he thrives on dangerous situations, in fact, despite his reputation. But that's neither here nor there. I don't think I've seen him really lose his temper since then, but it impressed the bullies enough that after that he became a general favorite. And then, of course, the mine made a fortune, and suddenly he was the most popular man in London. Only he's no fool, and has always known how little that really means. I've sometimes suspected that deep inside he's still that lonely, friendless boy from Cornwall I first knew."

She couldn't help suddenly remembering her own brief impression of him as somehow forlorn on the cliffs that day. The vision troubled her and made her feel a fool.

Mr. Harewood insisted upon her going to rest, promising to stay and keep an eye on Kinross. After a moment she agreed, needing some time to pull herself together again and rebuild her defenses.

To her surprise, she fell asleep and slept dreamlessly for several hours. It was almost dinnertime when she awoke, and she dressed quickly and hurried back to Kinross's room, half-afraid of what she'd find there.

She found Kinross sitting up in bed rather awkwardly trying to feed himself with his left hand, and he and Mr. Harewood laughing together as if they had not a care in the world.

Both looked around as she came in, and Mr. Harewood at least had the grace to look a little embarrassed. Kinross merely gave her his heart-stopping smile and said cheerfully, "Just in time to take pity on me, my sweet Nicola. My efforts to feed myself with my left hand are proving far from dexterous, and Gideon can only laugh at me."

She was glad to see Mr. Harewood had fashioned him a sling of sorts to rest his injured arm in, but she thought that despite his determined cheerfulness Kinross was looking decidedly ill. His cheeks were flushed, and his eyes overbright with fever. But when she went to put a hand on his brow, he immediately captured it with his left hand and brought it to his lips. "If I have a fever, it's probably brought on by your cool touch, my Celtic witch. And I seem to remember I haven't thanked you properly yet for saving my life today."

She retrieved her hand, her own color revealingly high by now, but retorted dryly, "If you have a fever, my lord, it is probably brought on by the wine you are so foolishly drinking. I would have thought at least one of you would have better sense. At the most, you should have been allowed only a little thin gruel and barley water for your dinner tonight." She eyed Mr. Harewood accusingly.

"Good God, you are even crueler than Gideon!" exclaimed his lordship, raising his wineglass to her. "In that case I'm grateful you weren't here, for I would almost certainly have gone into a high fever with such cold comfort to sustain me."

She soon saw that she would get nothing from him but such nonsense. When asked how he was feeling, he assured her he was already almost as good as new, despite the evidence to the contrary. When urged by both her and Mr. Harewood to send for the authorities, he retorted unanswerably that he had spent the morning closeted with the local authorities, and had no intention of repeating so worthless an exercise.

Nicola, who knew Sir Jonathan Trelissick fairly well, could not deny it, but in desperation at least tried to make him promise to post a guard during the night. He laughed and promised, if it would make her feel better, to have Fletcher sit up all night with a loaded shotgun, though he suspected the rest of his guests would hardly find that a comforting thought to take to bed with them. Certainly his aunt would never forgive him if his valet woke the household by discharging one of his barrels at a mouse, which was all the excitement he was likely to see that night.

She gave it up, knowing it was no use to try to talk any sense into him. Nor did Mr. Harewood prove a reliable ally, for he merely shrugged, his eyes sliding uncomfortably away from her own.

As for the rest of the household, they had decided between themselves in her absence that Mr. Harewood was to tell them at dinner that Kinross had been slightly wounded in a poaching accident.

Since she felt herself unable to face their questions, she gratefully remained with Kinross while Mr. Harewood went reluctantly off to change for dinner.

The evening passed pleasantly enough, Kinross dozing occasionally, and once or twice waking up to see her sitting in the chair beside his bed, the candlelight in her hair, and smiling as if it were natural to see her there. She told herself that for her own peace of mind, if nothing else, the sooner he recovered, the better.

She had no real expectation of any trouble during the night, for she hardly believed anyone would make an attempt on Kinross's life in his own home, but when she retired to her room she removed only her dress and lay on top of the covers, meaning to look in on him at least once in the night. She feared he would have a high fever by morning, and almost certainly needed to have some blood let, but he had refused her suggestion of some laudanum to help him sleep.

It was past midnight when she crept through the passage to his room, grateful that she didn't meet anyone. When she reached Kinross's room it took her a moment to realize that his door was slightly ajar, for faint light spilled out and she could hear voices.

For a moment her heart stopped; then she managed to assure herself it was merely his lordship's valet. But as she started forward again, a voice that was faintly familiar to her said more loudly, "I've been bleeding you for years, in fact, and neither you nor your father ever guessed. It was just my cursed luck 'that brought you to Cornwall after so many years. And even then I had no reason to worry, or so I thought. But you had to impress your latest fancy-piece by poking your nose in where you'd been content to let me do all the dirty work, so long as the money kept coming on time. Well, it's the last time your insatiable lechery will get you into trouble."

Nicola froze in horror, scarcely able to believe her ears. But Kinross's voice sounded unexpectedly calm and wholly unsurprised. "It was you, of course, out on the cliffs this morning," he said. "I began to suspect as much."

The other laughed harshly. "If it hadn't been for that bitch Nicola Lacey I'd have finished you off then. She and that father of hers have been a thorn in my side for years, with their pious concern for the miners and their trouble-making. I'm only sorry you're not going to live to marry her, for it should have proved interesting."

"So am I," said Kinross's oddly normal voice. "You meant to throw the blame on that local fool I so obligingly had released for you, of course."

"If not him, you seem to have been even more obliging in providing me a whole houseful of possible suspects, my lord!" answered the other mockingly. "By the time the local authorities sort through all the conflicting stories and accusations, I'll be safely in France."

"Unfortunately the joke is on you, Trevethy," pointed out his lordship quite pleasantly. "You were right to be contemptuous of me at the mine yesterday, for I was admittedly only out to impress Miss Lacey. But I found conditions there as appalling as she had warned me, I must confess. But even then, I asked to look over the books merely to prove to myself it was possible to pay a living wage and still keep the mine profitable. I had no suspicions about you at all. And when I told you at the ball last night that I had discovered some serious problems, which I presume is what prompted you to try to get rid of me, I was referring only to what I'd learned from the poor fool who'd tried to beat you to it. He was admittedly half-crazy, but he told me enough to make it clear to me I couldn't go on profiting with a clear conscience from such an operation as it stood. Not until this afternoon did I become suspicious and go over the books, with the help of Mr. Harewood—who incidentally knows everything I do. I'm just curious how you managed to get away with it all these years."

Nicola stood frozen, scarcely able to believe such a conversation could be taking place within ten yards of her. She had no notion where the valet was, but she was afraid to go in search of help and leave Kinross alone and unprotected, for she could easily believe Trevethy exceedingly dangerous. Her dealings with him had always been pleasant enough, but she had never particularly liked him, and thought him oddly hard to pin down on anything. Now that he knew the truth, she was not even surprised he had been stealing from the mine for years, given the absentee ownership and complete lack of interest displayed by its owners.

She was also afraid of driving him into precipitate action, and so compromised by pushing the door soundlessly inward, trying to see as well as hear the deadly drama being played out in the room. It made her blood run cold to think he had shot Kinross and had coolly meant to make sure of his job, and only Macduff's unexpected presence had prevented him. She dared not believe he wasn't deadly serious now.

The room was lit only by a single lamp on the bedside table, but by its light she could now see Trevethy, his back toward her. He looked even more menacing because of the shadows cast in the room, and she almost shuddered, the scene made more frighteningly real by the sight of his bulky figure.

Kinross was propped up against his pillows, his golden head gleaming in the lamplight and his right arm helpless in a sling. He looked oddly unafraid, but in his present state certainly no match for the other man.

He said now, mildly, "At any rate, you can never hope to get away, you know. On the other hand, I'm a very rich man, as you have reason to know. I am very possibly worth more to you alive than dead."

"My God, you're as weak a fool as I've always thought you," said Trevethy contemptuously. "You're going to support me, is that it? The way your kind supported my father when he lost his job as manager of Poldice, or his grieving widow and children after he killed himself in disgrace because he couldn't feed his family? I'll do it my own way, thank you. I suspect I'll be doing the world a favor to rid it of so useless a leech on society."

She could see now that he held a pistol pointed neatly at Kinross's breast. But Kinross, as if wholly indifferent to the fact, remarked evenly, "Perhaps so. But if you're fool enough to fire that pistol in here, you'll have the entire household down on us inside five minutes. You're not quite as clever as you think."

Trevethy began moving deliberately toward the bed. "Don't worry, I'm not going to shoot you. You will be found in the morning, smothered with your own pillows. Unfortunately you'll be quite alone, for perhaps the first time in your life."

She thought Kinross stiffened, but still he made no attempt to move or call for help. Her own heart was beating so painfully that she was almost sick, for she knew he would stand no chance against a healthy man, and one, moreover, armed as well. There was still no sign of the valet in the room, and she wondered if Kinross had foolishly sent him away, convinced the danger wasn't real. If so, he was learning his mistake, it seemed.

Nor was there any time to think. As Trevethy reached the bed, Nicola took a shuddering breath and boldly pushed the door open. "I'm afraid you reckoned without a witness, Trevethy," she said with an assumption of calm she was far from feeling. "You can hardly kill both of us that way."

What happened next, she was never afterward able to recall with any clarity. Surprisingly it was Kinross who swore, while Trevethy stiffened, then whirled, taken completely off guard for a moment. The next thing she knew Mr. Harewood had burst in from the dressing room, looking surprisingly unlike himself armed with a pistol; and Kinross, his own arm removed from the sling and holding a serviceable-looking little silver-wedged pistol, was saying warningly, "Be careful, Gideon! Don't take any chances of hitting Nicola!"

She felt frozen in surprise, but Trevethy was not so slow

to recover. Before she could gather her scattered wits he had lunged at her and pulled her in front of him as a shield, while Kinross and Harewood looked on in frustration, not daring to fire.

"I should have known you wouldn't be very long without your watchdogs, Kinross!" he said, holding Nicola before him and backing toward the open door.

Mr. Harewood was looking appalled, but Kinross said sharply, "You don't need her! Let her go and we'll let you walk away unmolested."

Trevethy laughed, and tightened his painful hold. "Thank you, but I prefer to keep my insurance. I won't harm her if you throw down your pistols, very slowly. But I'll admit I've a score to settle with Miss Lacey anyway."

She could see the horror in Mr. Harewood's eyes, and the indecision in Kinross's. She tried to say something to reassure them, but somehow no words came.

They were almost to the door, and she knew they'd soon be out it. After that she was afraid to think what would happen to her. As if aware of it, Trevethy laughed again, and added unpleasantly, "I'll admit I'm slightly curious as to what you saw in her in the first place. Unless the rumors are true and you'll bed anything in skirts. Is that it, my lord?"

"Far be it from me to defend his lordship," observed a new, slightly bored voice from the doorway. "But I believe Kinross's reputation is somewhat exaggerated. I suspect, in fact, he is not quite the fool I had always believed him."

26

After that, pandemonium reigned. Trevethy stiffened and instinctively swung around, taking Nicola with him. Sir Guy Percival, fully dressed and unarmed, stood nonchalantly in the doorway, a certain curiosity in his unpleasant eyes.

Trevethy instantly realized his mistake and swung back, but it was too late. A deafening explosion sounded in the confines of the room, and Kinross, looking surprisingly formidable, his blue eyes for once wholly devoid of humor, sat holding a smoking pistol. Trevethy stood staring at him in surprise, as if he couldn't believe he had been bested by such a fool. A slack expression was growing on his face, and though he still held his pistol, it was no longer pointed at Nicola, and he seemed to have forgotten it.

"Good God!" exclaimed an aghast Mr. Harewood. "Are you mad, you fool? You might have hit her!"

"But I didn't. Nicola, are you all right? Don't stand there gaping—get his gun, Gideon."

As if reminded of it, Trevethy lifted it as Mr. Harewood, too late, gave a shout of warning. Nicola, numbed by all that had transpired, grasped too late what was happening. Only at the last minute did she move, her limbs feeling as if they were asleep or underwater, and knock Trevethy's arm as he fired toward Kinross at point-blank range.

The flash and explosion momentarily blinded and deafened her, but when her senses cleared, Trevethy was dead and there was a spreading stain of blood on Kinross's shirt. She stared, feeling her old nightmare grip her, and for the first time in her life fainted dead away.

* * *

When she opened her eyes sometime later she was lying in Kinross's bed and he was bending over her, holding a glass to her lips. "Thank God, she's coming round," said Mr. Harewood's worried voice.

"Of course she is!" said Kinross, looking more worried than she had ever seen him before. "Here, sweetheart, try to drink a little of this. It will make you feel better."

The room seemed oddly full of people, but she was aware only of one of them. She perforce swallowed a little of the liquid in the glass, which made her choke, but clutched weakly at his coat and whispered foolishly, "I thought . . . I thought you'd been killed." Then she completed her humiliation by bursting into tears.

With great presence of mind Kinross thrust the glass he was holding into Harewood's hand and sat on the bed to take her into his arms, wholly ignoring the roomful of interested or shocked spectators. "Poor little love! Don't cry, sweetheart," he said soothingly, an unrecognizable look of tenderness in his eyes. "That's nothing to what I thought when I saw you fall. I was sure before I fired that you were in no danger of being hit, but that was cold consolation when you pitched over in a dead faint. I thought I'd murdered you."

She blushed, ashamed of her old weakness. "I'm sorry. When I saw the blood—"

His good arm tightened a little around her, and he dropped a quick kiss on her hair, apparently as oblivious of anyone else in the room as she was. "I know, my poor sweetheart. I'm afraid I broke open your handiwork is all. But my aunt has explained that you once witnessed a brutal wrecking as a child. It's no wonder you've been horrified of blood ever since. I'm only sorry I didn't know sooner. The last two days' adventures have hardly been conducive to getting over such a fear."

"No, I've been ashamed of it for years. But are you sure you're all right? I thought for sure he must—" She broke off and shuddered, unable to finish her sentence.

"Never better, thanks to you," he answered, smiling

down at her in a way that made her suddenly forget her former fears in a new worry. "I suspect if we look for it we'll find Trevethy's bullet somewhere in the wall behind me. I heard it go past, but it never came close to touching me."

She shivered again, and weakly closed her eyes, the room still having an alarming tendency to spin.

"If you two are mutually satisfied the other is all right, Miss Lacey is supposed to drink this, remember," observed Mr. Harewood a little sarcastically. He then added, rather spoiling his effect, "Are you certain you're all right, Miss Lacey? I thought for sure this fool had killed you with his heroics. Devil take me if I'll ever fall in with any of his harebrained schemes again."

"Good Lord, yes, I was forgetting," exclaimed Kinross, again awkwardly taking the glass back. "My aunt has gone for her smelling salts, but try a little more of this, in the meantime."

He held the glass again to her lips, but she turned her head aside, saying weakly, "Oh no, it tastes vile. I'll be perfectly all right in a moment."

His eyes lit again with their habitual laughter. "Does it? As I recall, you were heartless enough to want to condemn me to gruel and barley water earlier. But I won't make you if you'll promise to be good. You're getting a little of your color back now, at least."

She became aware that she was propped up in his arms, and tried to sit up. He easily prevented her, ignoring her protests that she was hurting his arm. But even as she became aware of the impropriety of their position, a scandalized voice she knew well cried, "*Nicola!* Kinross, I tell you frankly that even I can't condone her being found in your bed twice. And as for the rest of what's been happening here, I can only say I'm disappointed in you. Deeply disappointed. When your father was alive there was nothing so vulgar as attempted murders and musical beds and pistols being fired off in the middle of the night, scaring half a year off everyone's lives."

Kinross looked amused. "Yes, I know, and can only

apologize, Aunt. But I assure you I have every intention of marrying Miss Lacey, and have from the very beginning— not because I am required to but because I'm quite certain I can't live without her. Now there's really no need for any of you to remain. I can promise you the rest of the night will be undisturbed."

She looked in bewilderment between the two, plainly at a loss, but Lord Layton stepped forward and said stiffly, "I can assure you, Kinross, that I, at least, have every intention of returning to my bed without a moment's delay. I have observed quite enough of your escapades with Miss Lacey, and can only hope you will marry her without a moment's delay, for decency's sake. In the meantime, I think it won't surprise you to learn that my wife and I will be leaving first thing in the morning."

He bowed stiffly and stalked out, trailed by a reluctant and obviously avidly curious Miss Siddings. There was an awkward silence after they'd left, broken disrespectfully by Mr. Harewood. "I wonder what happened to the divine Judith, by the way? She either sleeps like the dead or couldn't face being seen at this hour unprepared."

Sir Guy Percival had been leaning against the wall, but he abruptly straightened, looking diverted. "I don't wish you to think I'm not enjoying myself, for I am, oddly. But I, too, will say good night. May I escort you back to your bedchamber, Mrs. Chudleigh?"

Kinross looked appreciative. "I haven't thanked you yet, by the way. I must confess I've been as guilty of under-estimating you as you have of me, Percival. We must have a talk tomorrow, as soon as I can again escape from the local authorities. It seems to be my lot in life to keep them busy these days."

"You will forgive me for not particularly looking forward to that talk," answered Percival dryly. "But I admit I have been guilty of thinking you the fool you're generally reputed to be. It is a mistake I won't make again, believe me."

When he offered Mrs. Chudleigh his arm in ironic gallantry, she looked torn. "But . . . but am I just to *leave*

her here as if it were the most normal thing in the world?''
she demanded helplessly.

Percival laughed unpleasantly. "From what I can tell, it
is. Certainly we are decidedly in the way, I fear, ma'am.
Kinross seems to be in no need of any help."

As she hesitantly accepted Percival's proffered arm,
looking ridiculous in her wrapper and papered hair,
Kinross assured her, "Don't worry, ma'am. I will escort
Nicola to her own bedchamber shortly, and Harewood will
remain as chaperon, if that's what you fear. But pray don't
let me keep you."

With another laugh Percival escorted a bewildered Mrs.
Chudleigh out and shut the door behind them.

Nicola, deeply humiliated, waited until they were safely
out of the room before saying in some agitation, "Oh, let
me up! How on earth will I ever face any of them again in
the morning?"

"You will face them as you always have, my love, with a
touching dignity and courage that makes a mockery of
their spite," said his lordship calmly, refusing to release
her. "And I meant what I said to my aunt: you will be
safely in your own bed soon. You're plainly exhausted.
But I thought you deserved some answers before you went
to bed."

"Oh yes," she said, preoccupied with the most recent in
a long line of surprises. "Did Percival really steal the
necklace?"

He laughed. "Don't look so shocked, my sweet. I doubt
he was any more than a go-between. And since he proved
very useful to me tonight, I must confess I am inclined to
say nothing, whatever Gideon's disapproval. That will
have to wait until I find out what he has to say in the
morning, of course, but I suspect he was coming to talk to
me tonight, which explains his timely presence at such an
hour. And I must be profoundly grateful to him, for I
don't like to remember that moment."

"But did he really steal it last night again?"

"Yes, which is what kept me from suspecting him as
much as you obviously did. Once he had it back, he had no

real reason to try to kill me except general dislike—which I'll admit has been mutual. I have been wishing him—and all the rest of them—at Jericho for a great while now. But to get back to the necklace, I obviously gave my suspicions away last night, somehow, but he must have known he was safe enough. Certainly to reveal the truth about the necklace would have been profoundly embarrassing to all of us, as he was no doubt counting on."

"But . . . but then it was *Trevethy* all the time?"

Kinross settled her more comfortably against his good shoulder. "So it would seem. Evidently he's been smuggling ore out of the country for years—you mentioned once, I remember, my sweet Nicola, that ore smuggling was one of the less popular local industries. Unfortunately he mistook my interest in the mine as suspicion, and when I asked to see the books, seems to have panicked. That poor fool in the village probably showed him the way, and I played further into his hands by not pressing charges. No doubt he had every hope that first time of being rid of me without the least suspicion being aroused in his direction. And he would have succeeded if it hadn't been for you and Macduff."

She couldn't help shuddering again, and he insisted upon wrapping a quilt around her. Mr. Harewood observed this operation with a mildly interested eye and remarked resignedly, "Yes, you always did have the most remarkable luck, Alex."

Kinross grinned at his old friend. "So I've been told. I fear it hasn't stood me in very good stead lately, however, with one notable exception."

"But why did you go to the mine in the first place?" she asked in bewilderment.

He grimaced. "Trevethy was nearer the truth than I like to admit on that, I fear. I did it because you had pricked my vanity with your accusations of my irresponsibility, and I couldn't honestly deny them. But what I saw there more than convinced me that you were right. It's little wonder you've despised me all these years."

She blushed fierily, and Mr. Harewood, obviously

fearing the discussion was in danger of wandering off onto irrelevant topics, said firmly, "Even so, you must admit that your interest was somewhat ill-timed. It came close to costing you your life, in fact."

"But are you telling me you guessed it was Trevethy all the time?" she demanded.

"As much as I'm tempted to try to impress you with my intuition, since my *amour propre* has suffered greatly at your hands lately, my love," he said in amusement, "I fear I wasn't sure of anything except that I was a great deal more unpopular than I'd ever imagined. And even when Gideon and I pored through the books this afternoon, we found little enough to make us suspicious. It's obvious if I'm going to run the mine myself from now on, I shall have to learn bookkeeping for my own protection."

"But . . . *are* you going to run the mine from now on?" She was feeling more and more bewildered.

He seemed to realize how near exhaustion she was, for he dropped another swift kiss on her hair before reluctantly putting her away from him. "Yes, but all that can wait for tomorrow. At the moment I think I should keep my word and get you to bed."

He insisted upon escorting her back to her bedchamber himself, though she protested that he was too weak to be out of bed. At her door he obviously started to say something else, but then contented himself with pressing his lips warmly to the palm of her hand before closing it around his kiss and gently pushing her into her room. It said much for the state of her exhaustion that she managed to sleep after that.

She again woke late, a little startled by how high the sun was in the sky and how normal everything looked after the shocks of last night.

But not everything was normal, for Trevethy was dead, Kinross had almost been killed, and she knew finally that she would have to leave, before what little resolve she had remaining to her was lost. She had not needed Mrs. Chudleigh to point out that Kinross would feel doubly obligated to marry her now, and she placed almost no faith any longer in her ability to withstand his almost palpable charm, especially when turned on full blast for her benefit.

As for Kinross's feelings, whatever they might be, she was afraid to trust what she had seemed to read in his eyes and behavior last night. He too had not been himself, and it would be folly to let her own yearning cause her to read too much into his concern and undoubted gratitude. Whatever had happened, the fact still remained that a marriage between them would never work out. They were too fundamentally different, and if she had learned belatedly that she had never known the real Kinross, in reality he fit into her world no more than she fit into his.

Again she had no desire to meet anyone, and so cravenly slipped out of the house by the back way and went for a walk along the cliffs, taking Macduff with her. She felt as if she were saying good-bye, and so could not get enough of the cliffs and the sea she loved.

She was standing looking out at the sea, lost in thought, when Macduff exploded with excitement beside her. She looked quickly around, her heart beating suddenly fast, to see Kinross walking toward her, fully dressed and looking as if none of the events of the last twenty-four hours had happened.

She had hoped to postpone this interview or escape it entirely, but she stiffened, turning to face him, grateful for the moment's respite she was afforded by the dog's exuberant greeting.

Kinross knelt to pet the dog, apparently undismayed by Macduff's enthusiasm. It was a circumstance that would have surprised her only a few days ago. But then, she had realized painfully in the last few days that he was a most surprising man.

At last he rose and smiled at her, the blinding smile she was least able to resist. "I thought I'd find you out here. How are you after your ordeal of last night?"

She closed her eyes briefly, then made herself answer calmly enough, "I'm fine. But I'm sure Mr. Harewood told you that you shouldn't be out of bed yet."

"He tried, but he is resigned to my folly. No nightmares, I hope? You should have told me what you went through so long ago."

She had no wish to be reminded of her shameful weakness, and abruptly turned away to stare back out over the water. "When will you be returning to London, my lord?" she inquired abruptly.

There was a moment's silence; then he said quietly, "That rather depends upon you. Are you so eager to be rid of me?"

She was trembling pitifully by now, and dared not meet his eyes. "I . . . have decided to go away as well," she managed. "My . . . my old headmistress has offered me a post at her school and I have decided to accept it."

There was an even longer silence. "I see. I know how much your teaching means to you. But don't you think you could be just as satisfied running your own school as teaching in someone else's? I have decided to build a school for the children of my miners, and was depending upon your help. I hope, in fact, that you will reconsider your decision."

She made a gesture of pain, hastily repressed. "My lord, I know what you are thinking—"

"I doubt that very much," he interrupted steadily.

She chose to ignore that. "You . . . you think that after last night you have even less choice in marrying me. But it wouldn't work, believe me."

She could feel him coming closer, though still she dared not turn. "You're right about that, at least," he said surprisingly, just behind her. "After last night I do have even less choice in marrying you, but not for the reasons you think. And I hope very much that it will work, for I fear my future happiness depends on it."

She was trembling so badly by now that she seemed incapable of thinking rationally. "Don't!" she cried involuntarily. "You always know just the words to say, but it's cruel—crueler than you know. I am trying to be sensible, for both our sakes, but you're making it very hard. You have determined to marry me, whether out of pique or chivalry, I no longer know. I only know that I can't stand much more!''

His hand was warm on her arm, and he turned her toward him, despite her resistance. "I have determined to marry you, my beautiful, amazingly blind Celtic witch, because I have fallen hopelessly in love with you, of course. I only hope I can manage to persuade you I am not the weak fool you obviously think me. At least I give you my word I will spend my life trying to convince you of the fact.''

"I know," she whispered. "I think I was always afraid of your power over me, and so fooled myself into thinking I despised you. And you make love as easily as you breathe. I didn't stand a chance."

She should not have been surprised, after that weak-willed speech, to find herself suddenly in his arms, being kissed rather violently. She just had time to notice that for once he looked nothing like his usual charmingly detached self.

"You little fool!" he exclaimed when both could breathe again. "I have admittedly made love to a number of women—if nowhere near the number you are obviously imagining—but can't you tell the difference when a man is deadly serious, as I am about you? I don't want to marry you because I compromised your reputation, but because I'm quite certain I can't live without you. Only I find myself in the damnedest coil—admittedly of my own making. If I say I love you, you accuse me of being a practiced deceiver. How the devil can I ever hope to convince you that I was never more earnest in my life? Shall I give away all my money to prove it?''

She said breathlessly, scarcely daring to believe what she saw in his face. "No, don't. We shall need it for all the good works I have planned. Oh, Alex, Alex!''

A much longer time later he said, her head warmly against his good shoulder, "Shall we restore Rosemullion together to what it should be—a home filled with love and laughter? But first I mean to take you on an extended bridal trip on your namesake. I hope your father's accident hasn't soured you on sailing completely."

When she frowned in puzzlement, he smiled and took her hand and led her along the path until they reached a vantage point overlooking the natural harbor below where he tied up his boat. She had never seen it before, and was bound to acknowledge that it was larger and more graceful than she had been expecting.

He smiled again and waited patiently until she picked out the name painted on its bow: the *Celtic Witch*.

He said softly behind her, "Kinrosses' origins have always been in Cornwall, and I intend for that to continue. Our sons and daughters will be natural sailors—and undoubtedly unpopular with their neighbors if they inherit their mother's crusading spirit. But perhaps by then you will have given all my money away and they'll be forced to stand on their own feet, which will be no bad thing. I almost envy them, in fact. But not quite."

And he set about proving exactly why not.

About the Author

Dawn Lindsey was born and grew up in Oklahoma, where her ancestors were early pioneers, so she came by her fascination with history naturally. After graduating from college she pursued several careers, the strangest and most interesting of which (aside from writing romance novels) was doing public relations for several zoos. She and her attorney husband now make their home in the San Francisco area.